A Brief History of Next Time

By
Colin Thompson

Simon & Schuster Books for Young Readers
New York London Toronto Sydney Singapore

SIMON & SCHUSTER BOOKS FOR YOUNG READERS
An imprint of Simon & Schuster Children's Publishing Division
1230 Avenue of the Americas, New York, New York 10020
Copyright © 1999 by Colin Thompson
First published in 1999 by Simon & Schuster UK Ltd
First United States edition 2000
All rights reserved including the right of reproduction
in whole or in part in any form.
SIMON & SCHUSTER BOOKS FOR YOUNG READERS
is a trademark of Simon & Schuster.
The text for this book is set in Melior.
Printed in the United States of America
10 9 8 7 6 5 4 3 2 1

Library of Congress Cataloging-in-Publication Data
Thompson, Colin (Colin Edward)
Future Eden : a brief history of next time / by Colin Thompson.
p. cm.
Summary: The human race has dwindled down to a population of
only a few thousand, and Jay and his all-powerful pet chicken,
Ethel, are determined to save what is left before it is too late.
0-689-83979-0
00-032237

FIRST
F
EDITION

For Anne

Future Eden
A Brief History of Next Time

The year is 2287.

Future Eden

Jay is fed up with the penthouse. It may have been a perfect place to live while things around him were deteriorating mysteriously; a place where he could be out of the way, self-sufficient with his roof garden and his chickens, a place away from the squalor and decay at ground level. But Jay is fed up with being safe, because being safe has meant being lonely.

We meet him on the day he decides to leave his penthouse. For the first time in years he enters the elevator and ventures down to ground level and out of the building to see what has happened to the world. But even as he takes these first steps on—what will become—his momentous journey, the utterly improbable happens: his pet chicken starts talking to him and reveals her true persona. Here's Ethel, an alien from a galaxy beyond galaxies. She's one of six companions who lead Jay to his destination, together with Douglas; Fluffy, The Oracle; Merlin, The Oracle's father; The enigmatic Blind Piano Tuner; and—of course—Kay, (Jay's soul mate and partner). We follow Jay's wild and wondrous path that will—if Ethel can live up to her task—eventually lead humankind back from the brink, back into a new Eden, maybe.

In Colin Thompson's *Future Eden* we find the sum of many worlds, some in the mind, some outside. He conjures up abstract constructs that could have come straight from Stephen Hawking. The author's grotesque humor reminds us of *The Hitchhiker's Guide to the Galaxy;* the story's characters would feel at home in Alice's Wonderland, in Emerald City, but also, perhaps, in *Gormenghast*. Here's a whole New World at your feet. A world that one day may become a reality if mankind continues on its path. Let's hope Ethel and her companions succeed and find the way to . . .

FUTURE EDEN

Chapter 1
Chicken

The sun breaking through the yellow clouds cast a sick light over the silent city. Jay turned his face toward the sky but the sunlight was as weak as the moon. The air, trapped under the clouds, was damp and heavy and the only way to keep cool was down in the basements of the deserted buildings. Up on the 127th floor it was even hotter than on street level.

Jay was getting restless in the penthouse. It was time to leave. At first it had been fantastic living up there, looking down on the city, searching the streets with binoculars for the last few signs of people. There was hardly anyone left now, just a few small dots huddling along the sidewalks searching for food and, very rarely, a car racing through the derelict streets. Cars never got far. Either the highways were blocked with abandoned vehicles or they simply ran out of fuel.

The gray landscape was dotted with green, which grew greener every week. No one swept the streets anymore, the wind blew leaves into damp neglected piles, and in the piles trees were growing. Their roots crawled into the drains, choking them, creating worlds for giant rats, worlds where it was hard to trap them. The rats hardly ever made it up to the 127th floor. Jay had only caught a couple of them, but they had made a welcome change from the endless diet of vegetables and eggs.

Jay remembered photographs of long-lost Aztec cities discovered in thick jungles and realized that one day this city would be like that. It was hard to imagine, hard to believe that

1

a whole city could disappear, but it would, though maybe not within his lifetime. He wondered if mankind would survive long enough to discover the ruins. After all, it had happened before, otherwise the Aztecs would still be there in their great cities. It was a beautiful thought, the idea of all that ugliness being reclaimed by nature, and it was amazing how fast it was happening. And it was happening everywhere. Even on the ledges of his 127th floor, plants were growing, green moss softening the edges of the concrete, eating into the stone.

At first, when the population had dropped below the critical mass and the infrastructure had started to collapse, people had pulled up the trees, as if by doing so they would keep the decline at bay. But after a while they gave up. Now, in the warm damp air that covered everything all year-round, the trees were thriving. In only a few months they could grow as tall as a man, and after a year as tall as a house, though from Jay's rooftop they still looked tiny beneath the rows of skyscrapers.

Here and there people had put up tents under the trees and were living in little encampments, returning to nature in fields of tarmac. It seemed a bit pointless to Jay, with all the thousands of empty apartments, but most people had turned their backs on the buildings, just entering them to collect things and hunt rats and cats. It was like they blamed the buildings for what had happened.

It had all happened almost without anyone noticing, or rather without anyone realizing what the eventual con- clusion would be. Long before Jay had been born, the population had started to fall. Right across the planet, for more than a hundred years, men's fertility had been dropping. And not just men—animals had become infertile too, though strangely not all animals. Dogs had almost died out, so had sheep and pigs and cows. It seemed that the animals mankind had close contact with had been particularly affected, except the cats. There were cats everywhere, wild, mean animals that had grown hostile to man, though considering one of the last books published had been *101 Exciting Cat Recipes*, subtitled *Your Friends Will Never Guess*, it was not surprising.

2

Jay had lived in the penthouse for a year. He felt safe there and for a while he had everything he wanted. There was actually very little threat below. He was young and strong, most people were friendly, and by and large aggression had died out as the population had dwindled. With so few people left, there seemed little point in fighting. Possessions and places had become far less important. Survival no longer meant the survival of the fittest. The key now was lateral thinking and working together.

Jay had been a loner all his life. He had no brothers and just one sister, who had been too young for company. It had suited him fine. He felt it had given him an independence that had helped him survive when his family disappeared, but now he was lonely and it was time to move on.

He'd known that for weeks, but it was such a sweet setup, it was hard to leave. It had taken a lot of effort to get there too. With no power in the city to run the elevators, all the tall buildings were deserted above the first few floors. But Jay had rigged up a generator, a neat system safely hidden on the roof of the elevator itself, so that when he was up there no one could steal it. Then he'd torched the first ten stories, so nobody would bother with the place. Even the cats didn't bother to explore the upper floors. He had everything he needed. Even chickens out on the roof garden. There was enough food for a year and if he grew stuff, even longer. He had everything, except someone to talk to. Friendship was a scarce commodity in the sparsely populated world, but then it had been all his life. He had learned to be self-contained, self-sufficient. But there were times when Jay felt very alone.

"It's time to go, man," he said to the chicken. It was too busy scratching in the earth to take any notice. There'd been four chickens at first but one of them hadn't realized how far up they were and had gone to have a look over the wall to see if the grass there really was greener. By the time it reached the fortieth floor it had passed out, and by the time it hit the ground it was in chicken heaven, where the grass was so green it blinded you. The person it landed on ended up in a similar place. Two of the other chickens thought they might be missing something and went after the first one. A few

3

minutes later, there was a small group of people at the bottom of the building. Two of them were dead and the rest were covered in blood and feathers. That hadn't been a good day.

Jay stood looking over the edge. It would be so easy. He just had to climb up, stretch out his arms, and he could fly like an angel.

Go on, he thought, *give it a try.*

He was tempted, but then he was always tempted by the voice in his head. It seemed as if he had been talking to himself from the day he was born, maybe even before. He had certainly done it before he could speak. Sometimes there were thoughts that he couldn't even understand. And these inner thoughts had coaxed him into all the stupid things he had ever done and then regretted, but they had also made him do all the exciting things that had given life its edge.

He wondered if the voice inside everyone else's head was the same. He couldn't imagine his mother having a voice that made her take risks. Her voice would have been calm and kind. Though of course she had deserted him. Maybe the voice in her head had made her do that.

There was a current of warm air rising up from the ground, carrying the smell of damp earth, a soft inviting smell that seemed to be calling him. He could see himself soaring like a bird, drifting over the rooftops like Peter Pan. It was so inviting. Just reach out and soar like a bird.

Jay lifted his leg to climb over and, as he did so, the last chicken flew at him. It fluttered in his face, making him fall back onto the balcony, and as he fell the spell was broken and he sat back against the wall with his heart racing.

"Idiot," he said at last. "What am I thinking of?"

The chicken just stood staring at him.

He had been so close to throwing himself to his death, it scared the hell out of him. It was definitely time to go.

"Hey, chicken, do you want to go to the country?" he said. "And when you start talking to chickens, it's definitely time to go," he added, "before they start talking back."

The chicken put its head to one side and peered at him, for all the world looking like it understood every word he said.

Jay packed a backpack with food, poured gasoline around

the apartment, stuffed the last chicken inside his coat, and left. It seemed a pointless gesture, burning the place—no one had ever come up in all the time he had lived there—but he felt it had become part of him, and rather than just leave it, he wanted to eliminate it, as if by doing so he would eliminate his past. It was time to move on, time for a new life untouched by the past. When the generator was running smoothly and the elevator was ready to go, he threw a burning rag through the open door and hit the button down.

The small generator would produce only enough power for the electric motor, so the lights and the illuminated buttons stayed dead as the elevator crawled slowly down in total darkness. The journey usually took about three minutes, except today. After two minutes everything stopped. Jay instinctively hit the door button, but he knew nothing would happen. The generator had stopped. He took the chicken out of his jacket, set it in the corner, and climbed up through the trapdoor. He pulled the starter cord but nothing happened. He pulled it again and again, but he knew it wouldn't start. It was out of fuel and the only fuel was spread around the carpets up in the apartment.

"Oh, shit," he said. "I forgot to check the damn gas tank." There was always something. No matter how sweet the plan, there was always something.

That wasn't really the problem. If he could get out of the elevator, he could walk down the stairs. The problem was that he couldn't get out. The floor above was too far up and there was no way down to the floor below.

Maybe I should have flown off the roof after all, he thought.

He dropped back down into the elevator and as he did there was a loud explosion above him. The fire in the apartment had reached the elevator shaft and had blown in the doors. Burning wood and hot metal flew down onto the roof above him. When he looked through the trapdoor opening, he could see the flames dancing like waving hands in the far distance. There was another explosion as the doors on the floor below his apartment blew in and a few minutes later the floor below that exploded. The fire was racing down the building toward him. A resigned weariness filled his heart, a weariness that was far too old for a twenty-two-year-old man.

"Well, we probably won't get burned to death," he said to the chicken. "The fire'll melt the elevator cable before it gets here and we'll, like, get spread across the basement floor."

"Oh, cluck," said a voice in the darkness.

Chapter 2

How Many Floors Must a Man Fall Down?

Jay froze. There was someone else in the elevator. It was impossible. There was no way there could be. He'd have seen him before he shut the doors. He crouched down in the corner and tried to look into the darkness. There was a faint glow from the fire through the trapdoor but it wasn't enough to see anything by.

"Shit, who's there, man?" he said as calmly as he could, the weariness he had felt minutes before now replaced by his heart pounding so loudly he could almost hear it.

"It's all right," said the flat, calm voice. "There's nothing to be afraid of."

There was another explosion and now the light was bright enough to see the four corners of the elevator. There was no one there. All he could see was the backpack, the chair, and the chicken huddled in the opposite corner.

"Where are you?" said Jay. "Like, who are you?"

"Don't worry, I'm a friend," said the voice. "I'm over here in the corner."

The chicken walked across the floor and stood in front of Jay.

"It's all right," it said.

"All right? All right?" said Jay. "Oh, man, I'm going to fall God knows how many floors to my death at any moment and a chicken's talking to me and telling me everything's all right. Yeah, great."

"It's actually sixty-four floors," said the chicken, "and

you're not going to plunge to your death. Calm down, I'm going to save you."

"What?" said Jay. "You're going to save me? A chicken's going to save me? Great, wonderful."

"I'm not a cluckin' chicken," said the chicken. "I would have thought the fact I'm talking would have made that obvious. Oh, God, humans, they never get any better. Dumb as cluckin' cardboard."

There were more explosions and the elevator shook as something heavy crashed down onto the roof. It was getting hot. Jay felt like there were explosions in his head, too. All his feelings were completely off the chart. Chickens don't talk to you. Five minutes earlier everything was cool, everything was going exactly to plan, and now it was all scrambled up like seriously knotted string.

This always frigging happens, he thought.

"Okay, okay, right, being totally calm," he said, being as calm as Cape Horn. "Okay, okay, I believe you, but if you're going to save me, I think you'd better do it, like, right now."

"Yeah, yeah, there's no need to panic," said the chicken that wasn't a chicken. "Hold tight."

The motor hummed into life, the lights came on, and the elevator slid smoothly down the sixty-four floors into the lower basement. The doors opened and the chicken walked out. Jay picked up his backpack in his shaking hands and followed the chicken out just before the roof of the elevator collapsed onto the floor in a pile of burning rubble. The chicken turned toward the fire, and the fireproof basement doors slid smoothly closed.

"You're safe now," said the chicken.

Jay collapsed against the wall and slid to the ground, clutching his backpack. He let out the breath he'd been holding in for the past three minutes, and stared openmouthed at the creature. Whatever it was, it looked exactly like a chicken. It waddled, it scratched, and it pecked in the dirt just like a chicken. God, it had even laid eggs for him.

Maybe I've died and gone to heaven? he thought. *And heaven is full of talking chickens?*

8

Jay was several stages beyond confused. He felt he was about to faint. He shut his eyes and took long, slow, deep breaths, but when he opened his eyes the chicken was still there. It raised its wing and spoke.

"I am not, as it appears, a chicken," it said in a calm, slightly patronizing voice that Jay, and everyone else who would hear it, gradually came to hate. "I have just borrowed this pathetic body. I come from somewhere far, far away, a galaxy beyond galaxies past the end of time, far beyond anything you could imagine. Not that that would be cluckin' far."

"But—," Jay started to say, but the chicken held up its wing for him to be silent. It was difficult for Jay to take this gesture seriously. Chickens are not natural figures of authority. "But a chicken?" he finally managed to say. "I mean, why not, like, a dog or a tiger?"

"Chickens are inconspicuous," said the creature, "and you find them all over the world."

"Yeah, so you mean all chickens are, like, aliens from outer space?" said Jay.

"Don't be ridiculous, of course not," said the creature. "You don't think the three who walked off the roof were relations of mine, do you? We'd hardly travel billions of light-years across space to fall off the tops of tall buildings, would we? Credit us with some intelligence. We're not human, you know."

It hated humans, they were so primitive, as dumb as dogs but without the cuddly appeal of Labradors to make up for it. They had started out with such promise, painting nice pictures in their caves and bashing one another over the head with bits of tree, but somewhere along the line evolution seemed to have gone on vacation. The alien felt bitter and cheated that it had been given such poor material to work with.

"Yeah, well, I reckon a chicken's a bit of a weird choice," said Jay. "Why not something fantastic, like an eagle? Are you all chickens?"

"Yeah, all six of us," said the alien. "And I can tell you it's cluckin' crap. The bodies are crap. This is the five hundred nineteenth one I've been in and they're all the same. Flying's crap, you spend half the time with your beak full of earth, and as for the egg-laying thing, well, I don't want to talk about it."

Jay had always been fond of chickens. After the machines that made artificial eggs had been invented, chickens had become quite rare, but Jay's parents had always kept a few in the backyard. Jay liked the ungainly way they walked, and their comforting broody noises made them very endearing to him. But this one was something different, something very different. In fact, *different* was too feeble a word to describe it. Jay wondered if he was dreaming and then he wondered if you could wonder if you were dreaming when you actually were dreaming, or maybe he was dreaming about dreaming . . . And then his head started scrambling itself again.

The alien from the galaxy beyond galaxies past the end of time told Jay that through the millennia its race had spread out to the very limits of everything, searching out planets with any signs of life. Over time they had found hundreds. And over time they had seen great civilizations rise and fall, suns collapse into black holes, and new stars grow from the dust of space.

"Wow, amazing," said Jay.

A strange calm that wasn't of his own making drifted over him and he thought he definitely must be dreaming, but he wasn't. It was the chicken untangling the thoughts inside his head and laying them out to dry.

"Yeah, right," said the alien, thinking just how pathetic the tiny little human brain really was. "I suppose you think it's a pretty interesting job, never a dull millennium and all that sort of garbage?"

All Jay could say was, "Wow."

"Anyway, it looks like everything's dying out," said the alien. "There seems to be more planets dying than there are being born," it continued, "so now we're rushing around like headless, uh, headless, um, ducks, trying to find out why and trying to stop it. Though why we're cluckin' bothering is beyond me. I mean, how much would the Earth suffer if you humans died out and the cockroaches took over?"

"Wow," said Jay.

"Yeah, yeah, wow. Is that all you can say?" said the alien.

"Anyway, that's why I'm sitting here with you in the basement of an empty burning block of luxury apartments in an almost deserted city on this crappy little planet where the human population has almost made itself extinct, when I'd much rather be at home in a hot acid bath with the one I love."

Jay stopped saying "Wow." The explosions that had been going on all the time the alien had been talking were getting closer and louder. And it was getting hotter, much hotter, and Jay could feel the muscles tightening in his chest.

"I think we ought to get out of here," he said.

"It's okay. We've got eight and a half minutes," said the alien.

"Look, uh, thank you for saving my life," said Jay.

"It's nothing," said the alien. "That's what I'm here for. Pathetic, isn't it?"

"And, uh, what am I supposed to call you?" said Jay. "I mean, I've never actually, like, met someone from another planet before. You know, I can't really call you chicken anymore."

"You can call me Ethel," said the alien. "And there's every chance you've met lots of people from other planets, you just haven't realized."

"Ethel? Ethel?" said Jay. "Come on, what sort of name's that for an intergalactic traveler?"

"Oh, yeah?" said Ethel. "And what's the matter with it? Anyway, you wouldn't be able to say my real name."

"Why not? What is it?" said Jay.

"Well, there are seven hundred thirteen letters in our alphabet, our true voices span ninety-six octaves, there are fifteen colors involved and seventy-two smells, seventy-one of which would probably kill you—"

"Okay, okay," said Jay, "I'll call you Ethel."

"Suit yourself," said Ethel. "You can call me Gladys for all I cluckin' care."

As if it weren't bad enough sitting below a towering inferno talking to a chicken that claimed to be from another galaxy, this one had to be bad-tempered and treat him like an idiot. When he'd woken up that morning, Jay had had the whole day planned out, and not just the whole day but the rest of his life for the foreseeable future. Pour the gasoline, pick up the chicken, light the fire, and head for the country and a new life. A small house surrounded by lush grass and trees, by a crystal-clear river, a patch of vegetables, more chickens, and the girl of his dreams. Except that there hadn't actually been that many girls in his dreams. The wonderful plan had worked for about ten minutes.

In the old electric days there would have been air-conditioning keeping the basement cool, but now the air was damp and stale and getting really hot. Brown snakes crept farther into the cooler shadows and giant cockroaches clattered their wings nervously. Behind the fire doors Jay could still hear explosions as the building continued to collapse above them. The doors themselves began to glow. Jay and Ethel moved off into the lower layers, where the parking lot had been.

"So where were you planning to go?" said Ethel.

She knew exactly what Jay had been planning, but it had been so disorganized, she thought she must have missed something when she'd read his mind—though the idea that she could miss anything in something as small and simple as a human brain was a bit of a joke, a bit like trying to hide a haystack in a needle.

"I dunno. I mean, I hadn't really planned it out," said Jay. "Just out of the city. You know, somewhere warm and peaceful, by the sea maybe." He wanted to add, "Somewhere where chickens don't talk," but thought better of it.

"Oh, yes, and how were you going to get there, walk?" said Ethel.

"I've got a motorbike hidden on the ground floor," said Jay, allowing himself a bit of a swagger and asking himself at the same time why the hell he was showing off to a chicken.

"You mean the ground floor of the blazing inferno above our heads?" said Ethel. "I don't think so."

Jay swore and sat down against the concrete wall. If he hadn't been wasting his time with the damn chicken, he would have got the motorbike out of the building by now. This was not how he had planned it. By now, he should be roaring through the streets toward the suburbs, his hair blowing in the breeze and the world opening up before him. Except all the gas for the bike was burning up in the penthouse. . . .

Shit always seemed to happen. He couldn't even burn a skyscraper down without screwing it up. No matter how carefully Jay planned things, something always went wrong. It never occurred to him there was a reason for it; it just seemed like bad luck. If he had been as neurotic as most of the world was in 2287, he would have felt like a complete failure. But he had a wonderful knack for shrugging his shoulders and moving on.

If Ethel had told him his failures were not his own fault, that all his life he had been under observation and the failures and mistakes had been a test, he probably wouldn't have believed her. So she didn't. There would be plenty of time for explanations later, and by then they might no longer be necessary.

Still, he told himself, *it's always easy to make gasoline.*

And in 2287 it was. The great urban myth of the pill you drop in a gallon of water that will run your car wasn't a myth. It really had existed way back in the 1950s. The myth had said that the man who invented the pill had either been paid vast sums of money by oil companies to give them the formula and keep quiet or been killed. They were both true, and for two hundred years the formula had stayed hidden, until the last drop of oil had run out. Of course by the time the Power Pill had come on the market there was almost no population left to benefit from it. If the pill had been made when it was first invented, the world might still be fully populated with happy, peaceful people living deep and meaningful lives.

Progress, thought Ethel, *can't live with it, can't live without it.* Then, "Hang on," she said. "It's okay. The bike hasn't blown up."

There was a muffled explosion somewhere above them.

"Now it's blown up," said the chicken with a strangled noise that was the best she could do by way of an ironic laugh heavy with sarcasm.

"How did you know it was going to blow up, man?" said Jay. "Can you, like, see into the future?"

"Of course not," said Ethel, too quickly for it to have been true. "I guessed, but I suppose having a gas tank in a burning building might have had something to do with it. Smart move."

In reality Ethel could see into the future, and the past, but she wasn't letting Jay know. He wasn't stupid. He'd probably work it out for himself eventually, but for now she'd keep it to herself. There was nothing worse than telling people that you knew what was going to happen when they didn't. They drove you mad asking you what you were thinking about all the time. Sometimes it could get so bad that they wouldn't even go into a room without pestering you to tell them what was in there.

"Oh, well, I suppose we'll just have to walk," said Jay.

"It's a long way out of the city," said Ethel.

"Well, can't you do something?" said Jay. "Can't you sort of beam us out into the country?"

"Yeah, yeah, big joke. I think you've been watching too much cluckin' *Star Trek*. Life's not like that," said Ethel, though she could have done exactly what Jay had suggested if she'd wanted to. But there were places to go and things to do before they went anywhere near the country.

"Well, I don't know what you can or can't do," said Jay. "I've never actually met a talking chicken before. There isn't a users guide, you know? Until fifteen minutes ago, when I looked at you all I thought of was eggs or casseroles."

"Don't mention the cluckin' eggs," said Ethel.

"Sorry," said Jay, wondering why he was apologizing to a chicken and wondering why he was wondering that when he should have been wondering why he was even talking to a chicken.

"I suppose you'd like me to shrink you down to a few inches tall, pop you on my back, and fly off into the sunset, eh?" said Ethel.

As if, thought Jay. He also thought the smartest thing to do would be to put as much distance as possible between himself and the bad-tempered chicken as soon as possible, but then the smartest thing was usually the most boring, so he seldom did it. All the voices in his head seemed to be shouting as loud as they could, telling him to run while he still had the chance. But from the minute he was conceived, this day had been preordained. There was no way he could run. The day when the creature from a galaxy beyond galaxies past the end of time would speak to him was no more avoidable than birth, death, and the stuff in between. This day was one of the most momentous in the whole history of mankind, though of course to Jay it was just another day. Sure, a talking chicken made it a kind of weird day, but there'd been others. Weird stuff happened all the time.

"Oh, yeah," said Jay. "That'd be great. Yeah, fly off into the sunset. Yeah, great."

"Idiot," said the chicken, but she did it.

It was the weirdest sensation Jay had ever experienced. He couldn't describe it, as he had never felt anything that he could remotely compare it to. As he got smaller and smaller, a strange yet oddly familiar smell filled the air, and the smaller he got the stronger the smell became. Then he realized what it was. He'd shrunk all right, but his clothes hadn't and he was three inches tall, standing naked surrounded by a giant pair of underpants that had seen better days, a great quantity of better days, in the middle of one of his own socks, inside one of his shoes, only now the sock was the size of a pile of blankets and the shoe was as big as a boat and the smell made him want to throw up.

"Oh, cluck, what a day," said Ethel, bringing him back to his normal size. "Hang on, I'll start again."

This time his clothes and backpack shrank with him. He climbed up onto Ethel's back and she started lumbering down the parking lot toward the exit tunnel. Now, everyone knows that chickens can't fly, and just because Ethel was being occupied by a superintelligent alien from the galaxy beyond galaxies past the end of time, it didn't change the laws of physics. As she ran down the tunnel flapping her wings, she remained firmly rooted to the ground. She just got slower and slower until she came to a dead stop.

"Oh, cluck," she managed to say, and then fell over. "There

are times when I think I'm too old for this cluckin' job," she said when she'd got her breath back, and stood up.

"How old are you?" said Jay.

"Older than you could ever imagine," said Ethel.

"How long have you been on Earth?"

"Well, you know the Last Supper?" said Ethel.

"What, Jesus and all that stuff?" said Jay.

"Yes," said Ethel.

"That wasn't real," said Jay. "He didn't really exist."

"Of course he did," said Ethel. "He just wasn't what the world thought he was. He was actually like me, a visitor to your planet, though not from my planet. We wouldn't tolerate a Goody Two-Shoes like that, but that's another story. The point is, do you know what they had to eat at the Last Supper?"

"Of course not," said Jay. "What?"

"Scrambled eggs on toast," said Ethel, "and guess who laid the eggs?"

Behind them the fireproof doors had stood firm against the inferno. They glowed deep orange and buckled slightly but they hadn't collapsed. The wall all around them was a different story. The concrete cracked like an eggshell and collapsed in a heap as the flames roared through the parking lot toward Jay and Ethel.

"Quick, man," shouted Jay. "We've got to get out of here."

Jay shot back up to his normal size. It happened so fast it made him want to faint, but there was no time. He grabbed Ethel and ran up the tunnel into the street. It was deserted. He ran across the road and took shelter in an empty office block as the skyscraper collapsed into a molten piece of twisted steel and concrete dust.

"Wow," he said, "some fire! Cool."

"Yes, you're good at fires," said Ethel. She was trying to be sarcastic, but being inside a chicken's body, she didn't really have the body language to carry it off.

"Thanks," said Jay.

"Mind you," said Ethel, "the past half an hour would have been a lot more cluckin' peaceful if you hadn't actually started the fire."

A lot of things would have been different if Jay hadn't started the fire. Jay would now be halfway out of the city on a great motorbike. The skyscraper would still be scraping the sky, and the chicken inside his jacket would still be a chicken.

A small group of people came along the street and stood in front of the burning building. Jay slipped behind a marble column out of sight. They looked, as most people did nowadays, like a multicolored mess. The factories that made clothes had closed down long before they had been born and hardly anyone had the knowledge or skills to make new clothes. Most of the tasteful stuff, the wool and cotton, the natural products, had worn out or rotted long ago, so the clothes were usually cobbled together out of the cheapest nylon, bits of old tracksuits and anoraks, shower curtains and bedspreads, a sleeve off this, a leg off that, with the odd bit of cat fur. High fashion was wearing fewer than seven different colors.

For the past century everything had been like that, not just clothes. No one made anything anymore; there were no skills handed down from earlier generations, just leftovers. People lived on their ancestors' remains. It was too late now. If only they hadn't burned all the books in the Big Backlash of 2099, when some smart idiot decided that all the world's problems had come from books.

This was nothing new. Men had burned books for centuries. The Chinese, who had had piped gas, printing, and umbrellas while Europeans were still discussing which shade of woad went best with bearskin, had begun the tradition in 213 B.C. Many people had kept the tradition alive. Goebbels, for example, had burned Jewish books in 1933. But in 2099 they had had the book burning to end all book burnings. All around the world people had burned all the books they could find, even ridiculous things like telephone directories. And not just books but microfilm, computer files, laser discs, any record of the past they could find, had all gone into the fire. In three weeks they had destroyed the stored wisdom of human civilization and covered the planet with yet another layer of clouds. From that time on, the sun had shone just that little bit weaker.

Not only had they thrown out the baby with the bathwater, they had thrown out the bath, torn out the plumbing, and then for good measure burned the house to the ground. At last they were free, free to freeze to death, unwashed, unclothed, and half starved, but free, free to die of simple diseases, free to walk tall and proud, unsullied by deodorants, free of man-made trappings like eyeglasses and pacemakers, free to walk into things, under things, and off things with no warning. The group that had just arrived outside was no exception.

"Listen," said Ethel. "Before we go anywhere, there are things I must tell you."

Jay moved back into the shadows of the deserted reception area and sat down against the wall.

"I'm not supposed to have spoken to you yet," said Ethel. "But I had no choice under the circumstances."

The street door opened and the people who had been watching the fire came in. There were five of them, a man of about thirty, two women the same age as Jay, and two identical children about eight years old. Jay couldn't tell from their dress or haircuts or smell whether they were boys or girls. He suspected that they couldn't either.

"Listen, quickly," Ethel whispered, "two things. One peck means no and two mean yes, and whatever you do, never let anyone know who I am or I'll have to kill them."

Jay stood up, tucked Ethel inside his jacket, and went over to the people, the first he'd spoken to in almost a year.

"Hi," he said.

"Jeez," said the man, jumping. "How long have you been there?"

"Not long," said Jay.

"Haven't seen you around here before," said one of the women.

"I was up there," said Jay, pointing over at the burning building.

"What happened?" said the man. "Something catch fire?"

"Yeah," said Jay, still proud of his inferno, "everything."

"Were you living there?" said the other woman.

"Yeah, man, right up on the top floor," said Jay.

"You were lucky to get out then," said the man.

"Not really," said Jay. "I started the fire and then came down in the elevator."

He explained how he'd made the elevator work and was just about to tell them about it getting stuck when he realized he'd have to tell them about Ethel.

"What did you burn it for?" said the first woman.

"It seemed like a good idea at the time," said Jay.

"So where are you going now?" said the first woman.

"Dunno," said Jay. "I had a motorbike, but it, like, blew up."

"Come with us," she said. "We live in the park down by the river. There's quite a few of us there."

She smiled at him and Jay felt a faint memory of desire. It had been a long time since he'd felt the closeness of another human being—not passion or sex, but just touching someone else, holding her hand, catching the scent of her hair. He realized just how lonely he'd become in the past year. Even loners get lonely.

God, she's beautiful, he thought.

Ethel pecked Jay hard in the chest. She had other plans.

This is probably the right place to talk about sex in the year 2287. When male fertility had first begun to really have a serious effect on the world population, sex became extremely important. Some countries even passed laws that said everyone between the ages of sixteen and sixty had to have sex at least once a day, preferably with someone of the opposite gender, whether they felt like it or not. They could have sex with people they wanted to, but they had to do that in their spare time.

Sex Police were organized to check up on everything from how often people did it to how tight men's trousers were. The egg test, in which uncooked eggs were put inside men's underpants, became a common sight on many city streets. If a man couldn't keep twenty-four eggs in his underwear without breaking them, his clothing was deemed to be too tight and he was forced to walk around naked below for a month. Populations in the colder parts of the world dropped even further.

None of these measures helped the world population to increase. In fact, sex became such a stressful occupation for most people, they did their utmost to avoid it. In the seedier parts of cities people went to brothels to drink tea and play Scrabble while computer experts created fake Polaroids of them having sex for them to show the Sex Police.

By the mid-2200s sex had become as dull and boring as it had been in England in the mid-1900s. It happened, but you kept your socks on.

By the time Jay was old enough for all this to affect him, the Sex Police had long ceased to exist. The population had dropped so low that all authority had fizzled out. Sex ceased to be an ordeal and became something people could enjoy again. The trouble was, there was hardly anyone around to enjoy it with and consequently Jay's sexual experiences were extremely limited. With one clumsy exception, no one else had been involved.

"Yes, come on," said the second woman, subtly easing the other one aside and coming closer.

She's even more beautiful, Jay thought.

He felt himself blushing and crossed his arms to cover his rising embarrassment.

"Well, I'd sort of planned on going to the country," he said.

Ethel pecked him again.

"What's that inside your shirt?" said the first woman.

"Nice shirt," said the second woman, obviously impressed. "Only three colors."

"Oh, it's just my chicken," said Jay.

"Chicken? Yeah, right. The last chicken I saw fell out of the sky, landed right on this guy, and killed him," said the man. "Stone dead he was, but we got enough bits to make a great soup."

"You ate a dead man?" said Jay.

"No, you idiot, the bits of chicken," said the first woman.

"Do you get eggs?" said the man.

"No, it's too old for that. It's like a pet, you know?" said Jay.

"A pet? What world are you living in, man? We eat cats and rats here. Do you realize how much soup a whole chicken would make?" said the man.

Jay folded his arms tight around Ethel and backed into the corner. The man was a lot bigger than him and if it came to a fight Jay didn't like his chances, especially as the two women were advancing on him too. He edged back around the column, but there was no way out.

I should give them the stupid chicken, he thought. *What's better, sex with two different women or getting beaten up?*

And as usual, Jay did the opposite of what common sense was telling him.

"No way," said Jay.

"Don't bo ridiculouo," oaid tho man. "You can cithcr hand it over or we can kick the shit out of you and then take it."

"Come on," said the second woman, stroking his arm.

"Oh, cluck," said a small voice inside Jay's shirt.

There was a dull *pop.*

The sun breaking through the yellow clouds cast a sick light over the silent city. Jay turned his face toward the sky but the sunlight was as weak as the moon. The air, trapped under the clouds, was damp and heavy and the only way to keep cool was down in the basements of the deserted buildings. Up on the 127th floor it was even hotter than on street level.

Jay was getting restless in the penthouse. It was time to leave. . . .

"God, I'm bored," said Jay. "Every day just seems like the same one over and over again."

There was another dull *pop.*

"Sorry about that," said Ethel. "Got the timing a bit wrong. That's the trouble with living inside chickens for all these years. Your skills get a bit rusty."

They were standing inside the office reception area. In front of them the man, the two women, and the children were all curled up on the floor as if they were asleep.

"Oh, shit, what've you done?" said Jay. "You've killed them."

"It's okay," said Ethel. "They just got very very tired and fell asleep, and when they wake up, they won't remember ever having seen us before. Come on, we have to cluck off out of here. And by the way, you did well in there. There were a couple of times I thought you were going to give me away, but you did pretty well."

"I have to be honest, I was tempted," said Jay.

"I know," said Ethel, letting Jay think he'd had some choice in the matter.

"If I had made a mistake, you know, like said something about you, couldn't you have just made them forget it?"

"Well, normally yes," said Ethel. "It's not difficult at all. But you humans have such pitifully tiny brains, it's very difficult just erasing a little bit. I usually end up wiping the whole thing out. Mind you, it's pretty hard to tell the cluckin' difference. I'd like to laugh ironically at this point but chickens haven't got the vocal cords for it. Oh, God, I want to go home. I'll be so cluckin' glad when this is all over."

Chapter 3
The Oracle

The street was deserted. The burned-out building was still smoking, but no one else had turned up to look at it. Things had grown like that over the years. People kept away from one another. No one wanted to get involved.

Stress, which had once been a personal thing—you either had it or you didn't—had gradually become part of everyone's lives, like television. You began to feel guilty if you weren't stressed, as if somehow you weren't trying hard enough, and of course that was very stressful. Combined with pollution, it had made 90 percent of men virtually sterile. By 2090, AIDS had already left large areas of the world almost empty and by 2170 sleepy sperm had pretty well emptied the rest. At least that's what everyone thought, or had been led to think by someone or something who or that shall remain nameless at this point in time.

As T. S. Eliot, the famous poet, had predicted a few centuries earlier:

> This is the way the world ends
> This is the way the world ends
> This is the way the world ends
> Not with a bang but a whimper.

Except by the time it had happened everyone was too numbed or bored even to whimper, and it hadn't actually ended, not quite. It was just sort of fizzling out, the last smoldering twigs around the remains of yesterday's bonfire. Jay was one of the twigs and now he was confused. He had put a lot of effort into getting his life as well organized and cool as he could and now there were chickens talking to him.

The past twelve years had been pretty chaotic and if you had any sense you kept your head down, never looked anyone in the eye, and kept out of people's way. Jay had been a child then and lived off his wits, but a lot of his friends hadn't made it. His family had fled to the country. At least that was what Jay had always assumed. Somehow in all the chaos they'd left him behind in the suburbs, the only living thing left in the street, apart from the chickens. Even the last few birds had flown away. Miraculously he had survived and actually flourished. Now he looked at Ethel and began to realize why.

"Have you been looking after me?" he said.

"Yes."

"Why?"

"It's my job," said Ethel.

"Yes, but why me?" said Jay. "Why not one of those people back there?"

"Chance," said Ethel. "Your mom and dad kept chickens. Theirs didn't."

This was not true.

"Oh," said Jay. He had hoped Ethel was going to say that he had been chosen to lead the world back from the brink, been chosen because he was special, the new messiah.

There was stuff that Jay knew that had been denied other people. Before the Big Backlash of 2099 and the book burning, everyone had access to everything, from how to build a patio set out of teak from ethically managed plantations to how to lance a boil when you're stuck in the middle of the Sahara with a jackhammer and no power outlets. The generations that followed knew less and less, and as knowledge is power, they had none of that either. But Ethel had looked after Jay and had filled the attic of his parents' house with three thousand of the world's most useful books. When Jay's parents had disappeared, he had looked for them in the attic and found the books. He had then spent two years reading, so that by the time he was twelve all the most important things mankind had known had gone into his brain. Unfortunately many of them had fallen straight out again and a large number of the books Ethel had saved had been in Latvian, which was as foreign to Jay as Latvian. But there was stuff in his head that no other living human had. He alone on the whole planet knew how to make a mortise and tenon joint, how much yeast to use to make a loaf of bread, and how to use a tourniquet to stop bleeding. He even knew how many roads a man must walk down before you can call him a man.

It was true that Jay had been chosen to be the new messiah, but there was no way Ethel was going to let him know it. He would become far too cocky. Ethel thought he was too stupid for the job, but who was she to question things? She had been given her instructions and if she ever wanted to return home to Megaton she'd have to do as she'd been told.

"No," said Ethel. "I'm afraid it was complete chance."

"I wish you wouldn't keep doing that," said Jay.

"What?"

"You know, like, reading my mind."

"Do you think I enjoy it?" said Ethel. "It's not exactly stimulating, you know."

"You really know how to make someone feel special, don't you, man?" said Jay, slowing down to a sulking shuffle.

"God, you cluckin' humans. Anyone would think you just had unlimited words. You're so dumb, it's amazing your species survived long enough to become extinct."

"I don't understand," said Jay.

"Of course you don't, you're a cluckin' human," said Ethel.

She went on to explain that all living creatures, apart from fish and solicitors, had exactly the same number of heartbeats during their lifetime, so staying laid-back and cool meant you'd live longer. In the same way, everyone who could speak, apart from trained parrots, had the same number of words and when you'd used them up you went dumb.

"Of course, a lot of people use up all their words long before they die and keep on talking," she added, "but they're just talking crap."

"That heartbeat thing's not true, man," said Jay. "It was just a dumb theory."

"Which is more proof of how totally stupid humans are," said Ethel. "Of course it's true. That is why the Greater Patagonian humming condor died out almost as soon as it evolved. Its heart beat at seventeen million beats a minute, so it died almost as soon as it was born."

"Well, the talking thing's not true, man, you're just winding me up," said Jay.

"You could be right," said Ethel. "If you're anything to go by, humans talk crap most of the time."

It hadn't been an accident that Jay's parents had kept chickens, or that Ethel had been one of them. Jay was the Chosen One, picked out of all the children on Earth. There were three other chickens that were not chickens on the planet and they each had a human to protect, though Jay was *the* Chosen One; the other three humans were spares, backups in case anything went wrong. None of the other chickens had made contact with their human companions. Ethel had spoken to Jay only because his life was in danger, not because it had been the right time to do so. That should have been a while away.

There would have been no point in telling Jay any of this. Humans could see things only in terms of their pathetically short life spans. They were quite incapable of seeing the bigger picture. Also, when they did think about the meaning of life, as they liked to call it, they always reached the wrong conclusions. For goodness' sake, they even thought man's fertility collapse and the subsequent drop in population to less than .01 percent were solely due to pollution. How could you explain anything to someone who could get even the most basic things that badly wrong?

There was so much Jay didn't know, so much that Ethel had to tell him, but she had to educate him slowly. Some of what she had to say would challenge fundamental beliefs that mankind had held since it crawled out of the primordial soup, beliefs that Ethel herself had put there.

"Come on," she said, "we have to collect The Oracle."

"The oracle?" said Jay. "What oracle?"

"*The* cluckin' Oracle," said Ethel. "Come on, you read about her in one of the books."

Another tiny wheel clicked in Jay's brain. The jigsaw had begun, though it would be many years before the last piece was put in place. They were sorting out the edge pieces and beginning to join them up. It would be hard work. She had no picture to give Jay for him to work from, so it would be quite a while before he even knew how far apart the corners were. For now it was enough to know things were moving.

How the hell does she know about the books? Jay thought.

He didn't need to answer himself. He didn't know how he knew, but he knew that Ethel had put the books there and she had put them there for him. The thought should have sent a shiver down his spine, but it didn't and that worried him more than the thought itself.

"What, like the old Greek legend?"

"Yes, that's the one," said Ethel. "*The* Oracle."

"Don't be ridiculous," said Jay. "That was just a story."

"And that is exactly why the world is in the state it's in," said Ethel.

"What do you mean?" said Jay.

"Look, it's cluckin' obvious. For thousands of years you've had this immense source of wisdom in your midst and you ignored it," said Ethel. "When the plague came or a world war looked like it was starting, did you go and ask The Oracle what to do? Did you cluck? Too arrogant you all were, and look where it got you. Left here on the verge of extinction."

Jay wanted to protest. Getting your whole race sneered at was bad enough, but getting it sneered at by a chicken was pretty depressing. Maybe he should have handed Ethel over to those people. He'd be having sex and a roast dinner right now instead of trailing meekly along behind a bad-tempered chicken. And why was he trailing along behind her?

Why indeed? he thought. *I could run away, go back and find those people. Down by the river, the woman said.*

"Don't even think about it," said Ethel, and Jay knew he had no choice but to follow her.

They turned onto a short street that led toward a park. Between piles of stripped and burned-out cars, half buried in ivy and covered in bizarre grooves that looked for all the world like something had tried to eat them, there was a well-worn path, obviously frequently used.

"We're not going in there, are we, man?" said Jay.

"Yes," said Ethel. "Pick me up."

"But isn't that, like, where the Fluorides live?"

The Fluorides were the last remaining descendants of the people who had thought toothpaste with fluoride was the greatest invention since sliced bread. And at the time it had been. Everyone had been blessed with wonderfully perfect teeth. They all lived long, productive lives without a day's toothache. Time ravished the rest of them, shrinking, wrinkling, chopping bits off, but they all went to their graves with teeth that shone bright and clear like fresh tombstones. Around the world millions of dentists, deprived of their overpaid elegant lifestyles, committed suicide, so that by the time the terrible long-term effects of fluoride were discovered and it was banned, there was no one left who knew how to treat bad teeth.

It took a few generations for people to realize there was anything wrong, and of course it was all blamed on pollution, stress, and a few other currently fashionable scapegoats. But people started getting shorter, not just a few inches but a lot shorter, and even when they tracked it down to fluoride and stopped using it, the shrinking kept on happening. People were no taller than two-year-old children, and as each generation was born smaller, their teeth turned out bigger, until they could hardly lift their heads, and of course breast-feeding was completely out of the question. Their perfect teeth leached the calcium out of their bones until the last generations had to crawl on all fours, resting their chins on small carts.

Now the Fluorides had almost died out. Their enormously distorted teeth and tiny bodies with bones as thin as twigs had made breeding a difficult and dangerous practice. They lived together in scattered groups in city parks, passing their remaining years trying to bite passers-by on the ankle in the hope of eating their bones. One subspecies who had gone to live in cemeteries had survived and even increased in number, until everyone realized what they were up to and began deboning their loved ones' bodies before they buried them. Cremation had, naturally, been outlawed a long time ago because of the smoke.

It was the Fluorides' teeth marks on the old cars and on the stone gateposts at the entrance to the park, and in the path itself, and in the tree trunks and the garbage cans and everything else that Jay could see.

"Don't worry," said Ethel. "There's hardly any left and they're very old and feeble."

"Yeah, right," said Jay, not convinced. *I don't want to be here,* he thought.

He kept seeing the two women from the office building and wanting to go back. For the past twelve years, since his parents had vanished, Jay had never had to ask anyone's permission for anything. He had gone where he liked when he liked and thought about no one but himself. Life had been hard sometimes but he had always survived and he felt that he had earned the right to answer to no one. Now he was trailing meekly along behind a talking chicken and he didn't like it.

"Anyway, if they come at you, just kick their cart away," said Ethel.

The park was beautiful. The grass that once would have been clipped and manicured into a travesty of nature was now full of wildflowers. They grew tall and spread across the overgrown paths. New trees, no longer torn out, were growing up everywhere. Where a few halfhearted sparrows had once lived there were now dozens of species: Parrots and cockatoos, doves and ducks, had all made their home there, safe from their old predators, the cats. The cats themselves had been threatened with extinction by hungry people, but cats are sly creatures and had taken to living in drains, where only the smallest children could reach them. The greenhouses stood broken and open to the sky like old skeletons, their once tame contents bursting out into the daylight. Nature, no longer repressed, fed and poisoned into submission, was giving vent to her feelings and sending her children out to reclaim the city.

As Jay followed Ethel's directions, he saw signs of the

Fluorides' presence here and there—flattened grass, huge teeth marks in the earth—and heard the occasional strange lisping gurgle. Unable to speak normally because of their gigantic teeth, they had long ceased to communicate with the rest of the world.

"I don't know why you want to go to the country," said Ethel. "Look at all this."

"It's not the same," said Jay.

"It soon will be," said the old chicken. "Come on."

She directed Jay around the back of a stand of trees to where a small pond sat hidden among some bamboo.

"Put me down, put me down," Ethel said, and walked over to the water's edge. She reached down and stroked the water with her wing, and as she did so a goldfish swam toward her and stuck its head out of the water.

"Who calls The Oracle?" said the fish. "Oh, it's you. Did you bring a jam jar?"

"No, I forgot," said Ethel. "It's okay. I'll send the boy off to find one."

Jay didn't like being referred to as "the boy," especially by a talking chicken, and doubly especially by a talking chicken talking to a talking goldfish. Things were getting altogether just too far-fetched to be believable, yet it was happening. It wasn't a dream. He wasn't drunk, like the time he'd found that stuff his dad kept hidden in the back of his shed. He was standing in a park of weird teeth on legs watching a chicken talking to a goldfish.

Tell me this isn't happening, he thought. *I want to be somewhere else.*

But Jay knew he couldn't be. He wanted to. He wanted to run, to try and go back a few hours to just before he got in the elevator, to the last time life had any semblance of reality, but it was as though Ethel had an invisible rope around his neck that made it impossible for him to leave.

"This," said Ethel, pointing at the fish, "is *The* Oracle. Oracle, Jay. Jay, The Oracle."

"A fish?"

"Yeah," said the fish, "The Oracle is a fish. What do you have against fish?"

"Well, uh . . ."

"Apart from birds trying to eat The Oracle all the time, and children with fishing rods trying to catch her, and the water freezing over in winter, and the pond getting awfully overcrowded with those common frogs, and the Fluorides trying to scoop her out with their teeth, and the lack of male company, and fin rot and toxic algae blooms. Apart from that, it's super," said the fish.

"I thought The Oracle was a woman," said Jay.

"Yeah, well, she was," said The Oracle. "When The Oracle arrived on Earth, a few thousand years ago, she chose a woman's body not a frightfully clever thing to do. She assumed that as women were the most levelheaded creatures on the planet, they'd sort of be in charge. It never occurred to her that men, with their tiny brains and stupid appendage obsession, would be running things. So Plan A was a bit of a cock-up really. Tons of people came to see The Oracle of course, to benefit from her staggeringly immense wisdom, but as soon as they saw she was a woman, most of them ignored her advice. Trouble is, it was too late by then. Once The Oracle had chosen to be female there was no going back. So when the first body wore out, The Oracle decided to try another species, and since then she has been working her way through every living creature on the planet and at the moment The Oracle is a fish."

"Why couldn't you, like, just stay a woman or become a man?"

"Well, The Oracle sort of thought she would see if she could do better than humans," said the fish. "Sort of give everyone a fair go. So every time the body she was in wore out she changed species. Sometimes the old body sort of got killed and The Oracle had to take over the nearest species, but as for being a man, thanks but no thanks, all that stupid testosterone and the hilarious dangly bits. Still, it's actually not much fun being a fish. The Oracle liked it best when she was a spaniel. That was super."

"We had a spaniel," said Jay, "in the old days, when my mom and dad . . ."

He went quiet. He hadn't thought about the past for months.

31

It always made him sad, so he tried not to do it. His plans to go to the countryside had vaguely included the dream that he might find his parents. Not that there was anything to suggest they'd gone to the country. They could be ten streets away for all he knew. It had been almost twelve years since he'd seen them. He wondered if they had ever tried to find him. He'd stayed in the house reading all the hidden books for two years, but they'd never come back in that time. They might not even be alive anymore, though there was no reason to think they weren't. There were no marauding gangs anymore. They'd fizzled out long before Jay had been born. People tended to ignore one another nowadays, avoid one another. Of course, out in the country it might be different.

"The Oracle knows that," said the fish. "She was that spaniel."

"Rusty?"

"Yeah."

"You're telling me that you used to be my dog Rusty?" said Jay.

"Yeah, absolutely, old chap, woof, woof and all that sort of thing," said the fish.

"Yeah, right. You don't expect me to believe that, do you?"

"The Oracle never lies. The Oracle cannot lie, and besides she can jolly well prove it," said the fish.

"Oh, yeah, like how?"

"Remember when you used to go and play down by the river and you built a hideout in those bushes? Remember what you used to do in there with those magazines that your dad had hidden with the booze in his shed?"

"Okay, okay, I believe you," said Jay, turning very red.

"Right, now you trot off like a good chap and get a jam jar while Ethel and The Oracle have a chat. It's been twelve years since they were both in your back garden. They've tons of catching up to do."

"So what am I supposed to call you now—Rusty?" said Jay.

"No, no, The Oracle has another name now," said the fish.

"What is it?" said Jay.

"The Oracle would rather not say," said the fish.

"Go on."

"You'll laugh."

"No, no, I won't," said Jay, "honest."

"It's Fluffy."

Jay laughed.

"The Oracle was a rabbit before she was a fish," said The Oracle.

"Yeah, right, so why didn't you, like, change your name?" said Jay.

"The Oracle has used them all up," said The Oracle, "even Sharon. That's when she was a hairdresser. The Oracle has used the lot."

"Look," said Ethel, "can we get a move on? It'll be dark soon. Do you want to be stuck here in the dark with the Fluorides?"

"Exactly. The Oracle's name is Fluffy and that's all there is to it," said the fish. "Now, toddle off and get a jam jar so we can get out of here."

As Jay walked off he could hear the fish saying, "Whatever happened to that nice young cockerel?"

He walked around the edge of the park, peering into the few remaining garbage cans, but there was nothing but dead leaves in them and nesting sparrows that looked up at him totally unafraid. He picked up a stick and kept his eyes and ears peeled, but there was no sign of the Fluorides. He saw a group of people like him in the distance, but he hid behind the bushes until they were out of sight. After the incident back in the office block he didn't feel like talking to anyone else yet. He wasn't sure when he would be ready, but it wasn't yet.

I want to go, Jay thought. *I could be at the river in ten minutes. What am I doing? I must be crazy.*

Jay tried to shut the voice out. He knew now that whatever Ethel instructed him to do, he would do it. His common sense told him he had no common sense. He had to be the only human in history who had ever been ordered around by a chicken. But there was something else that overrode common sense. There was a feeling of potential excitement, a feeling that he was on the verge of a whole new life, a life beyond imagination. He couldn't put it into words but there was an irresistible attraction that he couldn't resist. He felt adrenaline tingling in his veins and he wanted more of it.

He knew as he walked out of the park that this was his last chance to leave. He knew Ethel had given him the chance. He tried to bring back the brief memory of the woman in the office block, to recall her smiling face, but it had gone.

He went into a derelict café. Among the trash on the floor was a jar of pickled eggs, or rather a jar of murky green liquid with what looked like things that might once, in a former life, many, many decades ago, have been pickled eggs.

A family of cockroaches sat in a line on the counter staring at Jay. The biggest one, almost the size of Jay's fist, spat at him, so Jay emptied the slimy green eggs over it. The smell was overpowering. Jay could feel the acrid fumes in the back of his throat. The giant cockroach staggered around, rubbing at its eyes. It threw itself onto its back, thrashed around for a minute, and died. The other cockroaches gathered around it and stood silently for a moment before throwing themselves onto the corpse and eating it. Jay wondered how long it would be before humans were doing the same, recycling one another. Maybe it was already happening. They were certainly eating the cockroaches, though Jay had never been able to bring himself to. The eggs dissolved the counter, sank through the linoleum, and began to eat their way to the center of the earth.

When he got back to the pond, the chicken and the fish were still deep in conversation. Jay dipped the jar in the water and Fluffy swam in.

"Oh, God, I say, steady on," she said. "It smells like hundred-year-old pickled eggs in here."

"Don't talk about eggs," snapped Ethel.

As they walked back through the park, Jay caught his first sight of the Fluorides. A small group of them scuttled across the path in front of them like a troop of weird crabs. Only these crabs had faces that were almost human. Jay could hardly bear to look at them, but he couldn't look away. Their carts were old and half broken and their eyes stared up at him, full of tears. Their faces were covered with scratches and scabs from foraging in the undergrowth. They looked sad and pathetic, like the rejects from some mad scientist's experiments. Jay's heart went out to the poor sad creatures that many generations before had been the same as him.

There but for the lack of dental hygiene of my ancestors go I, he thought.

"Careful," said Ethel.

"But they look so sad," said Jay.

"Beware the Fluorides of March," said The Oracle.

"That's when they're the most dangerous," said Ethel. "It's an old hunting trick."

And as she said it, the nearest Fluoride opened its mouth, reared up on its tiny back legs, and threw itself at Jay, but before it could reach him there was a flash of brilliant light and it fell dead at his feet. In the panic, the other Fluorides scuttled off into the bushes and Jay dropped Fluffy's jar.

The fish was flapping around in the grass. Jay scooped her up into the jar and ran back to the pond for more water.

"The Oracle says thank you," said the fish as they were walking back.

"I've never, like, saved anyone's life before," said Jay, pretty pleased with himself.

"The Oracle is immortal, actually," said The Oracle, but seeing Jay's expression, she added, "Still, you did a good job. Another few seconds and The Oracle would have had to take over the nearest spare body and that was the dead Fluoride."

When they got back, Ethel was pecking around in the grass and the dead creature was gone.

"Where is it?" said Jay, wondering if maybe he didn't want to know.

"I sent it packing," said Ethel.

"What, you mean you can bring the dead back to life?" said Jay.

"Oh, yes," said Ethel, "piece of cake. One living cell, that's all you need."

"Wow, man, cool."

"I suppose," said Ethel.

"Well, The Oracle is impressed," said The Oracle.

"So if you had, say, like, a single hair, you could bring Elvis back to life?" said Jay.

Although Elvis had died long before Jay's great-great-grandfather had been born, some legends just go on forever, like Coca-Cola and the G-spot, albeit in stories that became more and more distorted with each passing generation. Though there were unconfirmed rumors that Coke was still being made by a group of people deep in the heart of America.

"Could, did," said Ethel. "Cluckin' ungrateful bastard."

This was not strictly true.

"So you could do it for, like, anyone?" said Jay.

"Oh, yeah," said Ethel nonchalantly.

"John Lennon?"

"Yeah, yeah, yeah," said Ethel. "Can we go now?"

"I want to go to New York," said Jay.

"One day, one day," said Ethel, "maybe."

Chapter 4
How Many Roads . . .

They left the park and walked north through streets of empty office blocks. Almost no one lived there now. The buildings were so close together, it was always gloomy and cold, with no sunlight. It was dangerous to be there too. The skyscrapers had been built at the end of the twentieth century by shortsighted men too old to care about tomorrow. They had been built with a life span of fifty years and now they were more than 250 years old and falling apart.

These streets had once housed the controllers of the world—the banks, the stock exchange, the moneylenders disguised as noble corporations. Their buildings, although designed to last so short a time, had been built to impress, to outshine their neighbors. There were no dark alleys here, no tenements, no poverty at all. Yet like everything else it had all come to an end. The lights had gone out years ago, the lights in the buildings and the lights in the minds of those who had worked in them. Prime real estate was now no more than streets of ghosts where only the desperate or foolhardy ever set foot.

"Did we have to come this way?" said Jay. He had always avoided the place. Everyone knew how dangerous it was and people always claimed to know someone who had gone there and never come back.

"Yes," said Ethel, "absolutely."

"But it's dangerous, man," said Jay. "You know, any one of these buildings could come crashing down any minute with us underneath it. It is not a cool place to be, you know?"

"You're perfectly safe," said Ethel, and as she spoke an eighty-five-story bank collapsed into the street two hundred yards behind them. Almost in slow motion, like it was too weary to fall down quickly, it disintegrated into a pile of rubble and dust.

"See," said Jay, diving into a doorway, "we could've been underneath that."

"No, we couldn't," said Ethel.

"Come on, if we'd been just a few seconds later, we would be dead now."

"Put me down," said Ethel. "I'll show you."

She turned and faced the fallen building, and as she did so, the dust cleared and the broken steel and concrete rose slowly in the air until once again the whole building was standing on its foundation, but instead of the crumbling wreck that had been there a few minutes before, it now looked like it had just been built. Every window shone like new. The steel doors sparkled in the weak rays of the setting sun that trickled down the street, and all the windows were alive with light. Of course it was partly an optical illusion. Sure, the building was standing again. Sure, it was as immaculate as the day it had first opened its doors for business, but the great brass door handles were only a vision planted in Jay's brain. Someone had stolen the original ones years ago and Ethel couldn't track them.

"Wow! Shit, man," said Jay.

"You see," said Ethel. "There was no way that building could have fallen on us. It was old and tired and ready to fall, sure, and I was happy to let it, but not with us underneath it, not until we were safely past. And please, don't say 'Wow' again, it drives me crazy."

"Uh . . . ," said Jay.

"Now come on, we're in a hurry," said Ethel.

"Hurry, what for?" said Jay.

"We need to get down that next street in three minutes," said Ethel. "A building's going to collapse and we have to rescue someone."

"Who?" said Jay.

"Your wife."

"What?" said Jay.

"Your wife," said Ethel.

"Don't be ridiculous, man," said Jay. "I don't have a wife."

"I know that," said Ethel. "That's why we're going to get you one."

"I don't think you, like, quite understand—," said Jay.

"Understand, understand?" interrupted Ethel. "Me, who can raise entire buildings . . . me, who can control time . . . me, who can shrink you to the size of a cluckin' mouse . . . me, who has the entire knowledge of twenty-seven universes stored in a very tiny part of my immense brain, not understand? I don't think so, sonny."

"Yeah, well, right, but you don't understand about love, man," said Jay.

"Listen, stupid," said Ethel, "before I came to your crappy little planet I'd been married eighty-seven times. I've mothered, fathered, and three other-gendered three hundred sixty-seven children. I know all there is to know about love, and believe me, sonny, it's just chemicals and hormones cluckin' around in your body."

"Don't be ridiculous, man, it's more than that."

"Oh, yes, what more?" said Ethel.

"Well, it's, uh . . . it's, like, uh . . . about love, sort of, uh . . . wanting to spend the rest of your life with someone. It's about the look in her eyes and the way she smiles and the smell of her hair," said Jay.

"Exactly, chemicals and hormones," said Ethel.

"No, it's not," said Jay. "It's about soul."

"Oh, yes," said Ethel, "and what's one of those, then?"

"You wouldn't understand, man," said Jay, beginning to feel miserable and rather lonely. *I bet the woman by the river would understand,* he thought, but that battle was long lost.

"Look, sonny," said Ethel, "I know what soul is. I'm in love too, you know. It's just that he, or she—it's been so long, I can't remember—happens to be a few trillion light-years away. Not that he or she even knew I existed. I sent him or her a bouquet of the finest, most radioactive plutonium, but did he or she take any notice, did he or she cluck?"

"Yeah, well," said Jay.

"Anyway, you'll see," said Ethel. "Now come on, we've got to hurry."

All through Jay's life, from the day he was born, the voice inside his head had tried to make him sparkle, make his adrenaline bubble and boil instead of just sitting there fermenting. Most people's consciences were, as their name implied, conscientious. They steered their hosts away from danger and illegal or immoral practices. Jay's had tried to do the opposite. It had led Jay down dubious paths. It had tried to teach him to take risks, even to the point of endangering his life. The flying idea up in the penthouse had just been the latest in a line of stupid ideas. Every time his inner voice had persuaded Jay to do something potentially suicidal, fate had always intervened. A door had slammed just as Jay had been about to stick his fingers in the light socket. The rope had snapped just before he had been about to walk across it over the raging torrent. It seemed fate had always been there. And now fate had a name—Ethel the cluckin' chicken.

The sun had gone below the horizon and the air was growing cool. The sky, flat yellow gray as always from side to side, glowed with the promise of a beautiful tomorrow, but then it glowed like that every night, summer, winter, spring, whatever—it looked the same every damn night. Like the population itself, the weather had fizzled out too. It promised a beautiful tomorrow but all it ever delivered was a carbon copy of today, over and over and over again.

The good old days, when the skies were blue and crisscrossed with the cobwebs of the vapor trails of planes, had passed long before Jay had been born. He'd seen a hot-air balloon once, watched it from the penthouse about a year ago. It had risen from the small park by the river and floated silently up into the morning sky. It had looked so peaceful as it drifted over the treetops toward him, and rather less peaceful as it crashed into the wall below him and plummeted to the ground. Now the skies were yellow and empty. Even the birds were too bored to venture up into them.

Colin Thompson

The occasional swarm of giant cockroaches, glowing radioactive in the dark, flew by like a small constellation, but apart from them there was nothing, not even any mosquitoes. The last of them had been wiped out in the Great Spray of 2070; 1,827,000,000 people had been wiped out in the Great Spray too, but the world government had told everyone that it was a small price to pay to save the world from mosquito bites. Everyone had just spread out a bit and filled up the gaps. Nature went even more out of balance and all the insect repellent companies went bankrupt.

"Here we are," said Ethel as they reached another fallen skyscraper. "She's in there."

"Who is?" said Jay.

"Don't you listen to anything? I told you, your wife, the woman of your cluckin' dreams," said Ethel. *And I should cluckin' know,* she thought, having spent a lot of time inside Jay's dreams, watching and taking notes at first, being disgusted a lot of the time, and more recently actually writing the scripts.

"Look, just drop all that, will you?" said Jay, but he had to admit he was intrigued.

"Yeah, yeah," said Ethel. "Put it this way. In the ruins of that collapsed office block the most beautiful girl you are ever going to see in your whole cluckin' life is trapped. She's injured and she's very hungry."

"So why can't you just lift the whole building up like you did back there?" said Jay.

"Because if I do," Ethel explained, "she'll be crushed to death."

The girl hadn't been inside the building before it collapsed. She hadn't even existed. As they had approached the ruin, Ethel had created her and buried her under a mountain of filing cabinets deep inside its broken walls. Why she hadn't just brought her into being out in the street or back in the park is a mystery, but then Ethel moved in a mysterious way, her wonders to perform.

"I'm not going in there," said Jay. "The whole thing could, like, collapse on me at any second."

Jay was about to say that his chest hurt but Ethel stared

41

hard at him with a look he would come to know well in the future. There was a silent *pop* and Jay heard himself say, "So why can't you just lift the whole building up like you did back there?"

"Because if I do," Ethel explained, "she'll be crushed to death."

"Okay, tell me what to do," said Jay.

This was how it would be for the foreseeable future. Ethel would say jump and Jay would jump. She would allow him to protest a bit but then she would tweak a few of his brain cells and her wishes would become Jay's, though even Ethel had her bad days.

Ethel stared at the ruins, and as she did so, great lumps of concrete and twisted girders lifted gently into the air and floated like feathers back over their heads into the empty street behind them.

"All right," she said. "You have to do the rest. Go through that door."

The door was on its side. Jay pulled it open and crawled down along the floor that had once been the wall, and as he did so he heard Ethel's voice inside his head. *Left here. Down here. Through that window, watch the broken glass. Right here. Don't kneel on those thumbtacks.*

Chapter 5

The Bells, the Bells

As he crawled deeper and deeper into the building, it grew darker and darker apart from a strange unnatural glow that was just enough to see by but no more. Jay stopped at a place where four corridors met, and listened. There was total and complete silence, except . . .

What have you stopped for? said Ethel inside his head. Her voice had grown weaker as Jay had crawled farther into the ruins.

"Shhh, man, I'm listening," said Jay.

Listening? There's nothing to cluckin' listen to.

"I can hear a bell," said Jay.

No, you can't, said Ethel.

"I can," insisted Jay. "It's beautiful."

It's inside your head, said Ethel. *You're imagining it.*

"I'm not. Someone is ringing a bell. I can hear it. It's down there," said Jay, crawling along a corridor where the strange unnatural glow wasn't glowing.

The bell was just a faint tinkling in the distance, but inside Jay's head it sounded like the song of an angel, a siren luring him away from everything, and I mean everything, not just Ethel and his mission to rescue the most beautiful girl he would ever see in his life, but even from life itself. The pull was irresistible, so strong that he almost forgot to breathe.

Don't go down there, said Ethel's voice, but her words seemed far away, lost on an alien breeze.

Jay was aware that the chicken did not want him to follow

the noise. But it was also obvious that she was not as strong as he had thought, unless it was just being farther away from her that was doing it. But whatever the reason, she seemed unable to stop him. Ethel made a few pieces of the wall collapse behind him, but Jay kept on going. The pull was too strong to avoid, though he had no intention of avoiding it and would have killed his own mother—if he had known for sure she was still alive and she had been standing in front of him, which of course she would have had to be alive to do—to get to it.

"I can definitely hear it now," said Jay, stopping outside a door marked THE FRIENDS OF THE EARTHMOVER. "It's in there."

Just leave it alone, said Ethel, far away, not just in distance but in time, too. *Anyway, the door's locked,* she added, summoning up all her power and locking it.

"That's all right, the key's lying on the floor," said Jay.

Cluck, said the chicken, and that was the last word Jay heard her say. If she had been there instead of three hundred yards away through a huge pile of steel and concrete, she might have been able to make Jay forget about the bell completely.

I must be losing my touch, she thought, but she knew it was nothing of the sort. There was another force in the world, a force greater than her own. It was masking Ethel's powers for reasons of its own. Maybe, and this made Ethel scared for the first time in living memory, maybe it had engineered the whole situation of making Ethel create Jay's wife in a collapsed building, rather than out in the park, which was where Ethel had originally planned to do it, just to lead Jay to the bell. Maybe Ethel, who had always thought of herself as Earth's puppet master, was just another puppet. And maybe that greater force had a puppet master of its own. Maybe they were all endless reflections in two opposing mirrors.

In the cool of early evening as she stood by the ruined building, the old chicken felt a shiver run down her spine, a shiver she had no control over. Things were about to happen in the world and the old chicken began to wonder if she had left it all too late. There comes a point in life when it's time to hang up your ballet shoes, retire from the world, and spend the rest of your days watching the sunset. Ethel wondered if that time was now. She wanted it to be but was afraid it wasn't. She wasn't going to be let off that lightly. She knew there was much hard work ahead, difficult times that would need her strongest powers and test her to the point of breaking, but she felt weary of Earth, weary of being stuck in a chicken's body, almost weary of life itself. If only she had someone to talk to.

Jay opened the door and walked into a room that looked like a museum display. There was an old wooden desk and chair with a cardigan draped over its back, and in the middle of the table was an old manual typewriter. He felt like he had gone back 350 years in time into a black and white movie. Everything was buried under centuries of soft dust like the down on a baby's head. Everything, that is, except the typewriter, which sat in a clear, dust-free circle shining like it was brand new. Actually, it was even older than Ethel, older in fact by several millennia than the first typewriter that mankind had made. The ringing that Jay had heard was the bell inside the typewriter, a small ringing that seemed to be calling him. Jay went over to it and as he did so the typewriter began typing.

Beware of strangers bearing
small gifts with yolks in them,

it wrote, followed by a carriage return and two line feeds. The keys danced under invisible fingers. Jay leaned forward to pull the sheet of yellowed paper out of the machine, but the bell began ringing frantically.

Things are not what they seem,

it continued. Jay waited. Nothing happened until he leaned forward to take the paper, when the typing started again.

On the other hand, they might be.

This time he waited for almost a minute before approaching

the machine and once again, when he did so, it started again.

Or not.

It seemed like ten minutes before it added,

Maybe.

"Is that it?" said Jay.

Yes,

wrote the typewriter. Jay reached out and pulled the paper from the machine. It felt ice-cold to the touch, so cold that it stuck to his skin, so cold that he felt his blood begin to freeze and a shiver run through his bones. As he tried to shake it from his fingers it grew warmer, taking its heat from Jay himself.

Throw it away, he thought. *Get out of here.*

But something made him fold the paper and put it in his pocket. It felt warm through the fabric, like it was alive. It seemed to be breathing in exact synchronization with his own heart.

Jay realized that all the time he'd been inside the office Ethel hadn't said a single word. It was like there was an invisible shield that she couldn't penetrate. He called out to the chicken, but there was no reply. She couldn't hear him, unless of course she was pretending. Maybe she had only been faking and had meant him to go into the room all along. For the first time he began to feel slightly uneasy about her, as though there was a lot more going on than he knew about. Which of course there was, but then, don't we all have that feeling from time to time?

When he got back to the place where the four corridors met, Ethel's voice said in a strange, gentle sort of way with the tiniest hint of menace, so tiny most people wouldn't have noticed it, *You shouldn't have done that,* and Jay became aware of the pain in his ribs returning.

Chapter 6
The Most Beautiful Girl You Have
Ever Seen in Your Life

"Okay, which way?" said Jay, deciding the best thing to do would be to change the subject and not talk about the typewriter.

Come on, hurry up, said Ethel's voice. *You're nearly there. Start calling.*

She looked inside Jay's mind to find out what had just happened but there was a tiny part that was now closed off. She circled around it, but without the magic PIN number there was no way in. This bore the hallmark of the Blind Piano Tuner.

"HELLO," shouted Jay. The pain in his chest was getting worse. It felt as if someone had reached inside him and pulled one of his ribs out.

"DOWN HERE," a voice, probably the most beautiful voice Jay had ever heard, called back.

Left. Along the corridor, said Ethel. *Stop. This is it.*

Jay opened a door in the ceiling that had once been the wall and climbed up into a room.

"Hello," he called again.

"Over here. I'm over here behind the filing cabinets," said the voice, and the voice was definitely the most beautiful voice that Jay had ever heard.

Careful, said Ethel.

It took Jay nearly an hour to clear a way through the filing cabinets. It was like one of those awful games where you have to remove a single stick without disturbing any of the others.

One by one he eased them out of the way until he lifted the last one and reached her. He felt a lump in his throat and the pain in his chest grew stronger.

Wow, I have seen heaven, he thought.

The girl was truly the most beautiful girl he had ever seen. She was the girl of his dreams, not in the love-story meaning of the words but really. When he had dreamed, he had dreamed of her. He had seen her face so many times, he could close his eyes and remember its every detail. The short dark hair making a ragged fringe over her forehead, the eyes the same color as the hair, it was all exactly the same as he had dreamed. It was almost like he had known her for years.

Jay himself had short dark ragged hair and the similarity didn't end there. They were both slightly built, with the sallow skin that came from ancestors who had traveled the world. Jay looked down at the girl's hands and even the tips of her fingers narrowed the same way that his did, with the fourth finger as long as the middle one. But it was the eyes that captured him. When he looked into them it was like looking into a mirror.

Since Ethel had cloned the girl from Jay's seventh rib, she was bound to look like his twin. Maybe that was why Jay had kept dreaming about her, maybe it was just vanity on his part.

"Are you all right?" he said.

"I think my leg is broken," said the most beautiful girl in the world.

Until Jay had asked her, she had been unaware of any feelings at all. When she thought about it later, she realized that she had no memories at all before that point.

"I'll go and find something to use as a splint," said Jay.

"My arm's broken too."

"I'll get two splints."

"Like, both arms."

"Okay, three."

"And maybe my ribs, too."

"I better get the chicken."

"What?"

"I'll explain later," Jay said, and turned to crawl back up to the surface.

"Don't go," said the girl. "I can't stand being here alone in the dark again."

"How long have you been here?" said Jay.

"I don't know. It feels like forever."

"We can't stay here," said Jay. "The whole place could collapse at any minute."

"All right, but don't be long."

"I won't," said Jay. "And by the way, I love you."

He touched her outstretched hand and felt his breath fade away. His heart danced and with each beat reminded him of the pain in his ribs.

Chemicals and hormones, chemicals and hormones, said Ethel inside his head, but even she had to admit there was something more. She felt excited that it all seemed to have worked so well. She felt jealous, too.

"I know," said the girl. "My name's Kay."

Jay had gone only a few yards up the corridor when he bumped into Ethel. She followed him back into the room and walked over to the girl.

"Oh, shit," said Kay. "It really is a chicken."

"Not exactly," Jay said, and tried to explain exactly who Ethel was and what had happened.

Kay found it difficult to concentrate on what Jay was saying, partly from pain and partly from hunger, but mostly because Ethel was standing on her chest staring straight into her eyes, and there are few things as disconcerting as a chicken standing up close to your face staring at you, especially when you know beyond any doubt that the chicken is far more intelligent than you are or ever will be.

"Yeah, right. You don't expect me to believe all that crap, do you?" she said, sitting up.

"Lift your left arm," said Jay, and Kay did.

"Lift your right arm," said Ethel, and Kay did.

"Lift your leg," said Jay, and Kay did.

"Oh, my God," gasped Kay.

"Yeah, yeah," said Ethel.

"I don't suppose you could, like, fix me, too, could you?" said Jay. "I've got a terrible pain in my ribs. I must have strained myself moving all the filing cabinets."

"Oh, cluck," said Ethel, "I forgot about the rib."

"And this is The Oracle," said Jay, picking up Fluffy's jar when they reached the outside again.

"Oh, I thought you'd brought me a snack," said Kay, who couldn't remember the last time she'd eaten.

"This will tide you over," said Ethel, laying an egg. "But I don't want to talk about it."

Jay thought about the words on the paper warning him about gifts with yolks in them, but he said nothing. Mainly because he couldn't think of what to say.

Chapter 7
By the (Massive) Powers
Vested in Me

They passed the old stock exchange. In its prime it had been a beautiful building covered in ornate marble, the sort of building that great wealth had put up to slap the rest of the world in the face. Now it was a sad broken shadow of its glorious past, but it hadn't been the passing of time that had wrecked this place. It had been the so-called Yuppie Riots of 2177, when the world finally decided it had had enough, when everyone decided, after more than two centuries of being screwed with fictitious wheeling and dealing, that it was time for it to stop.

The population had dropped to a tenth of earlier levels but still the money dealers carried on as though nothing had changed, until one weekend when everything, absolutely everything, devalued by 746 percent. The world's financial computers had decided that the population had dropped below the critical mass and had simply shut down. All previous crashes were renamed "tiny readjustments" and people who had gone to bed on Friday night as millionaires woke up on Monday and found they owed their brokers billions of dollars. Suddenly the wealthy were poor and no amount of money made any difference.

All around the world, from the London Stock Exchange to the Ulan Bator Investment Yurt, angry crowds stormed the money markets, wrecked all the terminals—or, in Ulan Bator's case, snapped all the counting sticks—and killed all the brokers. Within twenty-four hours 95 percent of the yuppies were dead and the rest had fled as fast as their Porsches could carry them.

In the next month most of the remaining dealers were tracked down. Unable to give up their Armani suits or ostentatious lifestyle, they had found it difficult to hide. Rumors sprang up of yuppies who had gone underground, slipped away with their live-in prenuptial-agreement partners to the depths of Patagonia, where they were forming the Ongoing Broker Liberation Front, surviving on betel juice latte and planning one day to go public. A few were caught in special traps, unable to resist the bait of a bulging Filofax wrapped in a pair of brightly colored suspenders, but the leaders were never found and after a few years they were actually put on the endangered species list, passing into myth with the Loch Ness Monster and the yeti.

Of course, without money as their central focus, governments all around the world had fallen too and for ten wild years anarchy reigned. The ridiculous thing was that hundreds of people had predicted what would happen, but no one with any power had listened to them.

By the time our travelers passed the old stock exchange it was almost dark. The moon shone weakly through the yellow gray haze that covered the world, its insipid glow too feeble to light up the road ahead, but with Ethel's help they picked their way through the deserted streets of rubble until they were clear of the skyscrapers and once again back in the more open streets of the old department stores and shopping malls. There were more signs of recent occupation here: the contents of shops dragged out into the streets and ransacked for anything useful, clear worn paths, and the occasional flicker of a small fire silhouetting the shapes of people. They passed through unnoticed, walking in silence, following Ethel into the darkness.

"Okay," she said at last, entering a large department store. "This place is empty. We'll spend the night here."

As she walked into the darkness the store lights came on one by one, and as the group passed them they went out again. They followed the chicken up to the third floor, to the furniture department, where they found some old mattresses to sleep on.

"I don't suppose anyone's got anything to eat, have they?" said Kay, eyeing Fluffy. "It seems like so long since I ate, I can't actually remember my last meal."

"What would you like?" said Ethel.

"What I'd like," said Jay, "is a great big steak, a mountain of french fries, and three icy mugs of beer."

"Okay," said Ethel, and turning to Kay, she added, "and what about you?"

"But I suppose," Jay continued, "I'll make do with the usual dandelion leaves and a bit of sun-dried cat."

"I'll have what he's having," said Kay. Ethel's egg had been the first thing she'd ever eaten and she didn't have the faintest idea what steaks or french fries or even sun-dried cats were.

"Okay," said Ethel again, and as they watched, a table slid across the floor, dusted itself, sort of beckoned two chairs, hid itself under a shining white tablecloth that seemed to materialize out of thin air, and covered itself in exactly what Kay and Jay had asked for, not the dandelion leaves but the steaks and french fries and even the beer. Jay had never actually seen any of these things before, except in one of his books. When he thought about it, it seemed rather cruel, considering the state of the world, that Ethel had included a ten-volume set of the world's greatest recipes, with full-color photos, in his three thousand books. He assumed she must have had a reason, but apart from being sadistic, he couldn't think of one.

"Some, uh, fried chicken, too, if you can manage it," said Jay, "nothing personal."

"It's the least I can do," said Ethel, "for your wedding breakfast."

"WHAT?" said Kay and Jay at exactly the same time.

"Actually, it's not the least I can do," said Ethel. "This is the least I can do."

And the tables, the chairs, and the whole sumptuous feast vanished into thin air and where they had been was a wooden box with two tin cans of muddy water and two very old paper plates covered in wriggling worms and cats' eyes.

"Actually, I suppose I could do less than that really," said Ethel, making the cats' eyes vanish.

"Yeah, right, very clever," said Kay. "What's all this about a wedding?"

"Can we, like, have our food back?" said Jay.

"Never mind the freakin' food, man," said Kay. "I want to know, like, what the chicken's talking about with all this wedding shit. What wedding?"

Kay was full of inner confusion, but there was no way she was going to let anyone know that. She was twenty-four years old, which was strange, considering that Jay was only twenty-two and she had been cloned from him. She had a head full of knowledge, tidy facts that Ethel had put there, but she had almost no memories of past events. Ethel had thought about copying Jay's brain in its entirety into Kay's head, but had decided against it. It would have created far more problems than it would have solved. So there was a large part of Kay's head that should have been full of life experience that was almost empty. It had seen less than a sixteen-year-old novice nun or a twenty-nine-year-old computer programmer. Like the computer programmer, the memory area of her brain was sitting alone in a dark room, but the screen was blank and it had no can of high-caffeine cola.

"You and him," said Ethel. "It's your wedding day."

"Don't be so stupid," said Kay. "We've only known each other five minutes."

Ethel stared at Kay and inside her head new thoughts appeared. Kay heard herself say, "But I haven't got a thing to wear."

"I think that long white dress is perfect," said Jay.

"Oh," said Kay, staring at her reflection in the mirror that had sidled up to her. "Cool."

Kay had been created angry—not deliberately, but suddenly coming into being under a pile of filing cabinets is not the subconscious's idea of birth and it was pissed. But now, as she looked at Jay, she felt the warm glow of love crawl over her. He was gorgeous. At that moment in time she had never actually seen her own reflection in a mirror. She had caught a faint glimpse as they passed dirty windows, but something about Jay looked so familiar and comfortable. She felt sure that she had dreamed about him at some point in the past. Ethel created that point and Kay remembered a beautiful dream that made her warm glow a lot warmer.

"We hardly know each other, man," said Jay. "Couldn't we, like, sort of leave it for a while?"

Ethel stared at Jay and the memories of dreams came into his head too. He heard himself say, "It's so weird how many things we've got in common."

"Yes," said Kay.

"Yes, isn't it?" Ethel said, and with a big flash of smoke brought the table, chairs, and food back again to distract them.

Fluffy stuck her head out of her jar and said, "Listen, chaps, pay attention. The Oracle has something terribly important to say, actually, a bit of ancient wisdom and all that."

"Go on, then," said Ethel.

"Oh," said The Oracle. "What, now?"

"Yes," said everyone in unison.

"Um, okay," The Oracle said, and recited:

> "This is the way the world ends
> This is the way the world ends
> This is the way the world ends
> Not with a bang but a whippet."

"WHIMPER!" shouted Jay and Kay.

"The Oracle whimpers for no one," The Oracle said, and went back down into her jar to sulk.

The incredibly short memory span of fish meant that she forgot about sulking before she was even back under the water.

"Yeah, right, good. Okay," said Ethel, "time to get married."

"But who's going to give the bride away?" said Jay.

"Yeah, and who's going to be the best man, man?" said Kay.

"The Oracle, of course," said The Oracle, sticking her head out of her jar again.

"Best fish?" said Jay. "I am not having a best fish."

In the darkness at the back of the store, something fell

over. Jay and Kay rolled over and ducked down behind a bed as footsteps began to walk out of the shadows toward them.

"Oh, God," whispered Kay. "This is not the wedding day I dreamed of. By the way, what's your name?"

"Jay."

The shape of two human figures could be seen silhouetted against the glow, tall and ominous. They walked side by side, stiff-legged and very upright. Ethel walked toward them and, as they came into light, she held up her wing.

"Stop," she said, and the figures did.

They were two mannequins, one male and one female. The male had only one arm and was completely naked except for a bow tie. By the look of the stains down his face and chest, birds had been sleeping on his head fairly frequently. The female had all her limbs but was bald and wearing pink slippers. She, too, had been slept on by many birds.

"Here we are, one best man and someone to give the bride away. I'm afraid they're the best I can do on such short notice," said Ethel.

"What about The Oracle?" said The Oracle. "What can The Oracle do?"

"You can be the bridesmaid," said Jay.

"Or part of the wedding breakfast," muttered Kay.

"All right," said Ethel. "By the powers vested in me—"

"Powers, what powers?" said Kay.

"More than you could ever know or even guess," said Ethel, and to prove her point the air was suddenly filled with thousands of white doves and the scent of roses. Slightly less romantic was the fact that Jay and Kay were standing ankle-deep in fried eggs that spread across the floor as far as the eye could see.

"Oh, cluck it," said Ethel, and most of the eggs disappeared. "Okay, by the powers vested in me, I pronounce you husband and wife."

"You may now kiss the bride," said The Oracle.

The male mannequin lurched forward and tried to fling his single arm around Kay.

"Not you, idiot," said Ethel. "God, I wish I smoked and

there were still such things as cigarettes. I could sure use a smoke right now."

The mannequin fell back into a chair and with his good arm removed his bow tie. The female mannequin sat on his lap and kicked off her slippers.

"I've always, like, dreamed of a honeymoon on some romantic tropical island, walking hand in hand along a golden beach as the sun set across a coal dark sea," said Kay, "not in a derelict department store with egg yolk all over my feet."

"I'm afraid this is the best I can do at the moment," said Ethel, and two potted palms and a selection of postcards from Hawaii appeared on the table.

Kay and Jay sat down to the greatest meal either of them had ever seen or even dreamed of. Most of what lay before them had been unavailable for more than a hundred years and exactly how Ethel produced it is not something we even want to think about. No matter how much Jay and Kay ate or drank, there were more and more wonderful delights that neither of them had ever even heard of, never mind tasted. In her jar Fluffy swallowed mouthfuls of green algae while Ethel pecked around on the floor eating the ants that had come out to investigate the egg yolks. The two mannequins were asleep, one of them gently snoring.

Ethel turned out the lights and they settled down for the night. A pale blue glow came in through the windows as the full moon made a sad attempt at lighting up the world through the haze that had covered the whole planet for as long as anyone could remember.

Jay and Kay curled up together on a pile of mattresses, silent and shy at first, neither of them quite sure what to say. Everything had happened so quickly and so weirdly. They were married, after a fashion, but they'd never even spent time alone together.

"Hello," said Jay.

"Hello."

They fell into the silence of the world around them. They were in the heart of one of the largest cities on Earth, yet outside there was total silence, no distant sirens or doors slamming, no half-heard voices or dogs barking, no garbage can lids clattering or even cats fighting. The only sound was a gentle *splash* as Fluffy swam slowly around and around in her jar. The world seemed more peaceful than it had ever been, on the edge of a new beginning.

"I feel odd with the chicken there," whispered Kay. "Like she's, you know, watching us."

Ethel was silhouetted against the window, as still as the night. She hadn't moved for an hour but Jay and Kay felt she was observing them, if not with her eyes—she was looking out at the street—then at least with her mind. Her body was sleeping but her mind never rested.

Jay and Kay dragged the mattress off to the back of the store, where they fell asleep in each other's arms.

The next morning they woke up to find the two mannequins lying in a jumble of disjointed limbs on the floor and Ethel still at the window staring out at the yellow sky. The sun was shining weakly, as it always did, casting halfhearted shadows into the room. Jay walked over to the window and looked down into the street. It was deserted. Like the business district, this was a part of the city that only the foolhardy or desperate visited and it wasn't hard to see why. During the night the whole front of the twelve-story store opposite had fallen into the street. Three trees lay broken in the rubble, their bright green leaves already beginning to curl up and fade.

"How long have you been here?" said Jay.

"About an hour," said Ethel.

"No, man. I meant, like, how long have you been here on Earth?"

"You remember reading about Stonehenge?"

"Yes."

"I built that, thousands of years after I arrived," said Ethel.

"What for?" said Jay.

"A good laugh," said Ethel. "Something to confuse the natives. It was cluckin' brilliant. I stuck it up one night right next to a village of dumb peasants. You should have seen their faces the next morning. And as for countless generations attaching amazing theories about solar clocks and mystical temples to it, well, that was just a bonus. Still, that's mankind for you—always looking for deep meaningful explanations for the simplest little thing, idiots. I mean, look at the Pyramids. How bright do you have to be to realize they are just the roofs of buildings that have sunk into the sand? Everyone knows what happens if you build on sand."

School as such had ceased to exist before Jay had been born, but he had read the history of the earth from its supposed creation up till the late twentieth century in the three thousand books from his parents' attic. There had been a lot of odd things that hadn't made sense and he found himself wondering if Ethel had had something to do with them. Why, for example, had the dinosaurs become extinct and why had the missing link never been found?

"Why did you keep, like, your real identity secret for so long?" said Jay.

"We weren't allowed to interfere. It's one of our basic laws," said Ethel.

"So why did you make contact now, then, eh?"

"Well, it was like this," said Ethel. "Billions of years ago, when we'd finished evolving and were getting a bit bored, we decided to go out and look for other forms of intelligent life. I'm using the word *intelligent* loosely here, you understand. Because everywhere was such a long way off and no matter what you do it's impossible to physically travel faster than the speed of light, some of us were chosen to send our minds out searching while our bodies stayed at home with our moms and dads. While we were away, they washed and fed them and then, when we found a planet like this one, our bodies were put in a spaceship and sent off to join our minds. Mine hasn't arrived yet and in the meantime, of course, we had to live inside something else, hence the cluckin' chickens."

This was 90 percent bullshit. The only true part was about her body being at home, looked after by her mom and dad. The rest was nonsense, even the part about her body being on its way in a spaceship, though Ethel believed it was. She would have gone crazy centuries ago if she'd known *that* wasn't true.

"So what do you really look like?" said Jay.

"Well, we're not those elegant slim aliens in flashy silver suits with big cluckin' heads and huge dark eyes like you see in those old science fiction movies," said Ethel.

"Well, no, I didn't imagine you would be," said Kay. "They look too much like us to be real. It's obvious they're made up."

"Oh, no," said Ethel, "they're real, all right, smug bastards."

"Why?"

"Well, they think they're so cluckin' beautiful. They're just about the vainest creatures in any galaxy anywhere, far worse than the Wonderful Fish or the Lovely Fairy Wrens," said Ethel. "Mind you, they're almost extinct now. They spend so long admiring themselves in front of mirrors that they've got no time left for anything else, like eating or producing children." She paused before continuing. "Anyway, the reason we have made contact now is that over the past couple of millennia, the number of planets with intelligent life has been dropping. Once there were about five thousand, now it's down to ninety-four. So after long, painful discussions, we decided we had to take steps, that we had to help."

"If you've, like, been here for centuries," said Jay, "and you could see the population was dying out and everything, why didn't you do something about it?"

"Two reasons," said Ethel. "Firstly, we're not allowed to change things without written authority. Secondly, because we live so far away from here, written authority takes twelve thousand years to get here. I am expecting it to arrive in eleven thousand eight hundred years or so. Besides, it wasn't pollution that made you all die out."

One of Ethel's greatest talents, the only thing she'd ever really been any good at in school, was creative lying. There was no way she was about to admit that anything that had gone wrong might have been her fault.

"Yeah, it was," said Jay. "Pollution made male fertility drop until, like, more people were dying than were being born."

"Nonsense," said Ethel.

"It's not," Jay protested. "Everyone knows that's what happened."

"Well, you are all wrong."

"Okay, so, like, you tell me," said Jay. "Why have we almost died out, then?"

"Boredom," said Ethel.

She explained that man's endless quest for eternal life had brought about his downfall. As people started living longer and longer, things they had known all their life no longer needed to be remembered and were wiped out.

"For example," said Ethel, "for ninety years you can look at grass and for ninety years it's always green."

"Except when it's dead," said Jay.

"Yes, yes," said Ethel. "The point is that after a hundred twenty years of knowing the grass is green, the human brain, small and pathetic as it is, says, 'Hey, I know the grass is green, I don't need to store that information anymore.' But instead of just erasing the information and using those cells for something more useful, the dumb human brain closed that bit of itself down. This kept on happening until there was so much of the brain shut down that the part that was left said, 'Hey, I might as well tidy things up and close down the rest.' And, hey, presto, dead humans."

"Yeah, but what about the sperm count?" said Jay. "That kept on dropping."

"Of course it did," Ethel explained. "Don't you think sperm get bored too? As people got more apathetic they had far less sex, so the sperm were left hanging around with nothing to do. Many died of old age, but most of them committed suicide. It's a documented fact. It hasn't just happened on Earth. It's called the lemming sperm syndrome."

"That's crap, man. Why didn't everyone die out, then?" said Jay. There was a horrible logic to Ethel's argument that was hard to ignore, but it went against everything Jay had known his whole life.

"Well, some people were so dumb that even after a hundred fifty years they still kept saying, 'Hey, wow, the grass is green,'" said Ethel. "Also quite a lot of people are color-blind."

"I don't believe you, man," said Jay.

Jay couldn't bring himself to admit that he and the rest of

mankind were all descended from people who were color-blind or idiotic.

"Oh, yes, well, what color's that?" said Ethel, pointing at a red piece of paper.

"Red."

"See," said Ethel. "It's green."

Most of this was more bullshit, but she had had the story well rehearsed for the day she would ultimately speak to humans. She had had it ready for so long that she almost believed it herself.

"But what can you do?" said Jay. "Mankind's on the edge of extinction. I think you've kind of left it a bit late."

"Well, we can get rid of all that crap for a start," said Ethel, pointing up at the endless expanse of yellow clouds.

She stood very still with her eyes closed. Jay watched for a while, but after a bit he grew bored and went back to bed.

Virtually nothing Ethel had told Jay was the truth, but she didn't think Jay was anywhere near ready to hear that she had created not only the entire human race but every other living and dead species on the planet. It would have blown his mind and, even worse, shown him that Ethel was not the omnipotent perfect creature she wanted him to think she was. One day he would be ready but that day was a way off yet. The truth was that Ethel had actually created every living thing on Earth, and this is how it happened.

Chapter 8
In the Beginning Was the Chicken

Long before the first life began on Earth, the planet of Megaton had risen, fallen, and risen again at least fifty times, until the population had finally evolved into a race of superintelligent beings far more clever than anyone else. This meant they had had to kill a lot of people on other planets, emptying entire solar systems of their populations, because no one likes people who are a lot more clever than they are. Well, some people do, but they are to be despised and usually get wiped out first because it's easier.

This meant that many galaxies that had once been home to ancient civilizations fell silent and lifeless, and once the Megatonians had begun their senseless extermination, they found it impossible to stop, until the day came when Megaton was the only planet left anywhere in all the galaxies, and all the other galaxies beyond them where there was life. Everywhere else was totally barren, devoid of not just intelligent life but stupid life and everything else, right down to the tiniest blade of grass.

A few million years passed and the Megatonians continued to evolve to the point where standing around whistling nonchalantly at what they had done was no longer good enough. So a High Council was set up and its first decision was that what they had done had been Very Bad. The second decision was that they had to do something to rectify the situation, to bring life back to all the deserted worlds. In the Hall of the High Council there was a huge notebook with all the planets the Megatonians had decimated written down in it. Just to give you an idea of how many planets there had been with life on them, the notebook was three miles high, two miles wide, and six miles thick and the writing was really, really tiny.

One by one people were sent to each planet with a packet of seeds, and life was started off all over again. Since the Great Annihilation many new stars had evolved, little bits of hot lava had fallen off them, and new worlds had been born. These new worlds were added to the bottom of the list, so by the time they were reached, all the really good galactic gardeners were busy and it was left to the dunces, apprentices, and dropouts to deal with them.

Earth was one of these planets and Ethel was one of the dunces. Well, to be specific, she was a dropout apprentice dunce, the most supremely useless student in the seven-million-year history of the Megaton Academy of Galactic Gardening and Home Economics, but Earth was the bottom of the list and she was the only one left.

She landed on a hot rock somewhere that ended up being Africa and planted her seeds. Of course, she wasn't in a chicken's body then. She wasn't in a body at all. She was just a sort of energy field floating around.

For the next 300 billion years or so things developed pretty much as described in the catalog. Bacteria and algae grew in the sea and gradually evolved into all sorts of wild and wonderful life-forms. As the gardener, Ethel had had some say in what had gone on—she had played around with a bit of cross-pollination here and there, sometimes because she felt things were not going the right way, other times because she was bored and wanted a good laugh. The poor duck-billed platypus was one of the few remaining examples of her quirky sense of humor, as of course were humans.

She could still remember the tears of laughter streaming down her face when she invented human reproduction. That, she felt, was her pièce de résistance. If she ever got back home to Megaton, she'd have a few laughs about that one. She'd even lived in both types of human bodies for a while, just to see for herself how hilarious the whole thing was.

But once man had arrived and settled down, Ethel grew bored. Practical jokes like Stonehenge, crop circles, and diarrhea soon wore thin and she became bored and irritable. Repeated requests to return home to Megaton were either ignored or turned down. There was always a reason why she had to stay just that bit longer. The truth was that Megaton was glad to be rid of her and didn't want her back.

"We can't keep putting her off," said the returns clerk.

"Oh, yes we can," the president of the academy said, and organized for dinosaurs to suddenly become extinct. "That'll keep her busy for a while."

Disaster after disaster was created—plagues, ice ages, wars—and with each one a little bit of guilt was implanted in Ethel's brain, until she became riddled with complexes and bad temper.

"There's no way she's coming home now," said the president, and to make doubly sure they performed the chicken trick, the most extreme measure reserved for the most extreme cases.

Sometime in the twelfth century, after a particularly riotous party, Ethel woke up to find herself, and her three sisters, who were visiting from Megaton, inside chickens' bodies and they'd all been stuck in them ever since. Sure, they could borrow other bodies, they could even float around without a body, but only for a while. No matter how hard they all tried to keep away, the chicken trick kept pulling them back like a terrible addiction. Ethel was convinced they would all remain as chickens until she had finished her work on Earth, and it was depressing, to say the least, looking at a future as a fat brown ungainly bird. She also had a terrible feeling that somehow the whole chicken thing was her fault, though she had been too drunk to remember what had happened. There was a vague memory of a lot of feathers and some brown paper bags, but nothing more, apart from a huge tub of Vaseline. That was all part of the chicken trick, especially the feeling of guilt.

The trouble was that Earth had gone seriously wrong. Not just the "natural" disasters created by Ethel's masters to keep her there but other things that were far more grave. Dozens of species had become extinct and loads more, even her humans, were on the verge of it. She could call home for another packet of seeds but that would mean killing every living thing off and starting all over again—exactly what her masters wanted—and staying on the wretched cluckin' little planet for billions more years. No, she had to fix things before it was too late. Also she had to admit, though she would never do so publicly, that for all its foibles she had grown quite fond of Earth.

Chapter 9

Rain

"What's happening?" said Kay.

"Dunno. The chicken's just, like, staring at the sky," said Jay.

The air grew warmer. Not the damp clammy warm that they'd known all their lives, which hung heavy in the air even in the middle of winter, but a crisp clear warmth that neither of them had ever felt before. It was like someone, on a bright spring morning, had opened the window after an all-night party and was stroking their skin with fine sandpaper.

They went over to the window. Ethel hadn't moved in almost an hour, but the sky had. The clouds, which really had not been so much clouds as one single endless cloud wrapped around the entire planet, were breaking up and through the gaps the sky was bright blue. The sun poured down, too bright for their eyes, lighting up the world with a brilliance that it had long forgotten. As the gloom lifted, the bits of cloud seemed to pile themselves up on top of one another, growing darker and darker against the new blue sky. A flash of lightning followed by a crash of thunder sent Jay and Kay running for cover at the back of the store.

"It's all right," said Ethel. "There's nothing to be afraid of."

"What the hell was that, man?" said Jay. "A bomb?"

"No, just nature," Ethel sighed wearily, and slipped a quick meteorology lesson inside their heads.

"The answer, my friend, is blowing in the window," said Fluffy.

"I am so bored," said Ethel. "I mean, I've been stuck here on this cluckin' little planet for millions and millions of years. I mean, a couple of days and you can see all there is worth looking at, never mind millions of cluckin' years. Christ, I've seen it all a thousand, thousand times."

"You couldn't have," said Jay. "Supposing you were in Australia when Kennedy was being shot, you couldn't have seen that?"

"Saw it," said Ethel.

"Come on, chicken, you couldn't have seen everything," said Kay.

"Listen, stupid, there are four of us, okay?" said Ethel. "Together we can see everything that cluckin' happens on this tiny little place, and what one of us sees, we all see."

"Wow, cool," said Jay.

"Bullshit," said Kay.

"Look, you dumb human, just because you can see only one thing at a time and it has to be right in front of your cluckin' face doesn't mean everyone else has to," said Ethel. "Compared to my brain, which is like a Rolls-Royce, yours is like half a pair of roller skates with the wheels missing."

They went back to the window and, as they looked out, it started to rain. For the first time in living memory it rained, but not the fine mist that always seemed to hang in the air, the mist that was the only source of fresh water for everyone, collected in huge plastic funnels several yards wide that sat on the roof of nearly every building like giant upturned umbrellas or vast fields of weird toadstools. This was real rain, and Jay and Kay had never seen it before. They ran out into the street and stood with outstretched arms and upturned faces as it poured all over them.

The air was filled with the sweet smell of a billion dormant microbes coming back to life, microbes that had lain sleeping since the last real rain more than 170 years ago, microbes that were ready to make up for lost time and evolve into new and exciting life-forms, to boldly evolve where no microbes had evolved before. Jay and Kay ran hand in hand through the torrential downpour. They stood in the middle of the street while the trash of 170 years floated around their ankles. They turned their faces to the sky and drank in the clear clean water. Ethel sat in the window looking down at them. They were perfect.

The sleeping world had been switched on again.

"I think it would have been better if you'd taken your clothes off before you went outside," said Ethel later as they huddled together, shivering in some moth-eaten blankets back upstairs in the bedding department of the old store.

To see a chicken create something is a weird experience that few are privileged to witness. Ethel would stand dead still with her wings hanging limply by her sides and a look of deep concentration on her face. Actually, to see a chicken with a look of concentration on its face is weird enough on its own. But to see Ethel standing there while a small tornado of inanimate objects whirled around her was an unforgettable event. Things flew across the room. Things flew down the street from blocks away and crashed in through the windows. Things even appeared out of thin air.

Then, when she had everything she needed, the things would seemingly throw themselves together in a mad frenzy that looked doomed to failure. But as the dust cleared, there, quite often looking all wrong, was the article she had set out to produce, and no matter how extraordinary it looked, it always worked. Well, nearly always. So it was with the dryer—there was no cable to plug into an outlet because there was no electricity. There was one of the mannequin's arms sticking out with green wires coming from it. Green wires were a favorite of Ethel's and seemed to be all over everything she created, sometimes even food and clothes. Yet ten minutes later Jay and Kay's clothes were perfectly dry and twelve minutes later all the bits and pieces that had made the dryer had gone back to where they had come from.

It may seem strange that Ethel would bother to dismantle her creation and send all the pieces back to where they had come from, but that was the result of centuries of secrecy.

Until she spoke to Jay, she had never revealed herself to be anything more than a chicken. So whenever she moved things around or created machines she needed, like the giant hovermower she had used to make the crop circles, she always tidied up after herself. Now it didn't matter, but the habits of centuries are hard to break.

While Ethel dried their clothes, Jay and Kay snuggled down together, less shy than the night before but still too shy to look at each other as they began to explore each other's naked bodies.

The storm lasted for two days and in those two days Ethel changed the course of history forever, and Jay and Kay got to know the sweet intimate details that newlyweds find out about each other, like their names and how old they both were, which pickles they liked best, which parts of each other's bodies to touch to send tingles down their spines. They were in their twenties, so any part of their bodies sent tingles down their spines.

The drains, idle for so long, had blocked up with dead leaves, cat bones, and antique hamburger wrappers, so the water ran down the street like a river. At first, as the dust of 170 years was washed away, the river looked like mud and smelled far worse, but by the second day it was clear and the world was clean again. Old lakes and riverbeds had been dry for so long people had built houses in them. The houses were now deserted for the most part, and as the rain ran down the streams into the rivers and then the lakes, the walls crumbled back into the ground they had been made from. Seeds that had rolled around in the dust for almost two centuries began to swell and put out roots into the rich mud. No place on the planet escaped the storm, not even the ancient deserts, where there had been no water for a thousand years. Everywhere, from the tops of the Himalayas to the salt pans of Saranjaya, plants began to grow, and grow like they had only five minutes left to do it in.

In the park, the Fluorides had struggled up into the trees as the water had risen and now sat sullenly chewing leaves or bits of themselves. In the city dozens of old buildings finally gave up and collapsed into the flooded streets, not falling like

70

before but sort of melting into the mud, where centuries later they would be discovered by future archaeologists, buried under layers of earth and trees. The flames in the remains of the skyscraper where Jay had been living were doused and a cloud of steam hung in the air, uncertain what to do next.

Chapter 10

The Perfect Hour

"There are things I must tell you," said Ethel as the four of them stood staring out at the rain. "And now is as good a time as any."

"What?" said Jay.

"We are not here together by chance," said Ethel.

"Oh, that's, like, so mystical," said Kay sarcastically.

"I thought you were here because you'd been sent here," said Jay.

"I don't mean that. I mean the four of us," said Ethel. "And when I say here, I don't mean here on this planet, I mean the four of us together at this place here and now."

And then she told them about the Perfect Hour.

"One day a long time ago—," she began.

"When you say a long time, do you mean by your timescale or by theirs?" said The Oracle, nodding toward Jay and Kay.

"The day I refer to," said Ethel, "is October eighteenth, 2042, three o'clock in the morning, to be precise. On that day, for exactly one hour, everything was perfect."

"Wow, cool," said Jay.

Kay was reserving her judgment. It seemed like a stupid idea. Nothing could ever be perfect. She wasn't even prepared to define the word *perfect*. Perfect for whom: people, fish, chickens? It was ridiculous.

"For whom?" she said.

"Everyone," said Ethel. "For that one single hour everything was perfect. There was no war anywhere in the world. No one got murdered. No one died. No one was in pain, not even a little headache. The sun shone everywhere except where it was nighttime or where there had been drought. There it rained. Nothing at all spoiled the moment. It was almost as if time stood still for sixty minutes. Quite simply, absolutely everything was perfect. The odds on that happening were so astronomical as to be incalculable. It was unnerving. It had never happened before. It has never happened since." She paused. "The sad thing was, hardly anyone noticed."

"That's right," said The Oracle. "The Oracle was there. It was so overwhelming, The Oracle thought she must be dreaming."

"That was my first thought too," said Ethel, "but unless everyone fell asleep at the same time, which is possible though even more unlikely, it couldn't have been a dream. No, I think someone or something made it happen."

"So what happened?" said Jay. "Why didn't it last longer?"

"If I remember correctly, someone stood on someone else's foot and one thing led to another and by the next morning seven countries were at war," said Ethel. "Whatever it was," she continued, "it only lasted an hour and it's never happened again, though there are vague rumors it's happened on other planets."

"Cool," said Jay. "So we're going to find whoever made it happen and, like, get them to do it again?"

"Yes," said Ethel.

That single word was to shape all of their lives forever. Of course, it was just one word, easy to say, easy to want, but hard to make happen. But if ever the time was right to try, it was then. The world was at a major crossroads and the lights were hovering on yellow. Though to the outside observer, the world looked like it was ready for bed, tired out, pooped, slowly vanishing under a quilt of endless green, almost devoid of the race that had molded it into its present form and ultimately screwed it up.

Ethel felt herself almost on the verge of maybe becoming prepared to possibly admit that she was actually a tiny bit fond of Earth and its inhabitants, though maybe *fond* was too strong a word. Humans were pathetic. They killed one another like there was no tomorrow, they poisoned themselves with progress, and yet there was something almost lovable about them. They were hers.

She felt there was nothing to lose and, more importantly, because there were so few people left, there was no time to lose. She felt in her heart there was a good chance that they could find who or what it was that had made the world perfect for that brief moment of time and get it to happen again. And maybe this time it could last forever.

Since it had happened she had racked her brains trying to discover who or what had been behind the Perfect Hour but she'd found nothing. Why had they done it and why had it lasted only an hour? And had it actually been someone who had done it or had it simply been an accident or a freak, a one in a billion? She had created Earth's nature, so it couldn't have been that. She would have known. She had a million questions and not one single answer.

"So it's, like, a quest?" said Jay.

"Mmmm," said Kay. "Okay, chicken, where do you plan to start this quest, if there is a quest at all, that is?" She thought the whole thing sounded very suspect. If Ethel could clear the entire sky and make machines almost out of thin air, why couldn't she make everything perfect herself? Kay didn't trust her. There was obviously stuff the chicken wasn't telling them.

"That is the first part of the quest," said Ethel, "to find the starting point."

"That's obvious, old thing," said The Oracle. "We start here."

"But from what you've said," said Kay, "you're not even one hundred percent certain that someone made it happen. Suppose it was just a fluke?"

"I'm still working on that one," said Ethel.

Everyone stood silently staring out at the rain, even Fluffy. A tree with two scraggy cats clinging to the branches floated by in the torrent, crashing and banging into other trees and buildings. It came to rest against the back of an old bus and the two cats leaped onto its roof, only to be thrown into the water a few seconds later when the bus toppled sideways and the tree floated away.

Ethel felt as though they were on the verge of something big. She couldn't put her finger on it, because she didn't have fingers, but she couldn't put her claw on it either. She kind of felt the four of them were coming together in a subtle symbiosis so that together they would be capable of more than any of them could aspire to individually. It was all too vague to be sure of, too ethereal to put into words. She was annoyed that Kay seemed to want to question everything. Yet maybe her suspicious nature would be to the group's advantage. Nor was the group yet complete. There were others still to join them. As yet there was no beautiful document, but the first sentences had been written.

Everything fell silent. The spiders scuttling in the rafters stopped in midstep and looked down at her. The very cobwebs and dust that had been moving ever so slightly as the warm air drifted slowly around the beams and timbers of the dark ceiling high above them hung motionless.

Time stood still for a split second and far, far away, in a galaxy beyond galaxies past the end of time, a voice spoke.

"Shit," it said.

I was right, she thought, *there is something there.*

The voice was a voice that she hadn't heard for thousands and thousands of years and in speaking it had given Ethel her first clue. Whatever had caused the Perfect Hour, even if it was still on Earth, had been aided and abetted, or even instructed and ordered, from a long, long way off. At some point they would have to leave Earth. But for now there were more immediate things to deal with.

"That's enough," she said, turning back to the window, and it stopped raining.

The sky cleared into a vast wide empty expanse from side to side, wider than Jay had ever seen. Distant mountains beyond the city that had been hidden for years now stood out as sharp as the trees across the street.

"Wow, blue," said Jay, staring up into it. "What a great color."

"That's the color it's supposed to be," said Ethel.

"Yeah, I've seen photos," said Jay, "but they didn't do it justice. I mean, they hardly prepare you for it. It's, like, so big."

"Okay, time to go," said Ethel, and they followed her out into the street.

Chapter 11

And Then There Were Five

It was hard going. The rain had covered everything with thick sticky mud that gripped their feet like glue. It clung to Ethel's legs until she couldn't even lift her feet to walk. Inside she might have been the most powerful being on the planet, but outside she was still only a chicken. Kay picked her up, cleaned the mud off her, and tucked her inside her shirt. Where the sun shone between the buildings, the mud was setting into hard adobe blocks, crisscrossed with great cracks like a giant web.

"Couldn't we, like, wait a couple of days until the mud's all set?" said Jay.

"There's no time," said Ethel. "We have to go now."

The four travelers struggled through the congealing mud, their silence broken only by Ethel's occasional "Left," "Next right," "Through there. No, there," "Not there."

The buildings were lower now, still mainly shops but with small single-story apartments above them. They began to see a few people, though they were all far off and no one approached them.

They came to a low black building with a bare featureless wall almost a block long with a single door at the far end. There were no signs that gave any clues as to what the building might have been, or any impression to show where a name might have been written, just a few pockmarks of bullet holes that barely touched the surface. All the other buildings they had passed were covered in ancient graffiti but these walls were smooth and bare. Although only one story high, the place sent shivers down Jay's spine. The air around it felt cold, like the touch of death. The piece of paper in his pocket moved. It was crumpling itself up. This was not a good place.

"Here we are," said Ethel as they reached the door.

"This place feels bad, man," said Jay.

"I think it looks cool," said Kay.

The door was as featureless as the wall, no handle, not even a keyhole, only really noticeable as a door because of the almost invisibly thin line where it fitted into the wall. Kay pushed it but it was locked.

"We can't get in, man," said Jay. "Let's go."

"Put me down," said Ethel.

She stood facing the door and from inside they heard the sound of wheels turning, wheels that had been standing still for more than a century. There was the sound of metal grinding against metal, a sharp *crack,* a sudden rush of cool air, and the door creaked open wide enough for them to enter. Ethel walked in, followed by Kay carrying Fluffy. Jay hesitated but then, hearing nothing, went in too. As he did so the door creaked shut behind him and locked itself.

"We don't want anyone else in here," said Ethel, somewhere in the darkness.

"It's always darkest before the spawn," said The Oracle.

"If only you knew how true that was," Ethel said, and made all the lights come on.

They were standing in a very lavish reception area. Thick carpet covered the floor, deep plush chairs sat around a glass-topped table covered in neatly lined-up glossy magazines. A water cooler bubbled in the corner and a coffee machine began to drip filtered coffee. Against one wall there was a wide desk with telephones and behind the desk in tall gold letters on a peach velvet wall were the words

Eternalia
"How to Live Forever"

in a typeface that Jay recognized at once.

Jay had never seen anything like it. He picked up a magazine. It was 185 years old yet it looked and felt brand new. Jay could even smell the ink. The whole place was like that. The air was fresh and cool. There wasn't a speck of dust anywhere, no spiders, no trash, and no signs of life. Everything was pristine, even the potted palms, which looked as if they had just been watered. This was hardly surprising, because they were standing in the reception area of the world's only surviving cryonic laboratory. Whoever had left the place 185 years before had switched off the lights and suspended the whole place in a time capsule.

Early in the twenty-first century, while scientists were still struggling to find cures for all known diseases and hadn't quite perfected the techniques to prevent aging, cryonic laboratories—or, as they had been known, sleeping hotels— had sprung up everywhere. At first they had been for only the incredibly rich, but over time costs fell until anyone could be frozen for the future. It finally reached the stage where every shopping mall had a cryonic store and there were more frozen bodies than living ones. When your granny died, you stuck her in a shopping cart, wheeled her down to the mall, and booked her into one of the discount chains that had sprung up all around the world. For a while, stores like Auntie Mae's Reincarnation Station, Stiffs R Us, and the more upmarket Phoenix: You'll Get a Rise out of Us were the biggest growth industry of the century.

Then at last the day arrived when scientists said they were ready, that they had ironed out all the wrinkles and at last could bring the stiffs back to life and iron out all their wrinkles. People rushed to thaw long-lost relatives and, as with every other medical procedure, the waiting list grew longer and longer. Fights broke out and bribery was rife. Hostages were taken and in all the furor and chaos nobody noticed that something was seriously wrong.

There was no problem bringing everyone back to life and at first everyone was wonderfully happy. Actually a lot of people weren't that happy, especially old men who had remarried younger women when their old wives had died and now found themselves in court for bigamy. And it seemed as if the New Living were younger and healthier than when they had died. And that was the problem, they were. A month after revival they were ten years younger than the day they had died. Six months later they were twenty years younger. It was fabulous. Old arthritic men threw away their canes and married women half their age. Except that after a year the women weren't half their age. They were older, and a year later the old men were teenagers and there was no way of stopping the rejuvenation process. After two years all the New Living, or Reborns, were dead. A few survived as cells frozen in laboratory dishes, but the majority passed their first birthdays, forgot how to walk, lost their teeth, threw up their breakfasts on their wives' shoulders, spent a few days attached to robot breast-feeders, then simply fizzled out.

The cryonic stores had been closed down as quickly and quietly as possible, all except this one, which had been the resting place of the most fabulously wealthy and talented people in the world. This one had been sealed up, waiting for the day when the problems would be fixed, which of course they never were. And it had sat there, sealed up and totally impenetrable, until Ethel the chicken had arrived.

Ethel concentrated and somewhere in the background machines began to hum.

"I really don't like this," said Jay.

There were so many shivers running up and down his spine, it felt like his skin was trying to run away. When Ethel told him where they were, he wanted the rest of his body to run away with it. It wasn't that he was squeamish. He'd seen some pretty gross things—God, he'd eaten pretty gross things—but there was something about knowing you were standing in a building packed with dead bodies that had been lying there for more than a century that scared the hell out of him. He had an unnerving feeling that Ethel was about to bring them all back to life, a huge army of killer zombies looking for breakfast and he would be it.

The elevator doors across the hall shuddered and creaked open.

"Follow me," Ethel said, and walked in.

The doors closed and the elevator began to descend. Jay

looked at the numbers. There was no up, only down, eighty-six floors of down.

"We'll start at the bottom and work our way up," said Ethel.

"Like, what exactly are we looking for?" said Kay.

"Brains," said Ethel, "working brains."

"Brains! Yuck, that is, like, so gross," said Jay.

"And other bits and pieces that are still in usable condition," said Ethel.

"Oh, God," said Kay. "You're going to make a monster, aren't you?"

"What's that smell?" said Jay.

"Oh, it's nothing. That's the bits and pieces that aren't in usable condition," said Ethel. "Don't forget, there's been no electricity to run the refrigeration machines for more than a hundred years. I think most of the stuff will have gone bad."

Jay started to speak, but the smell was so unbearable that he had to cover his mouth and nose. Kay looked green and went very quiet, the sort of quiet you go when you think if you don't move you possibly won't throw up but really you know that no matter what you do there's no way of avoiding it. Fluffy stayed at the bottom of her jar. And there were still thirty-four floors to go.

When the elevator reached the bottom, the smell seemed to have eased off a little. That, or they had all got used to it. The elevator stopped with an unpleasant shudder almost like it, too, was uneasy down among all the decay. Jay felt like they had descended into the depths of hell and all he wanted was to be outside in the new sunshine.

The doors opened and a single long dark corridor led off into the distance. There were doors on both walls, hundreds of them. Kay staggered out into the hall and threw up into a potted plant. Any hope Jay had had of avoiding it vanished and he threw up into another plant. Fluffy had nowhere to throw up but into her own jar. Only Ethel seemed oblivious to their surroundings.

She walked slowly down the tunnel, shaking her head and muttering. Finally she stopped.

"In there," she said, "a left arm."

"So?" said Jay.

"So, go and cluckin' get it," said Ethel.

"No way," said Jay.

"And don't look at me either," said Kay.

"You're cluckin' pathetic, both of you," said Ethel.

She was in a bad mood and to make herself feel better she gave Kay indigestion and Jay terrible gas and for good measure dropped a pickled onion in Fluffy's jar, though quite how the goldfish could have gone and got the arm, she didn't explain.

Of course she could have just made them go and get the bits she wanted, but she was too taken up with the task at hand. In the end she collected the bits herself. She dematerialized them in their tanks and rematerialized them forty-five floors up in the operating-room fridge. Jay and Kay followed her through the deserted building, floor after floor, as she stopped outside different doors and muttered, "Armpit," "Ear," "Toe," "Bottom," to herself.

"Okay, that's all the good stuff," she said at last. "It's cluckin' crap. The knees are different sizes, the brain's got a hole in it, the ears are the wrong color. Oh, cluck. So what's new? Story of my cluckin' life. I always get crap to work with. Come on, up to the lab. We'll just have to make do. Okay, back up to the fortieth floor."

"Life begins at forty," said The Oracle.

"You are so right," said Ethel.

In the operating room the air smelled of nothing. Like the rest of the laboratory, the place was spotless. As Jay and Kay watched, Ethel stood on one end of the operating table as all the bits she had managed to collect materialized in front of her and fitted themselves together. When the brain appeared to float across the room and squeeze itself into the head through the left ear, it was more than Jay could take and he fainted.

The creation was disgustingly, revoltingly hideous, far too hideous to describe in a single try, almost too hideous to look at, though by the time Ethel had conjured up some clothes and dressed it, it merely looked awful.

"Dr. Frankenstein, eat your cluckin' heart out," said Ethel.

"But it's dead," said Kay.

"I know, I know," said Ethel. "One thing at a time. I haven't finished yet. I haven't even stuck the cluckin' mustache on. You'd think I was making vegetable stew, the way you go on, not creating a living creature. I know it's only a cluckin' human, not an advanced form of life, but it still takes some expertise, you know."

"It's not going to be like Frankenstein's monster and, like, try and kill us all, is it?" said Kay, fighting fresh waves of nausea that threatened to make her collapse onto Jay.

"No, of course not," said Ethel. "It is entirely in my power."

"Yeah, right, so now you're going to make it alive, I suppose?" said Kay.

"Well, we need some lightning," said Ethel.

"Why?" said Kay.

"To bring it to cluckin' life," said Ethel. "Don't you know anything?"

"No, like, why are you making this thing at all?" said Kay. "It's, like, totally disgusting."

"We need it," said Ethel.

"Yeah, right," said Kay, "a freaky monster made of bits of leftovers is just what we need—not."

"You'll see," said Ethel.

She revived Jay, then flapped around the laboratory, ordering him and Kay to join up wires, attach steel rods to useful-looking hooks, and do the cleaning up. Far above them the distant rumble of thunder could be heard. They stapled bare copper wires to the creature's ears, lit the fuse, and retired behind the screen.

"Do you know whose brain you used?" said Kay. "Was it, like, some brilliant genius?"

"Well, it wasn't as though I had a lot of choice," said Ethel. "Most of them had dissolved, but I think this was the best choice."

"Who is it?" said Jay.

"Actually, it was the only choice. And if you must know, there are a few bits of it missing," said Ethel evasively. "I had to patch it up with bits from five other brains."

"Shit," said Kay.

"It's all right," said Ethel. "There's nothing to worry about.

Most of them were human brains. I only used a bit of dog and the tiniest bit of cat."

"Yeah, right, really cool," said Kay. "The damn thing'll keep chasing itself up trees."

The thunder was directly overhead now. Even so far underground they could hear it crashing violently through the heavens. Ethel walked out into the middle of the laboratory, flew up onto the operating table, and standing on her creation's chest, threw her wings into the air and let out a totally unchickenlike bloodcurdling scream that made the hairs on the back of Jay's neck, and all other parts of his body, stand on end—a not altogether unpleasant experience. As she did so a violent flash of lightning lit up the room and the creature sat bolt upright, throwing Ethel onto the floor. And in the split second that the room was alive with a million volts of power and light, Jay and Kay caught a brief glimpse of Ethel in the body she had lived in on Megaton and fainted.

When they came to, the creature was gone and Ethel was standing, ruffled and soaking wet, in the middle of the floor.

"Oh, cluck," she said.

"Where's it gone?" said Kay.

"I don't know," said Ethel. "I wasn't here."

"Oh, man, I knew this would happen," said Jay. "We're all going to die."

He wanted to run, to grab Kay's hand and rush out into the elevator and back up into the street, but the creature could have been just outside the door.

"Don't be so cluckin' stupid," said Ethel.

A few minutes later, the creature came staggering back into the room. At least since it had been brought to life, the green slime seemed to have stopped trickling out of its ears. Ethel had actually done a brilliant, almost invisible job of joining all the body parts together. There were none of those nuts and bolts or big cross-stitches that had been Dr. Frankenstein's trademark. It was just that the bits themselves were not all the same color. Its left ear was dark brown while the head itself was distinctly Caucasian, ending in a sharp line where it joined a deeply tanned neck. One eye was blue, the other dark brown and constantly pointing toward magnetic north. Yet it worked. In spite of all the dents and bumps and incongruous colors, the creature had a beautiful smile that was hard to resist. It walked across to Ethel, gently picked her up, and began stroking her feathers.

"Mommy," it said.

"Where have you been, you naughty boy?" said Ethel, showing a soft maternal side that no one had seen before, a side that even she hadn't seen before.

"Bathroom, had to do a wee-wee," said the creature. "Been waiting to go eighty-seven years."

"Okay, good boy," said Ethel. "Now concentrate. How many fingers am I holding up?"

"Purple," said the creature.

"What are you talking about?" said Kay. "You don't have any fingers. You're a freakin' chicken."

"I didn't mean it literally," snapped Ethel. "It's just what you say in these situations."

"Yeah, right, so you've done this before, have you?" said Kay. "Stuck bits of dead bodies together and made hideous monsters."

"Only twenty-three times," said Ethel. "Now listen to Mommy, that's a good boy. What is your name?"

Ethel thought back to the last time. That had been a dreadful mistake and by the time she had put it right her creation had grown a stupid mustache and conquered half of Europe.

The creature stood in the middle of the room, its mouth hanging open and its arms dangling limply at its sides. The activity in its brain can best be compared to a hot mud spring that sits there brown and steaming, its surface broken every now and then by a lazy bubble. It stared one by one at Jay, then Kay, then Ethel, and a huge grin spread across its face.

"Bathroom," it said.

"No. Try again."

"Sausage."

"No."

The creature looked around the room, trying to find a clue. It put Ethel down on the operating table and walked around examining everything with a frown on its face. Now and then it picked something up, turned it over in its hands, sniffed it, and spoke.

"Cabbage."

"That's the light switch," said Ethel.

"Bus stop," said the creature.

"No, that's your toe," said Ethel, "and spit it out."

"Pre-Raphaelite protobrontosaurassic tetrahedron," said the creature.

"No, that's a Post-Raphaelite protobrontosaurassic decahedron."

"Nipple."

"And that's the wastepaper basket," said Ethel. "Your name is Douglas. That's what was written on the tank the biggest bit of your brain came out of, so that's what we'll call you."

She had decided that the creature was a boy, even though there were bits of it that were definitely female. More than 50 percent of it was male and with her fixed logic, no matter what happened in the future, if it became the mother of numerous children, or even if it began to run around on all fours and gave birth to puppies, to Ethel it would always be a boy, her boy, and her pride and joy.

She was extremely gentle and patient with Douglas, slowly coaxing him through the early years of life. She tried to get into his brain but kept sinking in the mud. There were more bits missing than she had originally thought and the bits that were left were very confused. She had had to use a few paper clips to make some of them stick together and these were now acting like radio antennae. Douglas seemed to be picking up signals from somewhere else. If Ethel could manage to control this, it could be very useful.

"Lovely Mommy," said Douglas, lifting Ethel up and tickling her on the back of her head.

"Can we get out of here, man?" said Jay. "This place is, like, giving me the creeps."

He tipped The Oracle, who was looking decidedly green, into a clean laboratory flask and walked over to the door.

"Why the hell have you done this?" said Kay as they

walked back to the elevator. "I mean, like, do we need this walking potato?"

"Potato," said Douglas, "yum, yum."

"The creature, as you call him, happens to have some amazing talents that are vital to our quest," said Ethel.

"Yeah, right, like if we ever need to find some potatoes in a hurry," said Kay.

"Potato," said Douglas.

Ethel's species was genetically incapable of admitting it had made a mistake. Their history books recorded that no one had ever made a mistake and therefore no one ever could. This was creative history. All mistakes—and Ethel's race had caused some disastrous ones, like the time they muddled up piranhas and bananas and destroyed the entire population of an idyllic vegetarian planet in three weeks—had been either blamed on someone else or subtly twisted around into historic successes. The piranha/banana debacle was described as the greatest population-control program in history.

The upside of this attitude was that Ethel and her people had an almost supernatural ability to look on the bright side of everything, no matter how terrible the situation. For example, if someone lost his arm in an accident, Ethel would say how wonderful it was that from now on he would have to iron only one sleeve on all his shirts and, what's more, wasn't he lucky to have a spare sleeve to use when the first one got worn out? This had not made Ethel's species a lot of friends across the galaxies, although of course the philosophy had been adopted by politicians everywhere.

So even though her creation was little more than an ungainly multicolored walking half-wit, Ethel thought he was wonderful. And she wasn't pretending, she really believed it, even right down to her deepest, most secret thoughts. For everyone else this was unbelievably infuriating.

"There's a clever boy," said Ethel.

"Potato."

"Clever? Clever!" said Jay as the creature staggered around, banging into things. "It hardly knows which foot to put in front of which."

"I've seen snails with bigger brains," said Kay.

She and Jay were nervous of the creature. Although he kept smiling at everything, it was an inane smile that made him look like he had something wrong with his facial muscles rather than he was happy. As he was so very tall, he banged his head on the laboratory door and the entrance to the elevator and the exit of the elevator and all the light fixtures.

When they had arrived at Eternalia, opening the door from the street had broken the time seal, so when they got back to the lobby everything had decayed, and the magazines, the water fountain, the potted plants were all just piles of dust. Ethel opened the outside door and they walked out into the sunshine.

"Come on, this way," she said, heading farther away from the center of the city.

Chapter 12

The Exact Dead Center of the

Universe

Jay and Kay walked on ahead and had now reached the end of the street. Jay had never been in this part of the city before, and of course Kay had never been anywhere, though she did have a lot of Jay's memories that told her she had been various places. They talked about the future as they walked along. Jay told Kay about his plan to go to the country, the small house surrounded by lush grass and trees by a crystal-clear river, a patch of vegetables, more chickens, and the girl of his dreams.

"Well, I've found the girl of my dreams," he said, blushing. "All I need is the house."

Kay squeezed his hand, as shy as he was.

"It sounds like paradise," she said, and pointing back at Ethel, added, "Though I think I'd feel happier without the chickens. If they're all like her, I've seen enough of them for the rest of my life."

There were more trees and plants growing here, as nature crept in from the countryside to reclaim the city, and they sat in the grass and waited for Douglas, Ethel, and The Oracle to catch up with them.

Over the previous two hundred years, as the population had slowly shrunk, so the need for new buildings had shrunk too. At first, as places had become deserted, they had been knocked down and the rubble carried off to the edges of the cities and dumped in huge piles. The streets had become dotted with ugly barren expanses of flat concrete where the buildings had once stood. Some people had tried to make gardens in the empty spaces, but mostly they were just left to grow over with weeds.

Later on, as the population had grown even smaller, no one had bothered to clear the rubble away and the streets had begun to resemble the aftermath of war. That was when the silence had started, a silence that had become so infectious that not only had people begun to keep their voices down, even the birds had stopped singing.

Suddenly everywhere was becoming beautiful again as the world of humans vanished under the world of nature. The flat squares of concrete, now split and crumbling, had almost vanished under lawns of soft lush grass. The wind and visiting birds had carried seeds and planted them in the remains of the old buildings, so the walls were covered in flowers. In the gutters, where more water ran, trees had grown, reaching out across the street to one another, here and there turning the road into a green tunnel. Birds had returned and they had begun to sing again. The recent rain had washed the dust off everything. Fallen lampposts and trees had made dams. Water had collected into ponds, where swallows dipped for insects. Nature had lain idle for so long in the great cities that it now seemed to be playing catch-up as fast as it could. The whole world was becoming a truly beautiful place as the derelict metropolis returned to life.

Of course, apart from the clear blue skies, little of this was very surprising to Jay, and consequently Kay. It was all they had ever known. Sure, Jay had seen photos of the world when the population was up in the billions, but photographs can never convey the feeling of really being there. The endless streets of decaying buildings were evidence enough that millions had once existed in areas where now no more than a handful of people lived. For all Jay's life there had been so few people on Earth they all would have fitted into a large stadium.

Douglas had stopped with his arms around a tree and was stroking it.

"Daddy, lovely Daddy," he said.

"No, baby, that's not your daddy," said Ethel. "Come on, there's a good boy."

"Douglas, Douglas," said Douglas, sitting in the grass. He

leaned down close to the ground and very gently began to pick daisies. And then, one by one, he delicately pushed them up his nose.

"Yum, yum," he said. "Duggals like sausage."

"Here," said Kay, handing him a dandelion, "have a cabbage."

"No cabbage," said Douglas, laughing, "light switch."

Ethel, who had been pecking up slugs, wiped her beak on the grass and waddled over to the three of them.

"Stop teasing him, or you'll cluckin' regret it," she said, and then showed Douglas what to eat and what hole to put it in.

"Mommy clever," said Douglas with his mouth full of food.

"Up and down, like Mommy showed you," said Ethel. "Move your jaw up and down."

"Unnnhhh, mmmmuhh," said Douglas.

"Now swallow."

"Ooh," said Douglas, and then, in one of the rare flashes of clarity that showed just how brilliant his mind must have been when it was in full working order, he added, "Perhaps the universe is suspended on the tooth of some monster and we are but specks of plaque on its back molars."

Jay and Kay stared at him openmouthed, but Douglas just grinned and said, "Cabbage."

"Okay, which way?" said Jay. "Left or right?"

It would be months before Jay would be able to stop himself from thinking, *I'm talking to a chicken. This isn't happening,* before he'd accept that he wasn't in a coma, it wasn't all a dream, he hadn't somehow fallen into a parallel universe, or that all that stuff about heaven and hell really was true and he'd died and gone to hell and hell was spending eternity talking to chickens. In spite of this, he still found himself asking Ethel where to go.

"Left," said Ethel.

"But that's, like, back toward the city, isn't it?" said Jay.

"Yes, but there's somewhere we have to visit before we leave," said Ethel.

"Look, chicken," said Kay. "If you're so clever, why can't you magic us up some transportation?"

"Yeah," said Jay, "why can't you, like, turn a pumpkin into a cool hovercar?"

"Oh, yes," said Ethel, "and where am I supposed to get a pumpkin?"

"Well, can't you sort of magic one up?"

"Listen, it's the basic law of science that you can't get something for nothing," said Ethel.

"Okay, so if you can't make something from nothing," said Kay, "why can't you make a pumpkin from something around here?"

"Yeah, you could use Douglas," said Jay.

"Not pumpkin," Douglas said, and began to cry. "No Duggals pumpkin, Mommy."

"Of course I won't, darling," said Ethel.

"Mommy?"

"Yes, my angel?"

"What pumpkin?"

When Ethel told him, Douglas decided that maybe he would like to be a pumpkin after all, but Ethel told him that he was so wonderful already there was no way she was going to change him into a big orange vegetable.

They passed a derelict car showroom where, by a weird, almost miraculous coincidence, sitting completely untouched in the middle of the floor, was a Trabant Whispair Deluxe Turbo, the finest hovercar ever made. And miraculously it had been untouched by the ravages of time and passing looters. Ethel walked over to it and turned it into a giant pumpkin.

"Clever Mommy," said Douglas, stroking the giant pumpkin.

"Oh, yeah, right, great," said Jay. "A minute ago we had transportation, now we have enough of the world's most boring vegetable to feed us all for, like, a month."

"All right," said Ethel, "there's your pumpkin. Now, what was it you wanted me to do with it?"

Jay told her what he wanted her to do with it, but it would have been physically impossible unless Ethel grew to ten feet tall.

"Turn it back into a damn hovercar," said Kay.

"Well, that's not very imaginative, is it?" said Ethel. "That's what it was before. How about a nice suit or some solar-powered hair rollers?"

By the time they had finally got Ethel to turn the pumpkin into a four-seater-plus-one-fish-tank hovercar in a color they were all happy with, it was late afternoon. They climbed in and sat there.

"Go on, then," said Kay. "Let's go."

The hovercar lifted itself slowly off the ground and began to move forward. Douglas clung to the side of the car looking down at the grass and shook with fear.

"Vertical, Duggals got vertical," he said.

"It's vertigo, Douglas," said Kay, "and we're only a yard off the ground."

Ethel stared at her and Kay heard herself comforting Douglas. She even stroked his hair, until bits of it began falling off.

"Where are we supposed to be going?" said Jay, weaving the car in and out of trees that were growing closer and closer together. "It's getting kind of hard to find a way through."

He'd never actually driven a hovercar before. His parents had had one but he'd been too young to use it, and since he'd been on his own, he'd never seen one that was in working order. It was a great sensation, even better than the Nintendo 2048 total-reality-hologram speed-racer game. He'd driven a land car with wheels, but even the fusion-powered DeLorean had nothing like the excitement of racing down narrow streets a yard or so above the ground. There was no doubt about it, the antigravity engine was the coolest invention of the twenty-first century. If only they could have made them small enough to fit on skateboards.

"We're nearly there," said Ethel. "Park under those trees over there by the supermarket."

The supermarket was neither super nor a market, though compared to most of the other places they had just passed, it was still recognizable as a building. It also had a roof, which the hovercar didn't, and it was beginning to rain again.

There was something strange about the supermarket. It was the only building they had passed all day without a single broken window. In fact it was the only building Jay had ever *seen* without a single broken window. The factories that made things like glass had closed down long before he had been born. He could remember his dad and his friends going out late at night and coming back with windows to patch up their house. He could also remember trying to melt broken jars and pour them out into old baking trays to make a new pane when he had kicked a football through the kitchen window.

There were no plants growing on the building. The last few inches of concrete path at the foot of the walls were bare. Something unseen was keeping them away. And no matter what angle you looked at them from, it was impossible to see through the windows, even right up close. All you could see were reflections, though not necessarily of yourself and what was all around you. For all its being preserved in time, the paint was old, dead leaves had blown into the doorway, and the place had a dusty and insignificant air that made passers-by ignore it, which was exactly why it did have the dusty insignificant air. Almost every building on Earth had been picked clean years ago, even down to the nails that held the floorboards in place, but this one had remained untouched.

"What is this?" said Kay. "It looks weird."

"That's not surprising," said Ethel. "This is the center of the universe."

"What do you mean, 'the center of the universe'?" said Jay. "What universe?"

"Oh, cluck, *the* universe," said Ethel. "There is only one. Admittedly it's billions of light-years across, but it's all one single universe and this is the exact dead center. Or rather, to be precise, the white spot on the linoleum behind the meat counter is the absolute dead center."

"But I thought, like, the universe was supposed to be infinite," said Jay. "You know, like, sort of going on forever."

"Who told you that nonsense?" said Ethel.

"Well, everyone knows that," said Jay.

"Yeah, it's cool," said Kay. "It just goes on forever and ever and ever."

"Sorry, but that's a load of crap," said Ethel. "Even Douglas knows that."

"For sure," said Douglas. "You can only find truth with logic, if you have already found truth without it. And potatoes."

And, reaching up into the branches of a small tree, he picked out a brilliant butterfly, its wings shimmering like rainbows in the evening sun, and ate it.

"Yum, yum."

"Oh, yeah?" said Kay. "Well, if you're so clever, what's on the outside of the universe, then?"

"Itself," Ethel said, and walked toward the supermarket door.

"Yes," said Douglas, "itself and potatoes."

The door slid open, more like the entrance to an air lock on a spaceship than a derelict shop. Inside, the air was unlike anything Jay or Kay had ever smelled before. It stirred deep subconscious feelings felt thousands of years before by their primeval ancestors. It was the air of ancient times long past, times before smoke and pollution, before holes in the ozone layer, before air fresheners and bleach. It was the air that had hung around the swamps of giant horsetails and forty-five-foot tree ferns browsed by dinosaurs. Air that had fed the beginnings of life itself.

Inside, the building was exactly what it said outside, a supermarket. There were rows of shelves piled high with canned food, not just from Earth but from all over the universe, foods that Jay and Kay were the first humans ever to see, and at the back, along the wall where the fresh-food counters stood, behind the meat slicer that invited you to run your fingers along the edge of its almost irresistible gleaming blade, was the exact dead center of the universe.

Jay turned back and looked out of the windows, but all he could see, even when he went right up close, were more reflections, very few of which seemed to be the inside of the supermarket. It took him a few seconds to realize that what he was seeing were the thoughts in his head made into pictures. He remembered the previous night when he and Kay had been naked together and there they were, vague indistinct images blended with the shelves of food that were standing behind him. He tried to think of something else in case Kay saw the reflections, but of course when she looked she saw her own thoughts, which were almost the same as Jay's but from a different angle.

Ethel walked up to the exact dead center and stood on it. She closed her eyes, the lights dimmed, and she settled down with her feet tucked beneath her. The lights faded completely and a wonderful sense of calm drifted over everyone. Even Douglas, who had been running up and down the aisles looking for potatoes, stood still and silent, picking his nose. Up off the floor.

The scent of flowers filled the air, golden butterflies fluttered down the aisles, and all the sell-by dates on the cans updated themselves to three months in the future. It was a beautiful moment, jam-packed with five-star karma and the scent of exotic spices that teased the back of the nose with the promise of faraway places—Bombay, Bangkok, and Ethel's mom's kitchen back home on Megaton.

Ethel's mind drifted into the higher plane. Total emptiness was everywhere. Darkness darker than the total absence of light surrounded her as she drifted, free from the terrible restrictions of the wretched chicken's body, free from the restrictions of Earth, its atmosphere, and its endless niggling details. All the galaxies that had ever existed floated around her in perfect balance and harmony as she logged on to the whole of creation, entered her user name and password, and waited.

You've got mail.

There were seven messages. Four were junk mail telling her how she had been especially chosen to be offered the opportunity to become extremely rich, slim, or both in ten minutes. There were two that had been traveling around and around in the Möbius strip of the intergalactic Internet junk-mail room for almost three hundred years. One offered her cheap Viagra, the other revealed videos of Pamela and Tommy Lee, who by now had been dead for more than two hundred years but were still performing through the intergalactic ether, as they would forever. The final E-mail was from the Megaton High Council, Appeals Board, Subdivision: Minor Planets.

> Your request to return to Megaton has been denied. You may reapply 100 years from the date of this message.

It was always the same. Over the millennia Ethel's reactions had changed from depression to anger and now settled on erratic swings between both.

And then, as quickly as it had begun, it ended. The lights came back on. Ethel stood up, fluffed out all her feathers, and walked slightly away from the exact center of the universe.

"Oh, cluck," she said with a weary sigh.

Six aisles away, Douglas farted loudly and continued his search for potatoes.

"Wow, tranquil," said Jay when the lights came back on. It seemed like only ten minutes had passed but it had been almost a quarter of an hour.

"Yeah, that was so peaceful," said Kay.

"What happened?" said Jay.

"I logged on to the universe," said Ethel.

"What?"

"You know, collected my E-mail," said Ethel. "Most of it was junk."

"You mean the exact center of the universe is just a stupid computer?" said Kay.

"I wouldn't say that exactly," said Ethel. "I like to think of it as the Great Modem. You can plug in and connect with the whole of creation, every planet, every galaxy, every living thing."

"Every potato," said Douglas.

"Oh, wow, man," said Jay. "Can I have a turn?"

"No," said Ethel. "It would be too dangerous. Your brain's just not powerful enough."

Jay knew better than to argue with her. He decided to wait until everyone was asleep. He followed Kay down the aisles, collecting cans of food, which Douglas then tore the tops off of. This wasn't particularly successful, because Douglas, who had never actually eaten or seen a potato, thought everything was potatoes and promptly ate it.

Finally, they found a can opener and they went off into the back office with a cart full of food and cheap red wine.

The wine industry had survived long after many other sections of the economy had collapsed. In fact as things had got worse, wine production had actually increased. It was like smoking. No matter how hard up smokers are, they can always find money for cigarettes. So it was with wine. As society disintegrated, people drank more. As money and resources ran out, so production methods deteriorated. Grapes gave way to nettles. Nettles gave way to potato peels and potato peels gave way to anything that would keep still long enough to allow itself to be forced into the fermenting vats.

Jay and Kay were slumped together on an old mattress they had found behind some filing cabinets and they were not drinking a good vintage. There was a picture of a smiling rat on the label above the words CABERNET LAVEMENT.

"It must be good, it's got French writing on it," said Jay, trying to drink quickly enough to get too drunk to care. The alcohol was at war in his stomach, fighting a losing battle with a can of pickled beets and a pink slimy fruit from the AlphaCentauri Fruit Packers Cooperative. Muscles he had only read about were trying to send the sixteen slices of Spam-style algae loaf back up the way they had come.

He curled into a tiny ball and tried to sleep, and as he did so the alcohol gave up the fight, mutated with the pink slime and algae, and sent him into a higher state of being that devout Buddhists spend several lifetimes trying to achieve.

He felt himself leave his body and float across the room. He passed the sleeping Kay. God, she was beautiful. One day he would have to sit down in front of her and just look at her forever and ever. He drifted through the door into the store. Ethel was asleep among the remains of dozens of half-pecked graham crackers. Douglas was curled up on the floor surrounded by hundreds of half-eaten potatoes. He had his thumb in his mouth and would have looked very peaceful if the thumb had still been joined to his hand.

The piece of paper that had written messages on the ancient typewriter and that Jay had put in his pocket now floated in front of him where his hand would have been, had he brought his body with him. As he drifted along, the piece of paper drifted ahead of him. He looked down and written on it were the words

Follow me

As he looked at it more words appeared:

and all will be revealed.

Wow, said Jay inside his head, except his head was back in the storeroom, so he actually just thought *Wow* rather than said it. There was a cold aura around the paper that changed the *wow* Jay was thinking into a silent panic, but he was too drunk to care.

The words changed into

Well, maybe not all, but quite a lot and every bit of it will be really, really interesting.

Cool.

By now he was hovering above the meat counter, right over the exact dead center of the universe. Ethel's words echoed in his memory: "It would be too dangerous. Your brain's just not powerful enough."

"Whatdersheknow, stupichicken," mumbled Jay.

What are you waiting for?

Jay floated down to the spot where Ethel had sat and closed his eyes. Nothing happened.

Left a bit.

Inside his head, or rather inside his thoughts, he saw the words and moved slightly. Still nothing. Then it started.

He was far above the supermarket looking down. There was Kay, asleep in the storeroom. There was Ethel, shuffling from foot to foot in her sleep. There was Douglas, out like a light surrounded by empty cans. There was The Oracle in her jar, swimming in slow lazy circles. They say that fish never sleep and never grow old, they just keep growing and only die from disease or being eaten by a bigger fish. It seems a small reward for having to live underwater and for having a memory span of 2.3 seconds. And there, too, was Jay himself, curled up tight clutching a box of Alka-Seltzer. So where was the supermarket roof?

The shop grew smaller and smaller until it was no more than a dot. The dot grew smaller until it vanished and the curve of the earth appeared. The air grew cold and then he was out of the earth's atmosphere, floating in a vacuum in space, with broken satellites and space stations crashing and banging into one another in complete silence. Although they were more than two hundred years old, a few of them were still working, sending signals, readings from space, photos of long-deserted military installations, down to the planet's surface, though of course people had stopped listening generations ago. A sad dead monkey floated past, strapped into a tiny seat, its glazed-over eyes staring sightlessly out of a cracked porthole.

Jay wanted to look around, to see the vastness of space, but he was too scared to take his eyes off the earth, in case it disappeared and then he was never able to get back again. Then the whole planet vanished and he was alone. Except for the piece of paper. All alone in a sentence without a verb.

Ohshitman, was the first thought that went through his mind. It was also the second and third thoughts. The piece of paper drifted over and wrapped itself around his virtual wrist, squeezing it in a comforting way, and gently pulled him farther and farther away from Earth.

Oh, shit. Like, big, big double shit, was the fourth thought that went through his mind. The trouble was, he was sobering up, and as he did so the reality of what he had done and where he was began to sink in. He didn't know it but his body and his mind had become separated and he was scared witless. This was something he'd never imagined. There had been nothing in the three thousand books about out-of-body experiences, except as fiction. He had no information to tell him what to do next. There was only one choice, to get as drunk as he could and hope everything sorted itself out.

"I don't suppose you've got a drink, have you?" he said to no one. The possibility that he was actually talking to a piece of paper was even more ridiculous to contemplate than the fact that he had spent the last few days talking to a chicken and a fish in a jar. For an instant the words

You need to be stone-cold sober.

appeared on the paper, followed by

Don't worry, we're nearly there.

This implied, of course, that Jay was going to a specific place, which in turn implied that he might not be going back. It scared the pants off him. Except that his pants were thousands of miles below him in the supermarket storeroom, just about as far as they could be scared off already.

Now he was stone-cold sober and terrified. All the usual stuff went through his head. Why hadn't he listened to his mom, or more specifically why hadn't he listened to his chicken? Why had he drunk so much and why hadn't he concentrated more at school, or more specifically why hadn't he gone to school? And why had he come out without a warm coat on such a cold night and without some aspirin?

"I want to go back now, please," he said as inoffensively as he could.

I told you not to worry. We've arrived.

They had stopped. The earth looked about the size of a football. It glowed blue and white like an exquisite jewel. Humbled by the sight, Jay fell silent and just stared fixedly at it. There was Africa, there was India, and there, on the edge, was the beginning of Australia.

Future Eden

Now you can see why you are here,

wrote the paper.

> You are the only human ever to have gazed
> upon the earth from this exact spot. You must
> now consider what you can see. Take all the
> information from your three thousand books
> and lay it out in your mind. It contains
> the refined knowledge and experience of your
> entire species. Don't move your gaze from
> the planet. Look upon the world to see the
> whole tiny globe in its true perspective, a small
> insignificant dot, near a small insignificant sun,
> and its inhabitants no more than specks of dust
> on that dot. That is the true perspective. Consider
> this knowledge and you will realize how stupid
> mankind has been. See what centuries of petty
> squabbling, arrogance, and posturing have brought
> you to. You hover on the edge of extinction, on
> the razor's edge of no return. Look and learn.

Jay felt himself shrink to the size of a pinpoint. The poem
kept running through his mind:

> This is the way the world ends
> This is the way the world ends
> This is the way the world ends
> Not with a bang but a whimper.

The paper wrapped itself around his wrist and began to
move off into deep space.
"Why me?" he said. "Why are you telling me this?"

You are the Chosen One.

It would say nothing more. Jay asked it to explain—chosen
for what, by whom?—but the paper was blank.
With his free hand, Jay grabbed the paper and tore it off his

wrist. He screwed it up into a ball. He had caught it by surprise and could feel it wriggling in his hands, trying to straighten up. It put the thought into his head that there was something really important written on it, that he had to open it up and read it, but the spell was broken. Jay pulled back his arm and threw the paper away as hard as he could, and pushing down his fear with all the anger he could summon up, he shouted, "I WANT TO GO BACK!"

There was a brief flash of light and he was back in the supermarket, back inside his body, lying on the floor covered in rashers of bacon, mostly streaky but with a few slices of choice meat here and there. Ethel the chicken was standing on his chest.

"I told you not to go there, didn't I?" she said, jumping up onto the counter.

"I know," said Jay, staring at his feet and shuffling them around in the bacon.

"I knew you would, though. That's why I was waiting," said Ethel.

"But you were fast asleep," said Jay.

"You mean over there," she said, pointing to a chicken sleeping two aisles away. As Jay stared openmouthed at it, it slowly changed into a frozen chicken and rolled off the shelf.

"So, like, how did you bring me back?" he said.

"I moved the exact dead center of the universe a tiny bit to the left," said Ethel.

"Yeah, right, you mean that you, a chicken, shifted the whole of creation?" said Jay.

"No, no, of course not," said Ethel. "Well, actually, yes, I did. I took a few uninhabited planets from point A and moved them across to point B."

"Wow, man, that's pretty cool," said Jay. "I really wish I could believe you."

"Right, now cluck off back to bed and get some sleep. We've got a long day tomorrow."

"What's the Chosen One?" said Jay, and he told Ethel what the paper had written.

The chicken was visibly disturbed, though she hid it very quickly.

"It's nothing. It was just screwing around with you," she lied.

Jay was the Chosen One, the New Adam, the Messiah Two, whatever you wanted to call it, but it was far too soon for him to know that. He had a lot more learning to do before he would be ready, before he would be wise enough to carry the weight.

Jay wasn't tired. He walked to the front of the store and went out into the street. It was the first time he'd been outside at night since Ethel had cleared all the clouds away. The whole sky looked like those photographs of a city at night from an airplane, only upside-down, tiny lights from side to side. The night air felt so clean, and he realized that by taking away the endless yellow clouds, Ethel had taken away all the pollution, too.

I wonder where it's gone, he thought. It was a thought he immediately wished he hadn't had, because he had an awful feeling that one day he would go there and it would be like descending into hell.

As he looked up at the twinkling stars, something fluttered down from the sky. He reached out and caught it. It was a piece of paper, *the* piece of paper, and on it was written

Hi.

Jay ran back into the store, searching up and down the aisles until he found what he was looking for, a box of matches. He went back outside, held the paper in one hand, and struck a match.

It'll end in tears

appeared. He held the match to the paper but nothing happened. He lit two matches at once, and then three, four, ten, but the paper wouldn't burn. The box burst into flames, setting his shirtsleeve on fire and burning his hand.

Told you so. Aisle six, halfway down, top shelf, ointment and Band-Aids.

"Smug bastard," said Jay, batting his sleeve until the fire went out. "Oh, man, I'm talking to a piece of paper. I wish I'd never met that stupid chicken. Nothing's been cool since then."

Aisle twenty-seven, far end, men's shirts.

It was hard to imagine a piece of paper laughing, but Jay swore it did. He folded it into four and put it in his back pocket, where, in the darkness, the words

That's a good boy

appeared in bloodred crayon.

When he had changed his shirt and seen to his hand, Jay went back to the storeroom. He wanted to wake Kay and tell her what had happened. His heart was beating. For God's sake, he'd been in outer space, or at least his mind had, which didn't make sense, but then he had been pretty drunk. Maybe he'd just dreamed it. That would be the logical explanation, but he knew it hadn't been a dream. It had just been too real. All this Chosen One stuff was confusing too, chosen for what and by whom? He wanted to take Kay outside and show her the night sky, show her where he had been. It would be dawn soon and the stars would be gone. Staring at Earth from so far away and the words on the paper had made him feel very small and insignificant. He wanted to curl up in Kay's arms and feel whole again.

But Kay wasn't there. The mattress was still warm where she had been sleeping. Her image was dented into its surface, but there was no sign of her. Jay sat down and waited. She'd probably just gone to the bathroom, but ten minutes later there was still no sign of her. He walked around the store, but wherever he looked there was no sign of her. She couldn't have gone out of the front door, he'd have seen her, and the other doors, at the back of the store, were all locked. He searched through his pockets in case in some ridiculous way a key might have got there, but his pockets were all empty. Even the piece of paper was gone.

*   *   *   *

Meanwhile, life for Fluffy, who of course was more than a fish, had not been so uneventful. At first things had been fairly quiet. Jay carried her into the supermarket and set her jar on the meat counter. She swam left for a bit and then watched Ethel and later Jay stand on the exact dead center of the universe, and then, suddenly, life got more exciting, far more exciting than Fluffy really wanted it to.

When Ethel moved the exact dead center of the universe to rescue Jay, she hadn't given any thought to where she was moving it to. It hadn't seemed important, and if Fluffy's jar hadn't been sitting where it was, it wouldn't have been.

Fluffy felt herself—or, to be precise, felt her mind—fly upward. Looking down, she saw her body still swimming around and around in lazy circles. Proof, if she needed it, of just how mindless fish really are. Like Jay, she floated farther and farther away from the earth until it was no more than a dot. Yet inside her thoughts she could still see and hear the surroundings that her body was in.

"Oh, cluck," she heard Ethel say. The chicken was staring into her jar. She watched Jay walk outside and look up into the sky.

"Up here," she shouted, knowing it was a totally ridiculous thing to do. There was no way Jay could hear her, but it looked for all the world as if he was staring right at her.

If only The Oracle had some bloody arms, she thought, and waved her fins.

Something shot past her, making absolutely no whooshing sound in the eternal vacuum of space. It was a ball of scrunched-up paper.

And then the earth was gone and she was alone.

So what else is new? she thought. It had been a long lonely life being The Oracle. Sure, it had been fun at first, right at the beginning, with all those people hanging on her every word, and all those young men who couldn't take their eyes off her. She had been incredibly gorgeous, long brown hair, deep blue eyes, and a figure to die for. She'd always been gorgeous. When she was a rat, for example, she had had the longest, softest eyelashes any rat had ever had. But nowadays nobody cared. Sure, she was the most beautiful goldfish that ever lived, but how could you tell? The only people who showed any interest in her wanted to see her lying on a plate next to a pile of french fries. And she couldn't even remember the last time anyone had asked for any advice or even wanted to cuddle her.

"Jolly well, stuff the bloomin' lot of them, that's what The Oracle says," she said to herself. "The Oracle might as well be up here as back on that ungrateful bloody planet full of ignorant oicks."

And that got her thinking. Where had she come from? Every other living creature had a mother and father, but who were The Oracle's mom and dad, Mr. and Mrs. Oracle Sr.? As far as she could remember she had started off as a half-god on Earth, but she had no memory of being a child and growing up or having parents, and anyway, what other beings changed into different life-forms?

"I say, that's awfully clever. Why on earth didn't The Oracle think of it before?" she said to herself as she floated off into the dark space behind the Milky Way. "After all, isn't The Oracle just about the cleverest creature in creation?"

And she suddenly felt very, very lonely.

Chapter 13

The Gene Pool

Jay felt the sick feeling of panic in his stomach. Kay was the greatest love of his life and now he had lost her. Actually, she was the only love of his live so far, apart from that one time on vacation by the empty lake at the sand-skiing resort, but he'd only been twelve and what had happened couldn't really be described as love, even though he had loved it. And somehow he sensed that Kay had not just gone to the housewares department or outside to look at the stars, but was somewhere else far, far away.

"Don't worry," said Ethel, "she's not far away."

"But the piece of paper's gone too, man," said Jay.

"Well, I did tell you to leave it alone," said Ethel.

"I know, I know, man," said Jay. "But it was only, like, a piece of paper."

"Yes, well, now you know that's not the case, don't you?" said Ethel.

"Yeah, right. So what is it?"

"Well, hasn't it occurred to you that if I've come here from the other side of the universe, other beings could have done the same? No, it hasn't, has it?" said Ethel. "I wish there were some quick way I could make your brain work properly."

"What are you talking about?" said Jay. "My brain's a hundred times bigger than yours."

"Size isn't everything," said Ethel. "It's what you do with it. I mean, ninety-eight percent of the human brain just sits there drooling. It's like Bubble Wrap and in the middle of it there's a tiny two percent saying, 'Hello, clouds. Hello, trees. E equals MC squared.' If it weren't so sad, it would be hilarious. E equals MC squared, indeed."

"I haven't the faintest idea what you're talking about," said Jay.

"I rest my case," said Ethel.

"Would you like me to carry it, Mommy?" said Douglas, who had just woken up.

"Carry what?" said Ethel.

"Your case."

"Yeah, yeah," said Jay, getting more and more agitated. "Forget cabbage-head and screw the paper, can we just find Kay?"

"All in good time," said Ethel.

"Now is good time, man," said Jay. "Later is bad time."

"There's no hurry," said Ethel, but she was lying, or to be absolutely dead accurate, she was half lying.

"But the longer we wait, the farther away she'll be," said Jay. "Won't she?"

He wanted to pick Ethel up and shake her, but he knew that if he did, something terrible might happen to him, like getting turned into a potato peeler. The damn bird was being so frustrating though. She seemed to feel no sense of urgency at all.

"No," said Ethel, again only half lying, though she would have argued that she was half telling the truth.

"So where is she?" said Jay. "I can't find her."

"In the closet under the stairs," said Ethel, "with the spiders."

"Stairs, what stairs, man? There aren't any damn stairs," said Jay.

"Except for the ones down to the cellar," said Ethel, "but they were bricked up more than a century ago."

"If they're bricked up, how did she get down there?" said Jay.

"They've just been unbricked," said Ethel. "Follow me."

She led Jay down the aisles to the far side of the store, where it was dark and dusty. The shelves were filled with medical supplies and pots and pans and it was obvious that no one had been here for years, not even Kay.

"No one's been here for years, man," said Jay. "The floor's covered in dust and the only footprints are ours."

"There are other ways to travel apart from walking," said Ethel.

"Oh, very deep."

"Yeah," said Douglas, "you can roll, like a potato."

"Shut up," said Jay.

"You can fly," said Douglas, "like a flying potato."

They came to the last aisle. All the shelves had been tipped over and everywhere was ankle-deep in Band-Aids and fish slices. But even this seemed to have happened a long time ago, because everything was peacefully lying under a soft blanket of thick dust.

"Oooh, look. Oooh, potato peeler," said Douglas, diving into the dust and coming up with a big grin on his face and a peeler in each hand. "Now find potato," he added, walking back the way they had come. "I would be transported to heightened lands of pure blissful joy where E equals MC tripled and potatoes live free and unfettered, and although I haven't got where I am today, I soon will have . . ."

His rambling voice trailed off into the distance, leaving Jay and Ethel in a silence so deep they could hear the dust settle down and smooth itself back over the rest of the potato peelers.

"So where is she?" said Jay.

"Behind there," said Ethel, pointing to the only set of shelves still standing. It was full of pads of writing paper, and if Jay had bothered to look closely, he would have seen that every page was shivering in anticipation. The molecules of dust covering the pads shivered too, and under all the garbage on the floor pencils edged as far away as inanimate objects with no arms, legs, or brains could possibly move.

Jay tipped the shelves forward and behind them was the newly unbricked doorway that led down to the cellar.

"Take this," said Ethel, and a flashlight flew from the "Household Items A–H" shelves into Jay's hand. "I'll wait here."

Jay pointed the flashlight down into the darkness. The

stairs seemed to go on forever, down beyond the beam of light, down far deeper than any normal cellar, into a darkness far stronger than total darkness. On the right-hand side there was a wall of wet bricks running with unimaginable stains that cringed as the flashlight beam crossed over them. On the left side there was nothing, not even the darkness, just nothing.

"What is this place, man?" he asked nervously.

It was like a scene from one of his childhood nightmares, exactly like it. The penny poised on the edge of the shelf but didn't drop. Jay's own subconscious wouldn't let it. The idea that Ethel had created Jay's childhood dreams was too terrible to contemplate. If it were true, then it would surely mean that she could have created or at least controlled every part of his life. Jay's subconscious repressed the idea in case it was all just an illusion. After all, it was Jay aged twenty-two who thought the entrance to the cellar was like his childhood dreams. Surely it was possible that his dreams hadn't been like that at all and Ethel had just altered his memories. That was a far less frightening option.

"Do you remember the Nintendo 2048?" said Ethel. "You know, the one with the holograms you could climb into?"

"Oh, yeah," said Jay. "They were great. A friend of mine vanished into one of them. One minute he was skimming over the red seas of Mars, maximum weapons, maximum bonus, then there was a power outage, just a split second, and we, like, never saw him again."

"He wasn't the only one," said Ethel. "Dozens of people disappeared. And the ridiculous thing was that instead of the machines being banned, they sold ten times as many. Three hundred eighty-six people vanished in four weeks. It was all hushed up of course. The idea that virtual reality had actually become more real than real reality was too terrifying to comprehend."

"Wow," said Jay. "Did any of them ever turn up?"

Ethel pointed down into the darkness.

"What, you mean they're down there in the cellar?" said Jay.

"Sort of," said Ethel.

"What do you mean, 'sort of'?" said Jay. He knew that when Ethel said "sort of," what it really meant was either "definitely" or "not at all."

"It isn't a cellar."

"Well, what the hell is it?" said Jay. "And how did Kay get down there?"

"It's somewhere else," said Ethel, "and she was taken there while she was asleep."

"Who by?"

"Well," said Ethel, "I'm afraid I can't tell you."

She didn't know. She had her suspicions but she didn't know for sure and she didn't want Jay to know she didn't know. It was vital that he saw her as flawless. To him above all people she had to appear perfect, totally in control of everything, all-knowing, all-wise, and wonderful. If he was to grow and develop and help her save everything, then he had to have complete faith in her.

"Sometimes," said Jay, "you are the most frustrating person . . . uh, chicken . . . uh, creature I've ever met."

The piece of paper had been right. Earth and its population were a tiny insignificant part of creation. What it hadn't said was that Ethel the chicken was even more insignificant.

What made things so difficult for Ethel was that she had no one to talk to. Sure, she could communicate telepathically with her sisters, dotted around this pathetic little planet, but what was the point of that? Apart from Brenda, who was seriously strange, the other two were as pissed off as she was. She certainly couldn't talk to humans about it. There was no way she was going to let Jay know how she felt and as for Douglas, he was a great disappointment. Something would have to be done about him. Parts of him would have to be replaced.

"Go on, cluck off," she said, pointing her wing down the stairs. If she didn't get away from Jay for a bit, she might end up doing something she'd regret.

"Aren't you coming?" said Jay.

"No, I've got a few things to do," said Ethel. "You just run down there and get your wife. She's in the closet under the stairs."

"Can I take Douglas with me?"

"If he wants to go," said Ethel.

"Hey, Douglas, I've found the biggest potato in the whole world," Jay shouted.

Douglas came lumbering down the aisles, sending the shelves flying in all directions.

"Potato," he said, clutching his peelers, "where, where?"

"Down there, man," said Jay, pointing into the darkness.

"You must think I was born yesterday," said Douglas.

"You were, man," said Jay.

"Oh, yes. All right, then, come on," said Douglas, and they set off down the stairs.

The air grew cold and damp as they went down into the darkness. Jay could feel it stroking his skin as he passed through it, close and clammy like sides of pork hanging in a butcher's cooler, as if it were alive, or rather it had been alive until recently. It was like the air was checking him out. Douglas, blissfully unaware of any impending doom, speculated about the size of the biggest potato in the world and sang to himself.

"When we find the potato," he said, "do you think it will be so big I won't be able to lift it?"

"Yeah, yeah, probably," said Jay.

"What color is it?"

"Yeah, yeah, probably," said Jay.

"That's not a color."

Later, as the flashlight began to grow weaker and the doorway at the top of the stairs was no larger than a pinpoint, Douglas started to get anxious.

"I can smell the potato," he said, and began jumping up and down. "It's really, really big."

"Yeah, right, man," said Jay, and then, as Douglas started crying, he added, "There's nothing to worry about, man. Everything's cool."

He didn't really care that Douglas was scared. He was more worried that the creature would panic and rush back up to the store, leaving him alone or even knocking him off the edge of the stairs.

"But, but . . . ," Douglas sobbed.

"It's all right," said Jay. "Think of the awesome potato, man—the biggest, coolest potato that, like, ever existed."

"I am," cried Douglas. "And we won't have a saucepan big enough to cook it in."

"Shit, man," said Jay. "We'll cut it up into pieces." And he thought, *This is ridiculous. I'm beginning to believe in the damn potato myself.*

Which was a good thing really. It meant that when they reached the bottom step and found their way completely blocked by the biggest potato in not only the world but the whole of creation from the beginning of time he was partly prepared.

Douglas fell to his knees and held out his arms. "God," he said softly. "I have seen the face of God."

"Oh, shit," said Jay.

"This must be the gate of heaven," said Douglas, stroking the potato as if it had the porcelain skin of a newborn baby.

"No, man, it's a potato, a damn great enormous potato," said Jay. "And it's in the damn way."

"But . . . ," Douglas protested as Jay tried to push the giant vegetable out of the way.

"Look, man, it's a potato, a huge one admittedly, but it's still, like, just a potato, and it's in our way. Now come and push."

But it wouldn't move.

"Okay, we'll have to dig our way through. Have you got your potato peeler?" said Jay.

"Yes."

"Then start digging."

Douglas had a pocket full of potato peelers, but even with one in each hand, it took the pair of them four hours to dig a tunnel. Finally, sticky from head to toe, they wriggled through onto another flight of stairs that led them down to the cellar.

"Shall I turn the light on?" said Douglas.

"Don't be ridiculous, man," said Jay. "Do you really think there'd be a light down here? Anyway, don't you remember, there hasn't been any electricity for, like, eighty-seven years?"

114

"Of course I don't remember. Don't *you* remember, my brain's been sitting in a jar for two hundred years?" said Douglas. "Anyway, the light switch has fresh fingerprints on it."

"What! How on earth . . . ," said Jay.

Something strange had happened to Douglas since they had come down to the cellar. It had actually started as soon as they had begun digging through the giant potato. Its juice had covered Douglas from head to toe. Jay had hung back, letting Douglas do most of the digging. As he tunneled, Douglas had drunk the potato juice, licking the walls of the tunnel and mumbling. Now he was completely coated with the warm sticky fluid.

He had had odd flashes of intelligence before, little glimpses in his normal subnormal behavior. But something strange had happened that seemed to be turning him into an idiot savant with special gifts. His incredible sense of smell could be explained by the fact that part of his brain had once belonged to a dog, but for goodness' sake, if he could see fingerprints in the dark and even tell how recent they were, something pretty awesome was going on. Maybe he was right about the mystical powers of the potato. Jay didn't feel any different at all.

Douglas flipped the light switch and one by one hundreds of tiny lights flickered on high above them like a field of stars. The cellar was a huge cave with tunnels going off in all directions. Jay didn't realize that the lights looked like stars because they were stars. They were, as Ethel had said, somewhere else and what they couldn't know was that the somewhere else was the crucible, the very fountain of creation, the most sought-after place in the whole universe, the place where it had all begun. Here the first tiny seed that had started everything had been created. This was the only place anywhere where you didn't dare say, "I wonder how this was created?" because if you did, you went insane.

"Wow, man, I wonder how this was created?" said Jay, blissfully unaware of where he was. "This is, like, the most way-cool place I've ever seen."

It was a mystery how the crucible came to be on Earth,

hidden below a mysterious supermarket. If it was truly the fountain of creation, of every galaxy and every form of life, who had brought it there, and why and how? There were so many huge unanswerable questions, which fortunately for him were way beyond Jay's present mental abilities. Maybe it had been there forever and the earth had been created to hide it. Every idea just generated more questions. Hide it from whom?

In the middle of the cave was a smooth pool of dark water. In the middle of the pool was a small island and in the middle of the island was a small house with a delicate line of smoke rising from a chimney. If it had all been above them, in the outside world, beneath the new blue sky, it would have been idyllic, but here in the damp gloomy cave lit by the eerie glow of a clear night sky, it was menacing, very menacing, and yet totally irresistible.

"This is pretty," said Douglas.

"No, man, it's totally cool, but it's not pretty," said Jay. "It's weird."

"No, no, it's pretty. Look at the lovely little house," said Douglas. He was beginning to talk to Jay as if he were a child.

"No, man," said Jay. "I have a weird feeling about this place."

"You have a weird feeling about every place," said Douglas. "We can go to the house and have cake and tea."

"Where the hell's the closet under the stairs?" said Jay, walking over to the lake and turning around slowly. Then he said, "Oh, shit."

Looking back to where he'd come from, he saw that under the 3,070 stairs there were closets, hundreds and hundreds and hundreds of them, stretching off and up in level after level as far as the eye could see.

Jay felt his wit's end approaching. It was all getting too difficult.

"It's all that stupid chicken's fault, man," he said.

"Mommy saved your life, remember?" said Douglas.

"How do you know that, man? You weren't even, you know, like, you didn't exist then. She's just made everything so complicated," said Jay.

"You wouldn't have Kay if it weren't for Mommy," said Douglas. "And I'd still be disintegrating in jars."

"Yeah, right, I'm sorry, man. I just feel so helpless," said Jay. "I mean, I used to have it all together, but now it's all over the place."

He walked across to one of the closets and turned a handle. The door was locked. He tried another and another. They were locked too. He climbed up to the next row of doors, but every one he tried was shut fast. He put his shoulder to a door, but it was solid oak and barely shivered when he threw himself against it.

"Okay, so now what?" he said, looking down at Douglas.

"We need to get the keys."

"Yeah, right, so where are they? I don't exactly see a nail, you know, with a huge bunch of keys hanging on it," said Jay.

"Over there," said Douglas, pointing to the island, "in the house."

"Yeah, and I expect the house is, like, guarded by a dragon or some ridiculous witch," said Jay, "or another stupid chicken."

"Don't be silly," said Douglas. "There's cake and tea. I can smell it, chocolate cake all warm and yummy."

"So what's the catch, man?" said Jay. "I mean, like, if there isn't a catch, then why are the keys over there at all?"

"The pool," said Douglas. "You've got to cross the pool."

"Is it deep?" said Jay.

"Bottomless."

"So why can't we just swim across?" said Jay. "I know it looks cold but it's not far."

"Do you know what the pool is called?" said Douglas.

"Oh, go on, man, let me guess," sighed Jay. "The Black Lagoon and there's a giant sea serpent with fifty arms."

"No."

"Well?"

"It's called the Gene Pool," said Douglas, "and it makes you."

"Makes you? Makes you what?" said Jay.

"Makes you nothing," said Douglas. "It makes you."

"So, uh, what does that mean exactly?" he asked.

"Dunno," said Douglas.

"So you reckon it's all right?" said Jay.

"Probably," said Douglas. "Mommy wouldn't let anything hurt me."

"Well, why don't you swim across and get the keys while I try and figure out which door to open?"

"Okay," said Douglas, "but you have to come with me."

"Why?"

"Because I said so and I'm bigger than you," said Douglas.

He took off all his clothes, picked Jay up and took his clothes off too, sat him on his shoulders, and walked into the water, except that it wasn't water. And it wasn't cold either. The air in the cave was cold and stale, but the water that wasn't water was the perfect temperature, exactly the same temperature as the human body, so that while Douglas and Jay were in it, it felt as if it wasn't there. It was a very weird sensation. They could feel the resistance of the water that wasn't water, but because it was the same temperature as they were to a millionth of a degree, they couldn't feel the water that wasn't water itself. It was a thousand times better than getting into bed on a cold winter's night with the electric blanket on. It was fifty times better than getting into bed on a cold winter's night with the electric blanket on and cuddling up to the soft warm body of someone you love. It was ten times better than what sometimes follows getting into bed on a cold winter's night with the electric blanket on and cuddling up to the soft warm body of someone you love.

"Ooh, lovely, lovely, lovely," Douglas said as he swam slowly toward the island, feeling probably the most beautiful sensation he'd ever felt. The film of potato juice that had covered his skin now began to dissolve slowly and sink into his body. It permeated his muscles, swam with his blood to his heart and brain. It realigned broken connections. It rewired broken fuses. It turned on his lights.

Jay could feel it too. He was only wet up to his waist, but the urge to submerge himself completely was so strong that he slipped off Douglas's shoulders and swam beside him.

"Oh, wow, man," he said as they sat resting on the island. It was almost impossible not to run straight back into the pool, to give himself up utterly to the indescribable sensations.

"Coo," said Douglas, innocently uninhibited about his feelings and nakedness, even though he was not a pretty sight, with his body sections of different-colored skin.

"I suppose we better find the keys," said Jay.

"Yes, then we can swim back," said Douglas, "very slowly."

A few seconds after they went inside the house, there was a faint noise of rushing air, followed by a splash.

She wonders where she is, thought the creator of the splash. *She has a very strong feeling of déjà vu.*

It was Fluffy, The Oracle. She had traveled far out into uncharted space, which was about 99.99 percent of it. She had visited fabulous worlds with great civilizations and generally gone where no goldfish had gone before, and at every planet the message had been the same: "Piss off."

Space, she had concluded, was a very racist place, or to be exact a very fishist place. And the fact that she had been swimming in the pool for several minutes without anyone telling her to go away told her that she must have returned to Earth.

Then it came back to her, the déjà vu. This was the source of all life, the Gene Pool, the fountain of creation, and the place where, if you knew how to do it, you could become anything you wanted, maybe even immortal. The memories that had been wiped from her mind before she had been sent to Earth gradually began to re-form. She had nothing tangible to grasp yet, no mother, no father, no childhood, but she knew it would all come back and for now that was enough.

"I can't find any keys," said Jay. "Are you sure they're here?"

"Definitely," said Douglas.

The house had only two rooms, one up, one down. Neat furniture, a fire burning in the grate, pretty lace curtains, saucepans of food cooking on an old range, but no sign of anyone. It was like a set out of Disneyland, a cross between *Alice in Wonderland* and "Goldilocks and the Three Bears."

Jay kept expecting some animal dressed in clothes to walk in and start talking to him.

"The keys are in the closet under the stairs," said a rabbit in an orange shower cap. It had been sitting in one of the saucepans. "But then, isn't everything?" it continued. "Pass me that towel."

"This is getting totally ridiculous," said Jay, walking outside.

"Hey, what about the towel?" the rabbit shouted after him.

Of course, the rabbit in the saucepan was ridiculous. It had to be a hallucination. Maybe it was something to do with swimming in the pool. Sure enough, when Jay went back inside, there was no sign of the saucepan, just Douglas and the rabbit sitting at the table eating cake.

"Did you get the keys, man?" said Jay.

"They're in the closet under the stairs," said Douglas.

"Isn't everything?" said the rabbit. "Careful how you open it."

But it was too late. Jay had done it and was now standing ankle-deep in a small mountain of keys.

"Shit."

Douglas sifted through the pile, picking out the odd key. He put them together on a large ring and said, "It's one of these."

"How on earth do you know that?" said Jay.

"They're still warm," said Douglas.

"We're never going to find her, man," said Jay. "There's, like, hundreds of doors and thousands of keys. By the time we find her she'll have starved to death or suffocated."

Douglas told him that only twenty-seven of the doors had been opened in the past 780 years and the keys were the ones on the ring.

"Come on, then, man, let's go," said Jay.

"I'm having some chocolate cake," Douglas protested.

As Jay swam slowly back across the Gene Pool, surrounded by an aura of deep sensual awareness, he became aware that he was not alone. Something was swimming below him. It brushed his leg as it swam by and made his heart race in fear.

The way things had been going, whatever was in the pool with him was probably going to turn out to be some terrifying monster that would eat him very slowly. He told himself he should get to the shore as quickly as possible, but the magic of the pool filled his head with visions of peace and beauty. He rolled over onto his back and gave himself up to the wonderful feelings. He tried hard to be concerned about what was swimming below him, but never in his whole life had he felt such perfect calm and contentment—above him the sixteen heavens of the Mahayana Buddha, below him the eight hot hells and the eight cool hells, but here on the infinitely thin interface of the world was perfection. The water that wasn't water held him like a mother holding a newborn baby, a light yet perfectly safe caress that shut out all the sadness in the world. He felt as though he could stay floating there forever, drifting in a vacuum of immortality. It was almost impossible to leave.

"She wouldn't stay here for too long if she were you, old chap," said a familiar voice in his left ear.

"Fluffy?" said Jay, waking from his dream.

"The Oracle doesn't suppose you'd stroke her scales, would you?" said The Oracle dreamily.

"What is this place, man?" said Jay as he swam toward the shore. "It's, like, the coolest, most wonderful far-out place I've ever been to. I want to stay here forever and ever."

"Of course you do. Everyone does. Super, isn't it?" said The Oracle. "It's the Gene Pool."

"I have to get out and find Kay," said Jay, trying to convince himself.

Then he saw them, the images of thousands of people floating, like he had been, on their backs, faces to the sky, lost in total peace, their eyes wide in perfect contentment, the thousands of other people who had come to the pool seeking eternity and had found it. Only they were all dead, their spirits absorbed into the Gene Pool, their floating images no more than ghosts. Their eternity had also been their extermination. Their physical bodies had been absorbed into the Gene Pool itself and their spirits had been examined and filed away in one of the sixteen heavens or hells. Reincarnation? Yeah, right, there was no way the Gene Pool was letting them back into the land of the living.

Like a giant pitcher plant, it needed bodies to keep alive.

Over the millennia tens of thousands of life-forms from many galaxies, not just Earth, had swum to the island and eaten cake with the rabbit, but fewer than ten had made it back to the shore. Only rare and special people could enter the Gene Pool and leave it again. Jay swam toward the shore but seemed to get no nearer. Too much of him wanted to stay in the pool. But at last he began to move, to edge slowly away from the island, as though the pool knew it couldn't keep him.

Up in the supermarket, Ethel, who had been watching everything through Jay's eyes, breathed an enormous sigh of relief. At last things seemed to be going according to plan. She watched Jay swim back across the pool and knew beyond all doubt that she had chosen the right one. She waited. How would her creation, Douglas, survive the pool? She held her breath and waited and waited. Douglas was in no hurry. He was still eating chocolate cake and drinking tea with the rabbit. But Ethel needn't have worried. Douglas walked into the pool and swam straight back in record time.

"Come on, little fishy," he said, scooping Fluffy up into an empty jar that miraculously appeared on the bank, and carrying her out of the water that wasn't water. And of course in her jar Fluffy was still swimming in the Gene Pool. No one, not even Ethel, realized that Douglas had transferred not only The Oracle into the jar but some of the Gene Pool as well.

The Gene Pool had been unable to get Douglas into focus. His body being made from so many different people had confused it. It could feel ten people but they were all in the same place at the same time. But the body wasn't the real problem. It was Douglas's mind. The minds of all the species it had ever encountered worked in the same basic way, be they humans from Earth or bi-terapods from the outer rim of Fiasco. Of course, each species thought totally different things, came to different conclusions, had different dreams, but their brains all followed fundamental rules of nature. Nature was universal. It had to be—after all, it had all evolved from the one place, the Gene Pool, the crucible of existence. And this was where Douglas broke the rules. He appeared not to be following those rules and the reason he had swum back so quickly was that the Gene Pool had been trying to spit him out. It shuddered at Douglas's aftertaste and a circle of tiny waves rippled across its surface.

Ethel had observed all this and come to a very exciting conclusion. It was wonderful to know that she had chosen the right person to be the Chosen One in Jay, but this new development with Douglas was a real bonus. Somehow combining the parts of a human brain with little bits of dog's brain and just a touch of cat's had produced something far greater than the sum of its parts. She wondered if she would have got the same result with a different brain or a touch more cat with a bit less dog.

Jay took the keys from Douglas and went over to the doors. After half an hour he found a door that one of the keys fitted, but all there was in the closet were some old picnic chairs, an electricity meter, and some ancient gas masks. The next five closets were almost exactly the same. It was as though someone had collected all the closets under the stairs from every suburban home three hundred years earlier and put them all together in a time capsule.

It had happened in the late 1950s. In a small northern town hundreds of families had come downstairs one morning to find their under-stairs closets and everything inside them had simply vanished. Where they had been there was nothing, not even the closet door. Of course the authorities had hushed everything up at the time. Everyone had been given a new closet and boots and assorted junk, and been told it was something to do with civil defense and not to talk to anyone about it. The whole thing had passed quietly away into urban myth.

The seventh closet was the same too, except that there was a body slumped inside it, wedged between an ironing board and two umbrellas.

It was Kay and she was unconscious. Or rather, she was in a trance. Her eyes were wide open but they were completely empty. She was breathing very slowly and when Jay lifted her up she stood there without falling over. He took her hand and led her along, and she followed like a robot.

"What's the matter with her, man?" said Jay. "Has she, you know, been hypnotized?"

"The Oracle knows what has happened," said The Oracle. "Her mind has been stolen."

"Oh, man," said Jay. "It just gets worse and worse."

"It is nothing to worry about, actually," said The Oracle. "She's still alive. All you have to do is sort of find her mind and put it back. The Oracle says Ethel will know where it is."

Deeply buried memories from before his brain had been put into the cryonic jar were beginning to come back to Douglas. There were at least three personalities at war in his head. The human would win, but the cat would always be there, seeing in the dark, hearing a pin drop three rooms away, sharpening the human senses. The dog would be there too, catching the echo of scents long gone and fighting against the urge to chase himself up trees. Until he learned to put his personalities into perspective, just taking the best and discarding the rest, life would be complicated and confusing.

"I want my mom," he said.

"It's all right, old chap," said The Oracle. "The Oracle will be your mummy. She will look after you."

"I want my real mom," cried Douglas, "Ethel."

"Okay, okay," said Jay. "Come on, guys, let's not forget why we came down here. Time to go."

He would have liked to explore further. There were tunnels leading out of the cave and he wanted to have a quick look, maybe see if he could find the people, including his friend Kurt, who had got lost in the Nintendo 2048 worlds, but with Douglas in a state of insecure confusion and Kay doing a perfect impersonation of a zombie, it seemed that the top priority was to find Ethel. The lost gamers would have to wait. Someday he would return and swim again in the Gene Pool. He imagined swimming naked with Kay in the sweet sensual water that wasn't water. For a few seconds some pretty amazing images flashed through his mind, but he filed them away for later.

Colin Thompson

Jay picked up Fluffy's jar, took Kay's hand, and the four of them went back up the stairs to the store.

"Did you turn the light off?" said Douglas when they were halfway up.

"No," said Jay.

"Got to."

"Why, what does it matter?" said Jay.

"I don't know, but it does," said Douglas, and although it seemed quite pointless, they waited while he went all the way back down and turned off the light.

When they reached the store, Douglas carefully piled up the old bricks in the cellar doorway.

"I say, old chap, why are you doing that?" said The Oracle.

"I don't know. It's like the light," said Douglas. "It just seems like the right thing to do."

He stood the shelves up and pushed them back to hide the doorway, totally failing to notice that all the pads of quivering paper that had been on the shelves were gone.

So was Ethel.

Chapter 14
Going to Church

There was no sign of Ethel anywhere. They checked the exact dead center of the universe but all that was there was The Oracle's old jar, feeling strangely warm to the touch. They checked every shelf in every aisle, but she was nowhere to be found.

Things seemed to be going from bad to worse. Ethel was probably the only person, Jay reckoned, who could fix Kay and now she was gone. Douglas became hyperfrantic. He ran up and down the aisles, over and over again, looking for her, but all he found were a few feathers.

"Okay, okay, we'll go and look for her," said Jay, trying to calm Douglas down. "We'll eat, change our clothes, pack some food, and we'll go and find her."

He led Kay to a chair and sat her down. She sat still like a big doll. Her eyes, staring straight ahead, blinked from time to time but saw nothing. He put his arms around her and held her tight but she felt lifeless like a pillow. She seemed empty, like a shell, a beautiful empty shell washed up on a beach. Her breathing was so soft Jay could barely make it out.

"When you say her mind's been stolen," said Jay, "what do you mean? Is she, like, going to die?"

"No, no, old chap," said The Oracle. "Her body is fine. As long as you feed it and look after it, she'll live as long as you."

"So who could have done this? Ethel?"

"Well, she jolly well could have," said The Oracle. "But she created Kay. Why would she want to harm her?"

"Created her," Jay spluttered. "What do you mean, 'created her'?"

It was unbelievable. It was terrible. It couldn't be true. Ethel didn't "create" her. She'd been trapped inside that building with all those broken bones. Ethel would hardly have put here there. Yet every time Jay thought of a reason to tell himself it wasn't true, he knew it was. He knew in his heart that Ethel *had* created his perfect partner and made them fall in love with each other. He looked at Kay, wanting to hate her, to be disgusted by her very existence, but he couldn't. She *was* his perfect partner and he knew that he would love her forever.

"So if Ethel didn't do this, who did?"

"The Oracle doesn't know, but Ethel will," said Fluffy. "We must find her."

Outside the store, the transformation was nothing short of miraculous. Since Ethel had cleared the sky and the rainstorms had washed away years of dust, and the full force of a clear clean sun had warmed the earth, seeds that had slept since Jay's grandfather had been a child, or even longer, were waking up—and not just like it was spring, unless spring ran at a thousand miles an hour.

Thin roots had reached out across concrete paths and roads, creeping down through the cracks into the waiting earth. In the short time Jay and the others had been inside the store things had been growing like they were on speed. Nature had held down the fast-forward button in an attempt to make up for lost time. Plants that under the cool damp drizzling yellow skies had taken years to grow a few inches were now bolting as if their very lives depended on it. You could almost watch them move. They were alive not like plants but like creatures. Opposite the store a tree had flung its roots around an old telephone booth with such force that it had crushed it.

"Man, this is so beautiful," said Jay, taking in the lush primeval smell.

He knew little about the evolution of the world; all the old stuff like that had been suppressed to cover up just how badly wrong everything had gone. The three thousand books that

Ethel had hidden in his attic had covered a vast range of knowledge apart from this. But if Jay had read about prehistoric rain forests and evolution, he would have known that that was what he was in the middle of. Soon the cities would disappear under the new plants. Concrete would crumble to dust and the dust would be sucked dry by resourceful plants looking for nutrients. Everything that mankind had created on the face of the earth was being reclaimed by nature.

Inside the store the same change was beginning to take place. Seeds from a whole range of planets, packaged as food, were beginning to sprout on the shelves, bursting out of their packets and sending roots down into the ground. Fruit sitting in tidy rows split open as new trees began to grow. This was not good. It meant that soon plants from other galaxies would begin to spread across the world and, as always seemed to happen, they would be stronger than the native species and smother them. It was like a great irreversible chain reaction. And it was happening everywhere except the exact dead center of the universe. Around that the ground was bare. Green shoots reached an invisible barrier and then turned away, crawling back into themselves, leaving a circle of clear black-and-white linoleum tiles with The Oracle's old jar at the center. The water had turned green with microscopic plants, and hidden behind the green curtain, in the heart of the jar, something was moving. Leaving the jar right on the exact dead center of the universe was like going out and forgetting to lock the door.

"It's started," said The Oracle, looking down the street.

"What has, man?" said Jay.

"Everything. You know, old chap, tomorrow, the future," said The Oracle.

"Yeah, yeah, great. So where do we find Ethel?" said Jay, impatient to get moving.

Kay seemed to be breathing even more weakly than before and Jay was becoming increasingly anxious about her. Her appearance seemed too close to death for comfort, but he needn't have worried. Kay was in a state of catatonic hibernation that could last for years. Without her mind to make demands on her body, everything but the minimum vital survival routines had switched off.

"It's that way," said Douglas and The Oracle together, pointing in opposite directions.

"How many roads must a man walk down before you can call him lost?" said The Oracle.

"Yeah, right," said Jay.

"Well, you decide, old chap," said The Oracle.

"Okay, guys, let's get the plants off the hovercar and we'll go on the way we were going," said Jay.

As they pulled the plants off one end of the hovercar the green tendrils were beginning to grow back again on the other. As they watched, buds split, flowers opened, seeds ripened, fell, and took root. New plants were beginning to grow everywhere, even in the folds of the hovercar's seats. It took Jay and Douglas, working as fast as they could, almost half an hour to get the car clear and up off the ground.

Jay lifted Kay into the car and strapped her in. She sat bolt upright and still, like Sleeping Beauty, except that when he kissed her she didn't wake up.

"There's a chicken feather," said Douglas, pointing down into the tangle of plants.

"How on earth can you see anything through all that?" said Jay.

"I can smell it. It's my mom," said Douglas.

"I don't understand, man," said Jay. "How can you, like, see something by smelling it?"

"If the world acted only on things *you* understood, you'd still be in the womb, The Oracle would still be a goldfish, and Douglas would still be slowly decomposing in a bunch of bottles," said The Oracle.

"You *are* still a goldfish. You think I'm stupid, don't you?" said Jay.

Of course, Jay wasn't stupid at all. He had survived in this difficult world since he was a child. He had survived, thrived even, where many others had failed. The world he had created at the top of the skyscraper had been fabulous, far better than the environment all those poor souls down in the park lived in, surviving on roots and boiled cat. He'd had everything he could have wanted up there, except Kay. But now he was surrounded by events for which he had no reference points. Nothing he had read in the three thousand books, nothing he had experienced, had prepared him for talking chickens and fish, for strange creatures created before his eyes from bits of dead bodies. The rules were being made up as they went along and it was difficult sometimes to see where they were going. And on top of everything, the true love of his life was now no more alive than a cabbage.

Since he had lost—or, as he liked to think of it, misplaced —his parents, Jay had become singularly independent. He had had to, to survive. At an earlier age than most people, he had developed the ability to shrug his shoulders. It had got him through situations where others would have been totally stressed out and collapsed. Now it was different. For the first time in his life he loved someone. He couldn't look at Kay and just shrug his shoulders. Nor could he help her on his own.

"The Oracle cannot see the feather either," said The Oracle, "but she knows it is there."

"How?"

"Because Douglas can smell it," said The Oracle.

"Woof, woof," Douglas said, and laughed. "Turn left at this crossroads. There are more feathers around the corner."

Surely Ethel wasn't dead? Douglas could sense a lot of feathers. When they reached them, he looked down through the undergrowth and there, spelled out in feathers on the roof of a derelict panel van, was the word CHURCH.

The plants below were now a jungle. Looking down, Jay realized that without the hovercar it would soon be very difficult to find your way around. Even if you climbed a tall building, it would be impossible to see anything but the forest. All the old landmarks would soon be buried like Aztec ruins in a tropical rain forest. It was all so bright and clean and scary. The hovercar flew into a town square and at the far end was an old church with four spires.

"They're in there," said Douglas.

"They, who's they, man?" said Jay.

"My mom and the others," said Douglas.

"What others?" said Jay.

Douglas was sniffing the air. "One, two, three . . ." He paused. "Five. There are five chickens."

"Well, that should be all right then," said Jay, bringing the hovercar down by the door.

Why would Ethel have left them if not to look for Kay's mind? She was the only one who knew why they were in the supermarket or where they were going. It didn't occur to Jay that Ethel might have been taken anywhere against her will. She seemed too powerful for anyone to be able to make her do something she didn't want to.

"It's dangerous," said Douglas. "It smells dangerous."

"Yes," said The Oracle. "You have to be careful."

"They know we're here," said Douglas.

"Who?" said Jay.

"The chickens," said Douglas.

"If it's just chickens, what's the problem?" said Jay.

"I don't know," said Douglas. "But it smells really dangerous."

He hid his face in his hands, reverting to the child he had been before he had gone through the big potato. This was not good. Jay was not exactly well equipped for a fight. He looked around for something to use as a weapon but all he could find was Douglas and *he* was trying to curl up into the fetal position. Kay could do nothing and as for The Oracle, Jay could throw her jar at whoever it was in the church but that wouldn't do much for Fluffy.

"How do you know that, man?" whispered Jay.

"I can smell them, sensing me smelling them," said Douglas.

"Okay, old chap, off you go," said The Oracle to Jay. "We're right behind you and all that sort of thing."

Jay tried to protest but The Oracle said that if he didn't stop talking "they" would realize he was there too and that would take away the element of surprise.

"But shouldn't we make a plan or something?" said Jay.

"No time," whispered The Oracle.

"But—"

"Just go and have a little look," said Douglas.

The huge oak door of the church was open enough for Jay

to creep in. Inside, it was like the area around the supermarket. There was nothing growing. The plants had turned back at the door and Jay wished he could do the same. There were some stone steps just inside the door and Jay took off his shoes and tiptoed up until he was standing on a balcony looking down into the body of the church.

It was dark inside and getting even darker as the plants climbed steadily up the outside of the windows, cutting out the sun. There were strange figures of men with beards and sad women in blue robes painted on the windows. They all had what looked like white plates surrounding their heads. Obviously this place had been used by some sort of strange cult, or was maybe a restaurant.

Jay crept to the edge of the balcony and peered down into the gloom. There was garbage everywhere. For two hundred years, since churches had stopped being used, they had become home to outcasts and tramps. Long before the population implosion they had been sheltering there, disjointed bickering groups of forgotten people, escaping from the rain and the disapproval of the world. Since the great collapse they had stopped being a minority group. They had become part of the mainstream and had a few brief years of actually being better off than everyone else, because they knew how to survive on very little and the rest of the world didn't.

There were no tramps in the church now, just a few charred piles of burned sticks that had been their campfires.

At the end of the building there was a raised area, a sort of platform in front of some tall windows covered in more paintings. The windows were full of holes, where the tendrils of plants kept reaching in, but as soon as they entered, they coiled back out again. And there was Ethel, in a steel cage on a long table. Beside her were another cage, a big wooden cross, and two other cages, each containing a single chicken. The chickens looked so alike Jay couldn't tell which one actually was Ethel and they all sat so still that Jay thought they were dead.

And below, in the main body of the church, where all the rows of pews would have been, standing in a circle were thirteen hooded figures in brown cloaks. They looked like short fat monks. One by one they raised their heads to the roof, and where their faces should have been there was nothing, no eyes, no face, no soul, not even an empty space.

In the center of the circle, in a nest of thousands of scrunched-up sheets of paper, a huge black cockerel sat upright and stiff as a statue. His eyes shone with a yellow fire that pierced the gloom like two lasers. A mouse ran across the altar steps. Halfway across, it turned its face toward the cockerel and froze. The cockerel's laser eyes focused on the eyes of the mouse and the tiny creature exploded. The paper creased and uncreased itself in time with the cockerel's heartbeats. Jay knew he was gazing on pure evil.

Oh, shit, he thought.

The paper and the thirteen figures were moving. The whole mass of them was silently moving in a counterclockwise circle and in their midst the cockerel raised his head to the sky and let out a bloodcurdling scream that made the building shiver as though that, too, were alive.

Chapter 15
Nigel, Nigel, Burning Bright

Jay crept back out of the church as white as a sheet and told the others what he'd seen. The logical part of his brain, which had been having a bit of a hard time since he'd left the penthouse, told him the cockerel was only a chicken.

"What can chickens do?" his logic said. "They can't even fly properly."

But his logic was instantly overruled by recent experiences. No matter what powers she had, Ethel looked soft and cuddly. The cockerel didn't just look evil, the very air around him scared the hell out of Jay. And what about the hooded figures? They looked like empty blankets, but something must have been making them take on the shape of people, something must have been making them move. Jay's heart sank. He put his arms around the still, lifeless form of Kay as she sat stiff and upright in the hovercar and almost wished the earth would open up and swallow them both.

"Oh, hell, what are we going to do?" he said.

"The Oracle knew it would be something like that," said The Oracle. "The Oracle is getting the sort of feeling of an amazing amount of power coming out of there. Thirteen hooded figures, you say. That'll be the Thirteen Hooded Figures of Ancient Legends and Times Gone By."

"Yeah, but what are we going to do?" said Jay.

"We have to create a diversion," said Douglas, "so you can rescue Mommy. I'm sure if we can free her, we'll be okay."

"I couldn't even tell which one was her," said Jay.

"She's at the end on the left," said Douglas, sniffing the air.

"Maybe we could set the paper on fire, but what about the cockerel?" said Jay. "If he's powerful enough to catch Ethel, we'll never get past him."

"Tricky," said The Oracle.

For three hours, until late afternoon, they thought. Each of them came up with plans that would have worked but would have ended up killing all the chickens.

"And what about Kay?" said Jay. "Where exactly is her mind?"

"The Oracle thinks the cockerel has probably got it," said Fluffy.

"Does that mean, if we kill him, we'll kill Kay, too?" said Jay.

They thought for another hour, Jay and Douglas pacing up and down the square, The Oracle swimming around and around in her jar. And then, as the sun began to slip down behind the four spires, Douglas spoke.

"I know what to do," he said. "I've got a plan."

"Yeah, right," said Jay. "Spill it, man."

"Can't tell you. If I speak it out loud, they might hear it."

"Right, we'll, like, wait till it's dark, man, and then do your secret plan," said Jay.

He didn't know what the plan was, and considering how dumb Douglas was, he suspected it would probably put them all at risk and not even work, but neither he nor The Oracle had come up with anything, so they might as well give it a try.

While they waited, Jay lifted Kay out of the hovercar and laid her down on the grass in the doorway of an old house. He stood Fluffy beside her and flew back to the supermarket with Douglas, who said he needed to get something but he couldn't say what in case the creatures in the church heard him. The thing that had arrived in the supermarket via Fluffy's original jar hid in the back storeroom until Jay had gone. It was not ready for the world to know of its arrival.

It was really dark that night. The moon seemed to be too scared to come out. The only light was a faint yellow glow from inside the church, the light coming from the cockerel's eyes. High up in the church tower an ancient clock began to tick, and as it struck thirteen times Douglas and Jay crept back into the church, their footsteps hidden by the chimes.

As silence fell again, the paper stopped moving.

"Where?" said a sharp nasal voice. It was the cockerel.

"Shit," muttered Jay.

"Here, chicky, chicky," said Douglas, walking out into the middle of the floor.

The paper rustled and flowed like a shoal of fish, waving one way and then the other until it had piled itself up into four neat piles. The Thirteen Hooded Figures of Ancient Legends and Times Gone By split into two groups, one group of five and one of eight, and stopped moving. A thin blue line of force wrapped itself around both groups and crackled, filling the air with a smell of static electricity that was so strong Jay felt all his hairs stand on end.

Douglas seemed totally unaffected and unconcerned by it all and walked between them, staring straight into the cockerel's eyes. In his hand he was carrying a mug of corn.

"Here, chicky, chicky, nice corn," he said as innocently as he could.

"Stop right where you are," said the cockerel, trying to lock on to Douglas's eyes.

Douglas averted his gaze and stared fixedly at the ground. He'd heard what had happened to the mouse. "I've brought you some lovely corn," he said.

"Stay where you are, dog-brain," said the cockerel. "Corn, what sort of corn?"

"Nice golden corn, warm from the sun, remember?" said Douglas.

"Golden corn," said the cockerel, "all warm from the sun? I can't remember the last time."

Douglas threw a few grains of corn onto the ground and the cockerel leaped on them.

Jay tiptoed down the left of the church until he was safely hidden behind the altar. He reached up and managed to open Ethel's cage, then the other three. His hands were shaking so much he could hardly undo the catches. Ethel slipped down beside him and put her wing on his hand. As she did so, he felt most of his fear slip away. She pecked him gently on the knee to reassure him and then she concentrated. A large can of gasoline and a small box of matches materialized beside them. Then Ethel put her wing to her beak and motioned Jay to wait.

"Here, have some more," said Douglas, tipping out more corn and tickling the cockerel behind the head.

"You can call me Nigel," said the cockerel. "But don't try anything clever or I'll fry you, dog-brain."

"You are without doubt the most awesome and most handsome cockerel I've ever seen," said Douglas.

"Of course I am, stupid," said Nigel. "More corn. NOW."

Douglas said nothing. He tipped out the rest of the corn in a pile and, as Nigel stopped to eat, there was a flash of light followed by a furious commotion. The air was filled with the dust of dead bonfires and chicken feathers as Ethel and the three other chickens tore into Nigel. Two minutes later it was all over and Nigel lay dead in the middle of the altar steps, a kind of poultry version of Thomas à Becket.

As Nigel was torn to pieces, the thirteen hooded figures collapsed into thirteen piles of dust. During all the commotion the dust was blown into cracks in the ancient flagstones that covered the floor. When Nigel had stolen Kay's brain, he had divided it into thirteen parts and locked them inside the empty souls of the thirteen hooded figures. As Nigel died and the figures disintegrated, Kay's mind re-formed and returned to her. At the same time nature slipped out of hyperdrive and all the plants slowed down to normal speed.

Across the planet, deep in his cave, the Blind Piano Tuner felt the destruction of the Thirteen Hooded Figures of Ancient Legends and Times Gone By and sank into an infinite sadness. They had been his disciples. He had sent them out into the world and, over the centuries, they had moved through all the seats of learning, gradually bringing him back their wisdom, until the Blind Piano Tuner had learned everything there was to learn. Not just human knowledge but the wisdom of the animals, too.

And then the day had come when he felt there was no more to learn, that he had absorbed everything, and he had sent the

Thirteen Hooded Figures of Ancient Legends and Times Gone By to the church to rest, to wait until new wisdom came to the planet. It had been the first time since their creation that the thirteen figures had all been together in the same place and for two hundred years they had rested and waited. And then Nigel had come. He had cast a shield around the church that had hidden his activities from the Blind Piano Tuner, who was far more powerful than he was. He had overpowered the hooded figures, sucked them dry, turning them into zombies, into his own blind puppets, and now they were destroyed, no more than lines of dust between the flagstones. As Nigel had died, so had the shield collapsed and the Blind Piano Tuner saw his children turned to dust.

With Nigel gone, the sheets of paper became lifeless scraps. Jay and Douglas gathered them all up, emptied the gasoline over them, and set them alight. They burned like there was no tomorrow, as though there was an invisible breath fanning the flames, until all that was left was a fragile pile of black skeletons that would be washed away with the next rain. Under the pile, hidden from view, untouched by the fire, a single sheet remained, and on it were the words

Our day will come.

"Hey, where the hell is everybody?" said Kay, outside the church.

Jay ran out to her and flung his arms around her.

"What's the matter?" said Kay.

Jay told her what had happened, but Kay remembered nothing.

"The last thing I remember was drinking that awful wine and falling asleep," she said.

"You were like a vegetable, man," said Jay. "Are you, like, sure you're okay?"

"Nigel stole her mind," said Ethel. "Now that he's gone, she's got it back. She's fine."

"But why?" said Jay.

"To lure me to the church," said Ethel. "He knew he

couldn't overpower me, so he had to have something to lead me there."

"Hello, Mommy," said Douglas.

"Who's Mommy's little boy, then?" said Ethel.

Then Douglas wanted to meet the other chickens in case they were his aunties and suddenly everyone was talking at once and no one could get a word in edgewise. Ethel made food appear, turned some water into wine—a trick she hadn't used for centuries—and when everyone was feeling very relaxed, she sat them down and explained who Nigel was and how he had trapped her and the other three by a wicked and cheeky subterfuge and the very seductive use of the cry "cock-a-doodle-doo."

"Nigel was trying to catch all my sisters and fuse our minds together and turn us into the Four Chickens of the Apocalypse," said Ethel, "and finally clear the world of the last of the human race."

"So, like, who exactly was Nigel?" said Kay.

"Is Nigel, not was Nigel," said Ethel.

"But you killed him, man," said Jay. "We've just eaten him."

"What you ate was a dead chicken. Nigel is like us," said Ethel. "He was just occupying a chicken's body."

"So you mean he's still here, man?" said Jay.

"Oh, yes, he'll be floating around trying to find another chicken. He'll be back," said Ethel. "Still, as far as I know, almost all the remaining chickens on Earth are already occupied. He has to find another body within twenty-four hours or his mind goes back to Antimegaton. Trouble is, if he can't find a cluckin' chicken, he could end up inside anything. But when he does come back, we'll be ready for him."

"So who is he?" said Kay.

"He's sort of one of us," said Ethel, "but where we are good, he is evil. Where we are soft and cuddly, he will peck your eyes out. Where we are here to help save your planet and your sad little species, to help you grow again and maybe this time not screw everything up, Nigel wants to destroy all life and have the whole place for himself. We've sent E-mails home about him. Trouble is, with the distances involved, it can take hundreds of years for the mail to reach them."

"Oh, shit, man," said Jay. "Why can't anything just go right, without any hassles?"

As the night grew larger, the questions grew smaller. Kay, who seemed to be completely unscathed by her ordeal, lay back in Jay's arms. Douglas curled up next to Ethel and everyone slept. The Oracle stood guard by the door, one of the more useful aspects of never having to sleep. She was unsure what she was guarding against, but guarded against it just in case. Nigel could be anywhere, even in one of the slugs crawling through the undergrowth. While Ethel's chicken body slept, her mind, which never rested, scanned in ever larger circles and looked inside every slug just in case. Now and then one of the slugs was so fat and juicy she had to wake up and go and eat it.

There was something out there. Ethel could feel it, but it was vague, indistinct, and unfamiliar. It didn't feel like Nigel—he seemed to have vanished without trace—but there was definitely a new presence on the planet. It was probably nothing, but then again how many other things in the past centuries had started out as "probably nothing"? When beings from one galaxy visited another galaxy, why couldn't they just be nice and come in peace? Why couldn't they arrive with a box of chocolates instead of some cluckin' disintegrating ray gun or a bucket of mutant germs?

She wondered if it would ever end, if she would ever return home to the peace and comfort of her family, get out of this wretched chicken's body, give up the stress, and relax once more. She wondered if there would ever be a time across the galaxies when there were no longer any stupid little species hell-bent on destroying themselves and everyone else they came into contact with.

The next morning, before the humans were awake, Ethel bade her three fellow chickens good-bye. One went east, one west, and one south, leaving Ethel the way north.

"Farewell, sisters," said Ethel. "Stay in touch."

When everyone else woke up, no one was in any particular hurry to leave. The morning sun crept up through the new trees and filled the old church with shafts of multicolored light as it poured in through the stained-glass windows. The air was filled with the comforting smell of old furniture and jasmine blossoms. No one really wanted to do anything except lie back and relax. Jay thought if he lay there with his eyes shut that maybe all the bad stuff would disappear and there'd just be him and Kay left. Kay thought if she lay there long enough with her eyes shut that maybe all the bad stuff would disappear and there'd just be her and Jay. They had been together for such a short time and none of it had been what could be called normal. The only time they had relaxed was when they had been asleep. Every time Jay looked at Kay he felt a pain in his chest, not the memory of his missing rib but the feeling of love—which although he never wanted to lose it, he was scared that he might. Every time Kay looked at Jay she felt love too, though without the fear of imminent loss. She knew he wasn't going to leave her. When Nigel had stolen her mind, her thoughts had become disjointed, like in a surreal dream, but, as with so many dreams, she remembered nothing. One minute she'd been asleep in the storeroom at the back of the supermarket, the next she'd been lying on the grass with Fluffy staring at her from her jar.

Jay and Kay's dreams ran parallel and connected into one dream. There was an open clearing surrounded by trees. A crystal stream ran through the middle of the trees and in the bright soft grass stood a small wooden house with verandas on three sides and children playing. Ethel had put the dream into their heads, a glimpse of the future, a glimpse that over the coming years she would embroider to keep them with her on her quest, a glimpse that might one day become real.

Ethel produced breakfast, or rather, concentrated and breakfast slipped quietly in through the door. Plates of toast materialized, hot coffee warmed over a fusion-powered camping stove, marmalade with and without great chunky lumps of peel appeared, and for Douglas Ethel laid a soft-boiled egg and produced a pile of neatly buttered toast for him to dip in the yolk.

"Well, we'd better get going," she said when they had finished eating.

"Oh, why, man?" said Jay. "Why can't we just stay here?"

"Yeah, it's, like, so beautiful," said Kay.

They both knew they couldn't stay, but it was worth a try. The sunlight coming through the windows danced like leprechauns around the church and filled it with an air of great peace. The old building that had only the day before been the focus of so much potential evil now felt like the most comfortable place on Earth.

High in his cave, the Blind Piano Tuner closed his eyes and meditated. He saw his once beautiful apostles swept into the cracks between the flagstones and tried to collect them together. Soon he would need them again, but even with all his powers it would be a long, slow business to bring them back, for when he had managed to gather all the dust into one pile, he would then have to sort it out into the thirteen different apostles. Still, he had nothing much else to do. Ethel seemed to be getting along okay and he had contemplated all the wisdom of the world until he was sick of it. He had made every possible permutation of every possible thought. He had drawn every conclusion that could be drawn and, if he was honest with himself, apart from being able to levitate a few inches off the ground, he felt none the wiser.

To collect all his disciples' dust into one big pile meant the old church would have to be tilted up at an angle of forty-seven degrees, which is not something that happens to churches very often. What is almost impossible to believe is that about an hour after Ethel and the rest of them left the church, a small but violent and very localized earthquake did in fact briefly tilt the church to forty-six degrees. A severe thunderstorm and the ensuing rain two weeks later added the final degree, by which time some of the dust had been carried away by the wind and on the feet of mice. So when the dust was gathered, it had become the dust of the Eleven and a Half Hooded Figures.

There was only one being on Earth with the power to create such precise earthquakes and by a staggering coincidence it was the Blind Piano Tuner. This coincidence was roughly the same odds as the coincidence that would have been needed for the Perfect Hour to have occurred naturally. This is no coincidence.

"This isn't the right place for us to stay," said Ethel. "This is the past. We need to be in the future."

"You don't mean, like, time travel, do you?" said Kay. "You're not going to tell us you can do time travel, too, are you?"

"No," said Ethel.

"No what? Like, you can't do time travel, or no, you're not going to tell us if you can or not, or like, no, we're not going to?" said Kay.

"Or like, no, you can but we're not going to?" said Jay.

"We are not going to do cluckin' time travel," said Ethel.

"But you could if you wanted to, is that what you're saying, man?" said Jay.

"What I'm saying is we are not going to do time travel," said Ethel.

She'd never actually done time travel—well, not the big stuff that people usually think of when you say time travel, like zooming back to the Middle Ages or ancient Rome. Of course, she'd done the small stuff back on Megaton, like popping home to get her factor 900+ antiozone spray when she'd gone down to the beach without it, but then everyone did that. No, that wasn't true, humans didn't do it. As far as she could tell, they didn't know how to. That's why they carried handbags and personal organizers or tied bits of string around their fingers, so they'd never have to go back for something they'd forgotten. She'd altered time slightly now and then on Earth, moving people a few minutes here or there, including Jay himself, when things hadn't been going exactly how she wanted. No one had realized of course and it had been pretty small stuff.

It was so easy to time-travel, she didn't understand why humans couldn't do it. It certainly wasn't the environment—cockroaches were forever doing it. After all, all you had to do was shut your eyes, think of a number, and back you went, just like that. The truth was that Ethel wasn't very good at it. She had the unfortunate knack of never quite ending up where she'd planned. This was why she'd never tried any big time travel.

Time travel was why there was almost no crime on Ethel's planet. It was impossible to protect things from theft, so anyone and everyone was equally vulnerable. If you got robbed, all you had to do was travel in time and steal your stuff back again. In the end everyone got fed up rushing around for nothing, so they all stopped stealing. And anyway, everybody was fabulously wealthy already, so what was the point? It was the same with murder. If someone got killed, all you had to do was travel back in time to just before it happened and save him.

It did get a bit ridiculous once they figured out how to travel forward in time. Everyone stopped going to work. They just went ahead to the end of the week and collected their wages. Of course there was the problem of all that stuff where if you go back a hundred years and kill a mosquito so it can't bite someone who then dies of fever and that person is the grandfather of one of the greatest inventors/revolutionaries/maniacs of all time, that one tiny act of fly squashing can upset the whole course of the future. But most people had realized long ago that that was crap. You weren't altering the future, you were just moving sideways into one of the endless, infinite alternative futures. Whatever possible permutations there were in any situation all existed as different futures, and if you knew how, you could pop from one to another in an instant. Besides, there weren't any mosquitoes on Ethel's planet.

The only noticeable effect all this had was that while most of Ethel's race were capable of traveling vast distances across timeless galaxies, saving entire civilizations, controlling people's hearts and minds, and generally being very powerful and clever, they'd all been too busy to invent the wheel or panty liners with wings.

The upshot of everyone being all over the place, timewise, was that life had become terribly safe and predictable. It was one of the reasons they had started boldly going off to other galaxies.

It was ironic that Ethel, who more than anyone else could have benefited from some serious time travel, was so useless at it. If she had had the skills of most of her fellow Megatonians, she could have brought the dinosaurs back to life, found the missing link, lit a few forest fires just before the Ice Age, and probably tracked down the source of the Perfect Hour.

"But if you, like, go back in time, man," said Jay, "and kill a mosquito so it can't bite someone who then dies of fever and that person is the grandfather of one of the greatest inventors/revolutionaries/maniacs of all time, doesn't that, like, mean you could change the whole future of the world?"

"That's a load of cluckin' crap," said Ethel.

"But—," Jay started to say, but Ethel, who was getting very fed up explaining every little thing, cut him short.

"Look," she said, "basically it's like this. Life is like the outback of Australia, cluckin' enormous, and you humans' view of life is like a thread of cotton stretched out in an almost invisible line across the outback. There are billions and billions of lines of thread side by side and billions and billions more crisscrossing them, and each thread represents an alternative history. There are a billion, billion, billion versions of history out there, not just the one in your three thousand books. I mean, supposing you had a dead-straight road with a car going along it. Car comes along, car goes past, car goes off into distance. That's cluckin' history. Another history is car comes along, driver has heart attack, car drives off road, rolls over seven and a half times, driver dies. Another history is car rolls over seven and a quarter times or another is car rolls over seven and a quarter times but there is a small green spider in the ashtray. They're all cluckin' histories and they're all real. It just goes on forever."

"Yeah, but, like, only one of them would be the real history," said Kay.

"No," said Ethel, "they're all equally real, but one version is always the dominant one, the one that ninety-nine point nine percent of people live in. There are always a few weird people who pretend the earth's flat or the Holocaust didn't happen. It's like this. Suppose you went back to Mr. and Mrs. the Hun's bedroom about nine months before baby Attila was born and while Mr. the Hun wasn't looking you slipped a condom on him. That would be a new history, but it wouldn't change what happened, because it wouldn't be the dominant history."

What Ethel didn't tell them was that you could actually change things, because it was possible to make any one of the billions and billions of parallel histories into the dominant one.

"Come on, let's get going," she said wearily.

"Where are we going, man?" said Jay.

"Camelot," said Ethel.

Chapter 16
Camelot

They flew north, following what had once been the main road out of the city. They passed vast suburbs of almost deserted houses. Here and there a few wisps of smoke drifted up toward them, the only signs of human life among the emptiness. It was the same everywhere, the bright green leaves of a new spring had begun to cover everything. It was hard to tell where the city ended and the countryside began. Where gray streets had spread for endless miles there were now fields of green. It was very beautiful and the travelers, even Ethel, sat in silence, enchanted by it all.

They flew over a field surrounded by vast metal roofs and Jay realized that it was the airport, its runways and open fields now hidden by trees. The airport had been unused for more than a century but until recently it had barely changed. The runways had become crisscrossed with lines of grass where the tarmac had cracked. The few remaining planes had slowly turned gold with rust and collapsed as people had stripped them of anything vaguely useful, but apart from that, and the unseen changes caused by mice and insects, the airport after ninety years had looked little different from how it had after ten.

The airport meant they were at the edge of the city. Jay flew higher, turning the hovercar in a wide curve so they could look back at the great metropolis. Over the centuries it had grown and grown until it had covered an area larger than some small countries. The population of the city alone had

147

raced up to almost seventeen million and then in less than two hundred years fallen to no more than a few hundred.

Now the view had changed completely. The skyline of gray shapes, squares, lines, and sharp angles that had stretched away into a shimmering purple haze was now an almost unbroken sea of jungle. Even the tallest buildings were softened around the edges, like giant ungainly hedges.

"Oh, man, that is just so beautiful," said Jay, and everyone agreed with him.

"You are looking at tomorrow," said Ethel.

"I want to go back, right into the middle of the city," said Jay.

He wanted to revisit the places he had lived in as a child, to see the gray streets and run-down buildings clothed in their new colors. He felt old memories tugging at his sleeve, but he knew there was no going back, not even as a tourist. He felt in his heart, as they left the city behind, that he would probably never set foot there again.

"Later," said Ethel. "We have things to do."

Jay knew better than to argue with her. He turned the hovercar and they flew north again.

They continued for several hours over rolling hills and forests. The sun, hidden for so long, felt warm and fresh. It was clearing away a lot of old dead leaves and history. Hardly anyone said a word. Apart from Ethel and Fluffy, none of them had ever traveled out of the city before, so they were all too busy looking at everything to speak. Occasionally they passed over small groups of people who never once looked up, scared perhaps that if they appeared too friendly the travelers might land and spoil the delicate balance of their peaceful lives. In two hours they flew over half a dozen groups and not once did they see a child. Most of the time they saw old people, people too old to have children.

They climbed over a range of long, low mountains, and coming down on the other side, over an endless forest, Ethel felt a chill in her bones. The feeling she'd had before of a new presence on the planet returned and now she knew what it was. The visitor in the supermarket had begun to send its

148

Colin Thompson

offspring out into the world. The Virus had arrived and it was down below them on the forest floor. God help the poor humans living there.

They came to a wide river that, like them, was heading north. As it wove in and out of the forest, clearings appeared, clearings like the one in Jay's dream. There was the cottage with the thin line of smoke drifting lazily up from the chimney. There was the garden, bright with flowers, and there were people exactly like him and Kay. He was enchanted.

"Can we land?" he said. "It's all so perfect, man."

"No," said Ethol.

"Why not?" said Kay. "Just for a few minutes."

"Things are not what they seem," said Ethel.

"But it all looks so peaceful, the children playing in the river, dogs running around," said Kay. "Come on, please?"

"Do you not think it's strange that no one ever looks up?" said Ethel. "That no one waves? If you were down there, miles from any other human, and something flew overhead, wouldn't you at least look up, if only for a second?"

"Well, maybe they're shy, man," said Jay.

"No, they are not what they seem," said Ethel.

"What are you talking about?" said Jay. "We can see them."

"Okay, circle around and tell me what you can see," said Ethel.

"Okay, man, a little cottage, two blond children swimming in the river, four dogs—," began Jay.

"No, no," said Kay. "There are four dark-haired children and a naked man."

"What are you two looking at?" said The Oracle. "The Oracle can see seven white swans in the river and fourteen golden peacocks in a field of brilliant grass."

"What are you all looking at?" said Douglas, who'd been off in a world of his own.

"See what I mean?" said Ethel. "Things are not what they seem."

"Oh, man. So, like, what can you see?" said Kay.

"Reality," said Ethel, "and you don't want to know what it looks like."

149

"Okay, so, like, if they're not what we can see, what are they?" said Jay.

"The Virus," said Ethel.

"So is that, like, bad?" said Kay.

"The Virus," said Jay, "what's that, then, man?"

"It is the scourge of life," said Ethel. "I thought with Earth being so far from any other inhabited planet, it might not find us. A lot of life-forms don't know Earth exists."

"So what does it do?" said Jay.

"It goes to a planet and changes into whatever it is a person feels safest with," said Ethel. "You are then lulled into a false sense of security and approach it. Do you know what a spider does to a fly?"

"Yes."

"Well, the Virus does the same," said Ethel, "only in reverse."

"But spiders suck the insides out of things," said Kay.

"Exactly," said Ethel.

They all thought about that for a bit. Jay looked down and found it hard to believe Ethel. The scene looked so beautiful, so perfect. It was worse for Kay, seeing the Virus looking like humans. Jay was the only true human she'd ever met. Douglas looked human and large parts of him were, but he wasn't like her and Jay and didn't really count. She had existed for only a very short time, though she didn't realize it, and she had a deep need for human contact that the Virus could scan.

"Couldn't we, like, just land and see?" she said. "Maybe it's okay. You know, maybe we could just, like, have a meal with it and then go."

"I'm sure it would very much like to have a meal with us," said Ethel, "though not in the way you're thinking."

She concentrated and for a while made the filters slip from Jay's and Kay's eyes so that, a few minutes later, when the swans that The Oracle could see rose from the river and flew toward them, they saw the Virus for what it really was.

What they saw were no elegant birds but dark evil creatures who looked like scruffy cross-legged Buddhas about twelve inches high sitting in the air with brilliant eyes as sharp as lasers that seemed to be trying to pull them in like a *Star Trek* tractor beam.

"Move," shouted Ethel as Jay sat mesmerized. *"Now."*

Her concentration slipped and the Virus appeared as a flock of brilliant birds.

"What?"

"Let's go," said Ethel, flying across and covering Jay's eyes with her wings. As she did so the Virus vanished and Jay regained control of the hovercar.

They flew over at least two dozen Virus settlements and as they looked down each of the travelers saw something different. Each time what they saw was more and more enticing, until it was almost impossible to resist. Ethel could feel the creatures trying to break into her head, for it was only her willpower that kept them from landing, that and the blindfold Jay was now wearing. They tried flying higher, but the Virus filled the air with irresistible smells. Kay could smell the sweet scent of roses mixed with testosterone, while Douglas smelled chocolate cake. They even got into Ethel's head and she could smell the scent of new-mowed hay with just a hint of earthworm.

When the smells didn't work, the Virus tried to fill their heads with dreams. Kay saw visions of a mother and father sitting by a winter's fire, and brothers and sisters playing with her on the hearth rug. Ethel saw a proud cockerel, his feathers glistening in the sun as he raised his head and crowed to the new day. Jay saw vivid pictures that accompanied the smells and Fluffy saw a million tiny shrimps. As Ethel was not really a chicken but just borrowing the body of a chicken, the vision of a cockerel had no effect on her at all and she managed to keep control of the situation.

"Shut it out," she said, "it's not real. Just keep telling yourself it's not real."

And then they reached the end of the valley and the Virus was gone.

Ethel told Jay to take off the blindfold as they came down over the valley of Camelot. Through the trees they could see a small forest of towers growing up from dense undergrowth like the towers of a child's dream castle, and as they got nearer they could make out the castle itself, hidden among the trees. It was massive, the size of a small town. The towers grew up from everywhere and between them a vast expanse of flat roof covered with chimneys and smaller towers spread ahead as far as they could see.

Jay flew low, below the treetops around the outside wall of the castle. It rose sheer and featureless out of the ground as though, rather than having been built there, the very rock had been dragged up and shaped into a great outer boundary. Nor did this wall contain a single window or door. It was almost as though the castle and its moat had been sealed off from the rest of the world by this outer barrier.

Between it and the walls of the castle itself was a deep, black moat. Jay dropped the hovercar between the two walls and flew between black rain clouds over the surface of the water. There was no sign of life anywhere—no water lilies, no rushes, no fish, no birds, nothing save the black water that looked as cold as ice and the clouds. Above them and all around, the sun shone from a clear blue sky, but between the walls it was forever raining. It was the most chilling place Jay had ever seen.

The castle walls of golden sandstone were seven stories tall and almost bare of windows. Here and there, high up in some of the tallest towers, high enough to offer a view over the outer wall, were narrow slits, the castle's only eyes on the world. In the north side of the inner wall stood the main entrance, though to call it an entrance made no sense. The outer wall denied anyone access to it.

A drawbridge from nowhere made of timber as thick as a man was pulled up tight against an archway as tall as a house. The timber was old and decayed, pitted with deep holes and the marks of fire.

High on one wall hung the skeletons of dead men who had tried to catapult themselves into the castle and had died, impaled on the spikes of giant thorns that grew from the tops of the ramparts.

Jay lifted the hovercar until they were looking over the walls into the heart of the castle. In the center was a huge garden. Hundreds of trees that had once been as neat as rows of soldiers but were now wild and overgrown lined gravel paths that ran between lush lawns where fountains danced in sparkling ponds. Ancient roses climbed up the inside walls past the seventh story and onto the roof. The scent of the forest joined with wood smoke and the perfume of the roses. Flocks of brightly colored birds flitted between the trees like handfuls of jewels. As they approached, the air fell still and Jay had the strange feeling they had arrived in paradise.

"Here we are," said Ethel.

She pointed down and they landed on a chamomile lawn where seven white peacocks stood in a circle, fanning out their tail feathers.

"What is this place?" said Kay. "I've seen this in my dreams."

"So has everyone," said Ethel. "This is Camelot, the Castle of Dreams."

"Is there anybody living here, man?" said Jay.

"Yes," said Ethel, "one person, my oldest friend on Earth."

A door across the garden opened and an old man walked out. Jay and Kay had imagined that Ethel's friend would be a chicken too, not a human, though of course if they had been asked what sort of person would be living on his own in an amazing castle, the old man with his white hair and flowing beard and purple robes now walking toward them would have been exactly right.

"This is Merlin," said Ethel.

She was amazed at how old the wizard had become since she had seen him last. She barely recognized him.

"Welcome to Camelot," said Merlin. "By my faith, fair visitors, thy presence is most pleasing and auspicious."

"Hi, man," said Jay.

"Hi," said Kay.

"Hello, Papa," said The Oracle.

"What?" said Jay.

"Do not be foolish, little fish. I am not thy father," said Merlin.

"Is this not The Oracle," said The Oracle, "the fountain of all wisdom, the wisest woman who has ever lived? Yes, of course it is."

"Not necessarily," said Ethel.

"The Oracle is The Oracle," said The Oracle. "Everything she says is the truth."

Jay had read about King Arthur and Camelot. Several of the three thousand books had been about myths and legends and as far as he was concerned that's what it was, a myth. Camelot and everything connected with it was all just a story. True, it was a wonderful story, but it was no more than that. And even if there had been some truth to the legend, there was no way any of it would still be there in 2287. Merlin would have to be well over a thousand years old and Camelot would have been mentioned in lots of other books. The Oracle was the same, that was all just legend too.

But wherever they were, it was an incredibly beautiful place.

"You've just made all this, haven't you?" said Jay to Ethel. "You've, like, read our minds and created it."

"Yeah, right," said Kay. "There's no such thing as The Oracle or Merlin or Camelot."

"Yeah, it was all just stories," said Jay.

All these things were wrong. The Oracle was The Oracle, and although she had spent millennia alone with no memory of her parents, she knew deep in her heart as soon as she saw him that Merlin was her father. There was something in his eyes, something about the way he looked right into her. She also knew that she had no way of proving it, especially while she was a fish.

The place they were now standing in was indeed Camelot and the white-haired old man really was Merlin and Merlin was indeed the father of The Oracle.

"I believe you, Fluffy," said Douglas.

Ethel said nothing, even though she could have cleared everything up. She had been on Earth when Merlin and The Oracle had arrived, actually standing less than a mile from where their spaceship had crashed. She had been the first one to make contact with them and had saved them from the burning wreckage. The people who had sent Merlin and The Oracle to Earth had wiped out the part of their memories that held their pasts. The love and the childhood, the little things that make each person different from the next, were all erased. All that was left was the great wisdom they had been sent to Earth to dispense. Like Ethel, they had been sent to Earth because they had been failures. Merlin and The Oracle had been the worst wizard and oracle students in the entire history of the university of Morphine, their home planet. Their previous memories had been erased to stop them from trying to get home again. Morphine didn't want them back. People may wonder what Earth had done to deserve this, why they always seemed to get the dunces and dropouts. Earth had done nothing. It had just had the misfortune of being the last planet created that could sustain life and the farthest away from the central planet, Metropolis, proof if any were needed that there is no justice in life.

Ethel wondered if Merlin could remember the crash. It had been so long ago, and he had grown so old, she doubted it. Still, she had saved their lives, he ought to remember that. When she had seen him just now she had been deeply shocked at just how much he had aged. She hadn't seen him for, what, six hundred years, but it was incredible how bent and frail he had grown in that short time. And if his body had aged like that, she wondered if his mind had too.

"Greetings, noble chicken," he said. "Many score years and ten and ten more have passed since last I saw thee."

"You're looking well," Ethel lied, still unable to come to terms with how old he had grown.

"I beseech thee, little hen, lie not to me. Time has wrought its evil spells on me. See here how bent and frail I've become. Why, I spend half the time looking at my shoes," said the old wizard. "If I want to look up into the heavens, I must make to lie on my very back. Forsooth, I am weary with the ages."

"Why do you, like, talk so odd?" said Kay.

"Atmosphere," said Merlin.

"You could become young again," said Ethel, "if that's what you want."

"Nay, alas and alack and elastic," said Merlin, "'tis not for us mere creatures to control the mighty forces of nature."

"Oh, yes it is," said Ethel. "That's exactly what it's for us to cluckin' do. That's why we're here. And anyway, we are not mere creatures. We are above that."

"By Jove, father, nature interferes with itself all the time," said The Oracle. "It's called evolution."

"Nay, child, to make someone old young again, 'tis not evolution," said Merlin. "The very clocks of time click away for us all. And call me not thy father."

The thought of standing straight and not forgetting things all the time was very appealing, to be able to see the sky and watch the birds soar out of the trees instead of staring at slugs. Merlin remembered the old days, when the walls of Camelot had been like him, bright and young. Now they were both worn and old and had lichen growing in their crevices.

"It's just cosmetic evolution," said Ethel, "like cosmetic surgery. All we have to do is take you back to the Gene Pool. One swim and you'd be young again."

"'Tis well said," said Merlin cautiously. "But is not the Gene Pool many hours' journey from here?"

"Yes."

"Then I would not make it," said the old wizard, "for I should age so greatly on the journey that I should die ere we reached our destination."

"The Oracle could make you young again," said The Oracle, "but there is a price."

"Verily, is that not always the way of things?" said Merlin. "What is thy price?"

"Admit you are The Oracle's father," said The Oracle.

"I will think on it," said the wizard.

The sun had sunk behind the trees and the air began to grow cool. Sleek pigeons that had been feeding in the forest all day flew down into the garden and gathered in the bushes around Merlin. He held out his arms and they flew across to him. The old wizard leaned close to them as if in deep conversation, nodding his head from time to time, making comments, and asking questions.

The pigeons then flew up to roost in one of the tall towers and Merlin turned back to his visitors looking worried.

"Herein we are brought bad tidings. Thy arrival is timely. Something strangely contrived is abroad in the forest," he said. "Something disturbs the balance. The fundaments are uneasy."

"Do you know what it is?" said Ethel.

"Verily I do not," said Merlin, "for it is not something whereof I have encountered before. Though of course I could have forgotten thereof, my memory not being what it used to be . . . at least I do not think it is, I cannot truly remember, but I am sure at my age I should have a lot more memories than I have, but then it is perhaps a marvel that I endureth so long."

"Well, what's it like?" said Ethel. Maybe the old man could sense the presence of the Virus.

"What?" said Merlin.

He had reached an age where long sentences were becoming a problem. Two or three strung together were disastrous. For every fifty words spoken the old wizard could remember only the last twenty.

"You said there was something abroad in the forest," said Ethel, reminding him what they'd been talking about. "What is abroad?"

"I know not," said Merlin. "Pigeons, poor things, are not blessed with very big brains or great courage."

Ethel stared up at the tower and a single pigeon flew down toward her.

"I'm just going to borrow her body for a bit," said Ethel, "and fly around and have a look."

"Noble chicken, there is evil abroad," said Merlin. "Guard thyself against the owls."

"Ha," said Ethel. It was the closest she could get to a laugh. "Cluckin' chicken's body," she said, and moved over into the pigeon. "Cluckin' pigeon's body," she said, and flew off into the evening.

Merlin picked up the motionless chicken and tucked it into his robes, where it sat with the pigeon's brain, wondering how it had got dark so suddenly.

Chapter 17
The Virus

Back in the supermarket, the visitor who had arrived on Earth via The Oracle's old jar, having sent its offspring, the Virus, out into the world to start its colonization, had grown into something that can only be described as indescribable, formless yet hideous, as dark as night yet blindingly bright— and somewhere out there on a distant planet in an unknown galaxy there was a mother who loved it and wondered if it would ever get around to dropping her a postcard . . . nothing too demanding, just a few words to let her know it was all right.

Then it had formed a chrysalis, a disgusting wrinkled green chrysalis, hanging from the ceiling just inside the supermarket door, swaying imperceptibly in the slight breeze, feeling slightly guilty because it hadn't sent its mother a postcard, and oozing a thick brown liquid that dripped onto the floor and slowly ate through the concrete on its predestined journey to the center of the earth.

It rested. There was no hurry. It had followed its target across the galaxies and now it could rest until the target completed its mission.

Meanwhile, Ethel drifted slowly over the forest in the failing evening light. There was definitely something there, apart from the Virus, but it was out beyond the forest and indistinct. She had a vague memory of the Virus, someone had told her about it, or something like it, thousands of years

158

ago, long before she'd come to Earth. She hadn't been paying attention, so the details were vague. She had no idea what it was or where it came from. She thought it might have always been there, sort of dormant in the soil; maybe the sudden spurt that nature had taken when she cleared the pollution cloud away had triggered it.

A large owl was circling above her. Ethel could feel its eyes focused on her back. She cracked a branch in a tree below and in the split second the owl was distracted she slipped into its mind and changed bodies.

This is more like it, she thought to herself. *This is where I should be, not inside a potential fried dinner or a bird so stupid that when you take it out of a dark loft, drive it hundreds of miles out into the beautiful open countryside, and let it go, the first thing it does is fly straight back to the dark loft as fast as it can.*

The owl, now inside the pigeon's body, was flying around in confused circles. It didn't actually realize what had happened and was wondering where the plump pigeon had gone. It also wondered why it had suddenly lost about 90 percent of its night vision and flew straight into a tree.

Ethel lifted the stunned owl/pigeon into the safety of an oak tree and made it fall asleep. The last thing she wanted was it getting killed. Then she'd have to put the pigeon's mind back into an owl and goodness knows what problems that would cause. Something similar had happened on a planet in the Orion galaxy and in three short generations the whole population, with some of the most brilliant, beautiful peace-loving minds in all the galaxies, had been transformed from a race who had cracked the secret of time travel, learned how to grow jet-black roses, and outlawed leisure suits, into a bunch of gibbering nerds hopelessly addicted to lawn bowling and the Orion equivalent of Pop-Tarts. Ethel had been one of the team sent in to put them out of everyone else's misery. It had all been very messy. Just to be on the safe side, she fixed the owl/pigeon to the tree with six rubber bands that she'd transported from the supermarket.

Whatever the presence was, it was back toward the city. Ethel flew higher until she was just below the clouds. As she

159

reached the streets, the feeling grew stronger. It was something she'd never encountered before, and she had visited every planet with intelligent life and every planet with stupid life too. She reached back into her memory banks and flipped through the pages of *The Observer Book of Life*, but whatever it was wasn't listed.

It's impossible, she thought. *That would mean there's a planet we don't know about, and that simply isn't possible. Unless it's a mutation.*

Of course there were planets that Ethel didn't know about. Far beyond her galaxy, which was the galaxy beyond galaxies past the end of time, there was another galaxy, and beyond that another to the power of forever. But the new visitor wasn't from there. It was, as Ethel had imagined, a mutation, a terrible one in a billion, billion chance twists of fate that had once been the sweetest fluffiest stuffed animal in a gift shop in a theme park on a repulsively loving and caring, most creamy-sweet planet in the Milky Way, until that fateful day of the lightning storm and the exploding cotton-candy machine. . . .

She passed over the church and on toward the supermarket. Even before she reached the city, she had guessed that was where the intruder would be. It had to have come in through a portal, and apart from the secret one in Camelot that no one apart from Merlin and Ethel knew about, the only one nearby was in the supermarket. Unless of course—but no, that was too terrifying even to contemplate.

Portals are secret gateways between galaxies. They are invisible except when you turn around suddenly and see something out of the corner of your eye. Even then, unless you know you're looking at one, you'll probably just see something ordinary like an armchair or a toilet, the two most frequent things that portals are disguised as. They've been around as long as time itself. Hasn't everyone experienced the feeling of seeing something that, when you turn your head, isn't there? That is something coming or going through a portal.

She remembered Jay's words: "Why can't anything just go right, without any hassles?" How right he had been.

Out of the mouths of babes and cluckin' Earthmen, she thought.

She landed on the roof of the supermarket and concentrated. Not only was something there, it was trying to read her mind.

Who the cluck are you? she thought.

"I am the Visitor," came the reply.

"I've never heard of you," said Ethel.

"Oh, but you have," said the Visitor. "I am the one who created Moloch himself, the one who suckled Satan, the one who molded Beelzebub, the one who . . ."

The Visitor went on for ten full minutes, reeling off name after name of every evil being from every galaxy in every star system since the beginning of time. Its voice got deeper and darker until it seemed to be scraping the very inside of Ethel's skull. Yet Ethel wasn't afraid. She didn't feel particularly brave—bravery had never been one of her greatest traits—but something in her head told her the Visitor was a fraud. She heard the far-off voice of the Blind Piano Tuner telling her to be careful, telling her to act scared, but that if things went according to plan the Visitor's presence would be to their ultimate advantage.

"I can tell you're really evil," said Ethel. "So what is it that you want?"

"Everything," the voice said, and vanished.

And it had vanished completely, not just stopped thinking or talking, not just sat very still holding its breath, but vanished. Ethel reached out as far as her mind would go around the curvature of the earth, but there was no sign of the Visitor. She sent messages around the planet to her sisters, but even their mental network, which covered the whole planet like a giant cobweb, could find no trace.

"Oh, cluck."

It's bluffing, said the voice of the Blind Piano Tuner inside Ethel's head.

The only trouble was that Ethel was never really sure when the Blind Piano Tuner was bluffing. Either way things were not good. They didn't make sense. That the creature existed at all was improbable; that it had vanished so completely was impossible. Ethel had a bad taste in her brain, like it had been out all night abusing itself with forbidden substances and had given her a hangover. Of course it could just be a hologram, a practical joke from one of her friends on Megaton. But it wasn't, it was real. In fact it was more real than real.

The Visitor was still there. It had gone nowhere. It had just spread its mind so thin that Ethel couldn't see it. It had divided itself up into smaller and smaller pieces until there was one tiny piece in every living thing on the planet, from the last solitary whale to the tiniest ant, even inside Ethel herself, and then it had hidden inside their heads in a quiet dusty corner that was never used. There it was safe and there it could grow. It had spent a long time traveling to Earth, the last planet on its list, and now it was so near its goal, it wasn't going to go away because of some dumb chicken pretending to be an owl.

As she flew back to Camelot, Ethel decided not to tell the others about the Visitor. Life was complicated enough without any extra hassle. It seemed like the quest for the Perfect Hour was being delayed over and over again. It was time to move on, to actually take steps forward without taking steps backward.

She'd just pretend that she'd been mistaken and what they'd all thought was something sinister had in fact been a bad thunderstorm. There was no point in worrying them about it. If she couldn't do anything, there was no way any of the others could. Reluctantly, she moved back into the pigeon and then into the old familiar chicken body. How ungainly it felt after the sleek elegance of the owl, all fat and useless. She fell asleep and dreamed of her home planet with its caressing acid rain and beautiful black ozone-free skies.

Chapter 18
Fire Dreams

"It was just some sort of magnetic storm," she said to everyone at breakfast the next morning. "Nothing to worry about."

Douglas, of course, never questioned a thing Ethel told him and the others were only too happy to believe her too. Life was messy enough already without any more complications.

They were sitting in the Great Hall of Camelot, or to be exact, one of the great halls. There were 127 rooms that could have been described as great halls, though this was the only one that Merlin himself called "the Great Hall."

"Apart from the other Great Hall, that is," he said. "But verily, thou couldst not breakfast there."

"Why not?" said Jay.

"'Tis full of stuff," said Merlin.

"What sort of stuff?"

"Never thou mind," said the old wizard, buttering toast in a way that made it very obvious he wasn't going to discuss it.

Camelot wasn't your average castle, not that there were many of those left. Years before, when the roads had still been open, people had passed through the valley on several occasions and not once had any of them seen anything that remotely resembled a castle. There had been an eight-lane freeway, which had vanished beneath the encroaching grass, two truck stops, a gas station, and a derelict giant fantasy theme park. Basically, the once beautiful valley had been a hideous eyesore, a relic from the early twenty-first century, when everyone over the age of fifteen had been required by law not only to own two cars, but to drive them every day of the week except Sunday, which of course had been the one day when most people had wanted to drive their cars, to escape the traffic and pollution of the cities with a day out in the country.

This absurd situation had come about because the oil companies discovered massive oil fields that they had not factored into their future plans. Suddenly there was the awful prospect of very cheap fuel, so, wielding their power, they told the major governments to pass the Two Cars Each legislation. By the time they discovered that the vast oil reserves weren't even as vast as 10 percent of what they'd been told by their engineers, who were direct descendants of the man who had invented the Power Pill and were out for revenge, it was too late and all the oil ran out in a couple of years, leaving the world a quieter and slightly cleaner place.

Camelot had been there all the time. It had been smack-dab in the middle of the theme park but had always been mysteriously closed for repairs, surrounded by an invisible thing that could only be described as a spell disguised as a very tall hoarding that made you forget you'd ever seen it.

What made Camelot unique was something that you couldn't see unless you lay down on the grass at the foot of the outer wall and peered very closely. An almost invisibly thin line ran along the stonework right around the outside of the entire twenty-five-acre building. It was jet-black and no thicker than a human hair. It looked like a damp-proof course but was actually a force field. When you were inside, it meant you weren't on Earth but on a vaguely similar planet at the back of the Spirochete galaxy—Merlin's home planet, Morphine.

Though Merlin had created the entire castle and shielded it within the force field, it had not been completely impervious to invasion. Nature was at work, slowly eating into it. In one corner of the vast castle, the corner where no one had been for years, giant plants, mutated by centuries of pollution, had grown into voracious feeders with superhungry roots feeding off the house itself. Several rooms were so overtaken by roots as to be uninhabitable. The branches of the plants were home to strange animals that lived nowhere else on Earth. Because Merlin had lived alone in three rooms at the other end of the castle for centuries he was completely unaware that any of this was happening. Yet for all the plants' voracity, the force field remained untouched, holding Camelot and everything inside it. The very air was more than one thousand years old.

When Merlin had crash-landed on Earth and Ethel had saved his life, he had taken the force-field engine from his wrecked ship and made it stretch its field until it was as big as possible, and once safely inside it he had built his castle. As long as he stayed inside the field he would never age a single day, nor would anyone else.

"Tell me why you have aged," said Ethel when they were alone together in the Great Smoking Room. "I thought the force field was supposed to keep you young."

"'Tis my fault and I will tell thee why," said Merlin. "Needs must I leave Camelot from time to time."

"Of course," said Ethel. "To do all those great deeds in the legends."

"Verily, there was that," said Merlin, "but they took mere moments."

"And you had to help those knights on their noble missions as well," said Ethel. "That must have taken a bit of time."

"Nay," said Merlin, "no more than fleeting days. Most of the time they came here unto me and I will tell thee it vexed me sore at the time. Thou know, thou invite a score or so of so-called noble knights to partake of bread and wisdom at the Round Table, and do they ask thee back so they may return thy hospitality? Nay. Nor did they offer to help with the washing of the dishes or the throwing of the slops over the castle wall for the local peasants. Forsooth, it really got my goat."

"So why have you grown so old?" asked Ethel.

"Love."

"Love?"

"Yea, verily, I have been visiting my true love," said Merlin. "Not the wretched Lady of the Lake, who enchanted me with her witchcraft and did shut me in a rock to die. Nay, my true love is the Lady Gladys, daughter of Beryl and wife of Sir Geon."

"Well, why not get her to come here?" said Ethel.

"Sir Geon guards her like a very hawk," said Merlin. "On my peril, she cannot get away. Well, not for long enough to be of any use at my age."

All this had happened hundreds of years earlier. The old wizard hadn't left Camelot in more than five hundred years, but, as with lots of old people, his timelines were badly tangled and he spoke of ancient events as if they had just happened or were even still happening.

The stuff in the other Great Hall that Merlin had referred to was centuries of junk he had collected in a vain attempt to repair his ship and go home. Even if he had collected the exact things he needed, he would have been quite incapable of repairing his craft. He was one of the most impractical people who had ever lived, so impractical he had had to have diagrams above each basin telling him how to use the taps.

Camelot was proof of his lack of abilities. It was all over the place. The superficial image was of a truly beautiful place, but looking closely you could see that half the windows were sideways, towers were wider at their top than their base, doors opened inward making access almost impossible, and doors opened outward in places that meant you could fall to your death with one false step.

But like most impractical people Merlin thought he was a great handyman and he had collected endless bits of useless junk over the passing centuries, convinced that one day he would rebuild his ship and fly back to Morphine.

The two old friends sat in silence staring into the fire, each seeing his or her own dreams in the flames. Ethel dreamed of her home planet. Megaton was the most beautiful world in all of creation, so beautiful that she felt it must be the womb of creation itself, the center from which all other worlds had evolved, the place where the Gene Pool had come from. She was quite wrong. Megaton was neither the most beautiful planet nor the womb of creation. It never had been, but Ethel had been away from home a long time and absence makes the heart grow fonder.

Merlin, whose memories of his home planet had been erased before he had left, just stared into the fire and dreamed of the day he would return to wherever it was he'd come from. His lack of memories would have made him believe that he had always lived on Earth, if it hadn't been for the crashed spaceship. He had been inside it. He remembered that, and that meant he had come from somewhere. As he had grown older, his short-term memory had begun to play tricks on him and had developed ever growing holes. This wasn't much of a problem considering he had led a very quiet life for the previous two hundred years. But as his short-term memory had faded, so his long-term memory had grown stronger, until he could even remember how many sugars King Arthur took in his tea. The old wizard lived in the hope that one day his memories would return. Then he would rebuild his beloved spaceship, *Desperalda*, and go home.

Ethel and the old wizard were weary with the weight of time. The millennia just seemed to go on for thousands of years. The warmth of the fire filled the room and surrounded them with a peace that neither had known for ages. Ethel nodded off on the arm of a chair while Merlin puffed away on a big homemade cigar of dubious origin.

"I wonder," said Ethel at last, "I wonder if it will ever end."

"That boy," said Merlin, "verily, I think he hath great potential."

"Jay?"

"Nay, not the Chosen One, the other one, thy creation, Douglas," said the old wizard.

Ethel was surprised that Merlin could remember the Chosen One. They had not spoken of it since the twelfth century, when Ethel herself had learned about it from the Blind Piano Tuner. Even she had had to be reminded of it from time to time.

"Douglas?" said Ethel. "I think not, old man."

"Thou will see, signs will come to pass," said Merlin.

"If only."

"Verily, I can sense something," said Merlin. "Maybe when all the segments meld together, when the joins close up. In those times maybe then the vital force will begin to flow and thou will see greatness."

"I wish I had your optimism," said Ethel. "Right now I

think the whole thing was a really bad idea. I was too late getting to the laboratory. Nearly everything had disintegrated. If only I could have got there sooner, while the bodies were fresher, but I couldn't leave the boy. It was too risky."

"I understand," said Merlin. "He has to be thy prime consideration at the moment."

"Yes," Ethel sighed, "but it's a terrible strain keeping them all under control."

"He knows not, does he?"

"No, he hasn't a clue, though I have told them about the quest, about the Perfect Hour," said Ethel. "But with everything that's happened recently it wouldn't surprise me if they've forgotten all about it. We'll talk again tonight, now we are all together at last."

"Yea, 'tis timely," said the old wizard. "And thou did well with the girl. She seems very promising and she is passing fair betimes and mighty comely, too, bearing more than a passing resemblance to my lady Gladys."

The old friends dozed off again and by the time they awoke the morning had vanished and it was time for dinner.

Chapter 19
We Are Not Here by Chance

"I suppose you're wondering why we're here?" said Ethel when everyone had gathered in the Great Hall.

"Forsooth, I live here," said Merlin, pretending he didn't know what the chicken was talking about.

"The Oracle is visiting her father," said The Oracle.

"Don't start that again," said Ethel.

"I just want to be wherever you are, Mommy," said Douglas.

"Good boy," snapped Ethel. "But it so happens there is a reason why the six of us are gathered here in Camelot."

"'Tis well said, old bird," said Merlin, who had totally forgotten the conversation he'd had with Ethel in the Great Smoking Room. "Now, who will partake more of my almost wonderful soup?"

"For cluck's sake, listen," said Ethel. "We are not all here by chance."

She stood very still at one end of the table, a feat in itself considering it was the Round Table, and stared at everyone. One by one they stopped eating and drinking and looked at her.

"That's better," she said. "Now, pay attention even if you've heard some of it before."

When Ethel had first told Jay and Kay about the Perfect Hour, Douglas hadn't existed. Nor did he know anything about the past two hundred years, since his brains had been sitting in a glass jar seventy stories below the earth's surface all that time. So Ethel told them again how for one hour during October 18, 2042, everything on Earth had been perfect. She told them how mankind had been wiping itself out like there was no tomorrow and taking half the other species on Earth with it, yet in the middle of it all, for no apparent reason, and unnoticed by most humans, the Perfect Hour had happened. It was almost as if someone or something had pressed Earth's pause button and given everyone a brief glimpse of paradise.

"That is awesome," said Jay.

"The trouble was," Ethel continued, "people were so wrapped up in survival, they completely failed to notice it. You see, the snowball effect had just started. The population wasn't dropping by a few hundred a week but by thousands, tens of thousands even, and people were too frantic to notice the sunshine after months of clouds or the rain after years of drought or that their back stopped aching for an hour or even to realize that for that hour no one at all died. Everyone was too busy looking in at their own little piece of life to see the whole world anymore."

"Wow," said Kay. "That is so sad."

There was a nagging feeling in her mind that somehow everything Ethel had just told them hadn't happened quite as she'd said it had.

"And thou wouldst find who created thy Perfect Hour?" said Merlin.

"Exactly."

"You know what's the coolest thing about it?" said Jay. "The fact that it happened. I mean, not who made it happen, but the fact that it happened at all."

"*Exactly!*" Ethel exclaimed. "It means there is hope for the world."

"So, are you trying to make it happen again?" said Kay.

She was dubious about the whole thing. All the others, including Jay, seemed to be swallowing everything Ethel said without question. With Douglas that wasn't surprising. After all, the chicken had created him and he worshiped her. Merlin seemed half out of it, he was so old, and The Oracle was only a stupid fish. But Jay just seemed to blindly believe everything Ethel said too. If she was so amazingly brilliant, thought Kay, how come she got caught by Nigel? How come she made such a mess of creating Douglas, and why the hell couldn't she just re-create this Perfect Hour? Kay didn't trust her. There was something she wasn't telling them.

She doesn't trust me, thought Ethel.

She looked inside Kay's mind and read her doubts. She tried to change the young woman's thoughts, but met with a resistance that surprised her. If she could persuade Kay to trust her, that resistance could be useful. Otherwise Kay might be a problem. For a split second the thought that she might have to kill Kay crossed her mind, but she brushed it away. For now she would just keep an eye on her.

"Earth's only hope is for us to find out who or what created the Perfect Hour," she said.

"Verily, noble chicken, I will quest no more," said the old wizard. "I have had more than enough of that for several lifetimes."

"You have no choice," said Ethel. "We are all part of this and unless we work together we have no chance of succeeding. That is why I have brought us all here to Camelot."

"The Oracle knows what you mean," said The Oracle. "We are a sort of gestalt thingie and The Oracle is the brain."

"No, I'm the brain," said Ethel. "But we all have a part to play in the quest."

"Quest?" said Merlin. "Could thou just runneth it past me one more time? It is many long centuries since last I quested."

"The Quest of the Perfect Hour," said Ethel.

"Ah, verily," said Merlin, who had forgotten and hadn't the faintest idea what Ethel was talking about.

"So where do we start?" said Jay.

"That is the first quest," said Ethel, "to find the starting point."

"Yeah, right, but from what you've said," said Kay, "you know, you're not even a hundred percent certain that someone made it happen. Suppose it was, like, just a fluke?"

"I've thought about that," said Ethel, "and I think I know how to find out."

Even though she felt uneasy letting the others know about the existence of time travel, Ethel explained that she would go back to that magic day in October 2042 and have a look. She didn't say that she was no good at time travel and had never traveled more than a few minutes before, certainly not 245 years. She was scared. It was like walking out onto a tightrope blindfolded and she had no way of knowing what lay beneath the tightrope or how far it was above solid ground. It could be a few inches above a feather mattress or a thousand miles over a fiery abyss.

"Yeah, right, then what, man?" said Jay.

"What I'll do is count everyone on the planet, just before the Perfect Hour, and then count them all again just after," said Ethel. "Then we'll know if anyone visited Earth."

"So what will that prove?" said Kay. "If you do find someone was here, you still won't know who they were or where they went. And how do you know they even left?"

"Are there any more potatoes?" said Douglas, not realizing, as no one else would for many years to come, the frightening importance of his question. Nor did anyone, apart from Kay, seem to notice the ridiculous flaws of logic in Ethel's plan. The person or creature that had caused the Perfect Hour may never have left Earth, or may never have been there in the first place and just done everything by remote control, or it may all have been a fluke, or the whole thing may never have happened and just been created and put into everyone's mind by Ethel.

"We've got to start somewhere," said Ethel. "Do you have a better idea?"

Kay said nothing.

"So, like, what should we do, you know, while you're away?" said Jay.

"Stay here and amuse yourselves," said Ethel. "Maybe, dare I suggest, try and learn something. Call me a silly old chicken, but I love the idea that I might come back and find you, say, possibly a fraction of an inch higher up the educational achievement scale."

"What?"

"Oh, cluck, why can't they ever give me decent materials to work with?"

"Verily, there is plenty for thee to do here, Jay," said Merlin. "Forsooth, I have all the combined knowledge of mankind and some intelligent species, too, at the very tips of my fingers. Great galleries of history, seven perfectly tuned pianos, and fine treasure-houses of things shall thou enjoy, and great places of wonder. And there shall be strawberry yogurt for dessert."

Chapter 20

Skateboarding on Thin Ice

There was a dull *pop* and Ethel vanished out of her body. The chicken body stood stiff and lifeless, just like Kay had been when her mind had been hijacked. Merlin picked her up and stuck her on a shelf next to some dinner plates. Jay wished he could have felt more surprised, but so much had happened recently that nothing seemed strange anymore. He was surprised at how quickly you took even the most fantastic things for granted. Talking chickens, talking goldfish, bits of paper that seemed to know what you were thinking, it was all quite ridiculous, yet it had happened. It wasn't one of those oh-and-it-was-all-just-a-dream situations that you read about in books.

"Do you think this is all maybe, like, just a dream?" he whispered to Kay.

"No, do you?"

"No, but I keep thinking I should. I mean, like, a week or so ago everything made sense. You know, chickens laid eggs. The sky was yellow. Now look, the sky's blue and animals keep talking to us and making us do things. Everything's just got so uncool and complicated, you know?"

"I can't even remember a week ago," said Kay.

"What, nothing?"

"No, not a thing," said Kay. "I've tried. Like, I really have, but the first thing I can remember is lying under those filing cabinets just before you turned up. I mean, I've got memories but they're just, like, knowledge, not stuff that's happened to me."

"'Tis not wise for the young to give themselves over to the dwelling on the past," said Merlin.

"How long do you think wonder chicken will be gone?" said Kay sarcastically.

"No more than the time it takes," said Merlin.

"And what the hell's that ringing noise?" said Jay. "It's been going on since we arrived."

"'Tis just the phone," said Merlin. "Forsooth, it has rung eternal these many long centuries."

"What ringing?" said Kay. "I can't hear anything."

"Nay, not everyone can," said Merlin. "'Tis only there for those it wants to reach."

"What do you mean?" said Jay.

"Ask not for whom the bell tolls, it tolls for thee," said the old wizard.

"Doesn't it ever stop?" said Jay.

"Nay," said the old wizard.

"Doesn't it drive you crazy?" said Jay.

"Verily, after a few years the sound flows over thee like a babbling brook, like a twittering bird, like a giant tortoise breaking wind, like a banana tumbling down a thousand stairs, like the sound of one hand scratching," said Merlin. "Though in truth there are times when it flows like concrete into the very depths of the soul."

"I'm going to look for it," said Jay. "It's driving me up the wall."

"Thou must cross the garden to the Tower of Dreams," said Merlin. "For it is there the bell tolls. Now fare thee well and take care."

Jay walked out into the garden, into the bright sunshine of another perfect day. At first the ringing seemed to come from everywhere, but as he concentrated he pinned it down to the tallest of the three towers on the opposite roof. He crossed the lawn and climbed seven flights of stone steps up to the roof. The ringing was definitely coming from high up in the tall tower, so he walked across to the great oak door at its base and went in.

As he entered, Jay realized it was the first time since he had left the penthouse that he'd been alone. For twelve years he had been on his own and although he had been lonely from time to time, he had been happy with his own company. There was never any need to think before he did anything. He could scratch himself where and when he liked. He could talk to himself or spend whole days in complete silence. As he thought about it now, he realized that he'd never been alone. Ethel had been there all along and heard every word he'd thought or said.

As he walked along the corridor toward the ringing bell, he felt his old calm returning. He loved Kay, he wanted to spend the rest of his life with her, find the cottage in the country, make babies and all the rest of his dreams, but right now being alone couldn't have come at a better time.

The tower looked huge inside, far bigger than it had looked from the outside. A central spiral staircase of gray stone led upward into the darkness that appeared to have no end, and on every fifth stair there was a door. The ringing now was a distant echo coming from the very top of the tower, so Jay began to climb. Around and around he climbed past door after door until he felt he was on an endless Möbius strip in some weird Franz Kafka novel.

Bright lights crept out from under some doors, yellow like the sun, lights that changed shape as if someone or something was moving behind the door. Ethel had said that Merlin was the only person living in Camelot. Steam seeped out of keyholes. Wonderful smells that even his deep memories, inherited from earlier generations, had never encountered caressed his nose, trying to lure him in. And music enchanted his ears with the promise of paradise. Jay wanted to open every door he passed, but knew if he did he would never reach the bell. Up in the distant darkness lightning crackled, yet through it all the phone kept ringing, ringing, sometimes tantalizingly close, sometimes far, far away, but always there leading him farther and farther up into the Tower of Dreams.

The ringing was very close now and constant. It came from a door that was twice the size of all those around it, tall and wide, of dark oak carved into lots of small panels and held to its frame by great curling hinges of black steel. As Jay pushed the door open, the ringing grew louder. This was the right room.

Jay found himself inside the biggest room he had ever seen, far too big to be inside the tower, too big to see the far walls even on a clear day when there was no mist, and there wasn't today. This was the Grand Ballroom, undoubtedly the largest ballroom ever built, so large there are no words large enough to describe it.

Where other ballrooms have potted palms this one had potted forests with monkeys living in the branches and a crop of coconuts that in its best year had produced enough milk to bottle-feed seventeen orphaned elephants four times a day for eighteen months. Far above, hidden in clouds, massive chandeliers sparkled like miniature galaxies and in the distance, mingling with the ringing of the phone, the call of lonely seagulls echoed in the still air and Jay thought he could hear waves beating on a distant shore.

When the greatest ball ever had been held there—and it really had been a grand affair, with thirty-two kings, thirty-three queens, and the entire population of several small countries apart from the caretakers—there had still been enough room for all the Horse of the Year shows from seventeen galaxies. Fifty-seven orchestras spread around the perimeter of the room had provided the music and still there had been places that were in total silence. It is said that if Lake Titicaca was filled to the brim with floor polish, there would barely be enough to clean the parquet of the Grand Ballroom for a year. After the ball it was two years before the last guest found his coat and left, though an urban myth says that to this day there are still forty-seven people endlessly wandering in search of their hats. This was a room of physically impossible proportions, a veritable pocket galaxy.

The Grand Ballroom was deserted now, emptied of all its finery, its plants and curtains, totally bare but for the fifty-ton chandeliers up in the clouds and, somewhere off in the mist, a telephone that wouldn't stop ringing. Dust had gathered on the floor, covering the parquet like a sheet of gauze. The last waltz, played more than eight hundred years before, still echoed faintly around the high ceiling, slipping in and out of the clouds and keeping the great spiders that lived in the ornate plasterwork awake.

And in the middle of the room, on a small table, was the telephone.

It was just a dot in the distance, but after half an hour's walking the dot became clearer. Jay could see the table. After another half hour, he could see the phone was red. And then, as he approached it, the ringing stopped.

He sat down in the dust and stared at the phone. It sat there silently on its table being a phone. A black cable hung down from the back of it and wove its way lazily off into the distance like a sleeping snake.

Jay had never seen a telephone. There had been references to them in some of the three thousand books, but they hadn't seemed very interesting so he'd skipped over them. He picked up the whole instrument and as he did so the ringing started with such suddenness that he dropped it. As it hit the floor the ringing stopped, there was a few seconds' silence, during which Jay thought he'd probably broken the thing, and then a faint voice came out of the smaller part of the machine. Jay picked it up and held it to his ear.

"Hello?" he said instinctively.

There was silence, though there was someone there. He could feel it.

"Hello?" he said again.

Nothing.

"Hello?"

In his cave below the glacier the Blind Piano Tuner put his handkerchief over the mouthpiece and spoke: "Welcome to Yesterday," he said in a stilted mechanical voice. "To help us serve you more quickly, please choose from the following options: To speak to yourself aged four, press one. To speak to yourself aged five, press two. To speak to yourself aged six, press three. To speak to yourself aged seven, press four. To speak to yourself aged eight, press five. To speak to yourself aged nine, press six. To speak to yourself aged ten, press seven. To speak to yourself aged eleven, press eight. To speak to yourself aged twelve, press nine." There was a pause and then, "To speak to the operator, press zero."

Jay just stood there openmouthed. There was a sheet of paper folded up under the phone. He unfolded it and read:

Hello again.

It was the same typeface as before. He folded it up and put it in his pocket. He picked up the receiver, held it to his ear, and listened. His mind went completely blank. He hadn't known what to expect from the phone—maybe something relevant to the situation, but certainly not silence. The whole thing was so stupid. No matter how he juggled the contents of his brain, there was no way he could put any of it together to make sense. None of it would fit in with the rules of life that he had in his head, but then that was why he had been taken there, to learn new rules, or, more precisely, to learn that there are no rules.

The world's entire combined telephone systems had collapsed years before Jay was born. It had been just before everything else collapsed like a wall of dominoes. One day the whole of the Internet had simply imploded and all the billions and billions of bits of trivial information stored on thousands of hard disks around the world had simply vanished into a microscopic black hole in a small rock carved in the shape of a tiny gargoyle on the topmost turret of Camelot.

Communications ending had been the spark that meant the end of civilization as everyone had known it. It had been a significant date, recorded in almost every country of the world, even England, where people had always gone to endless lengths to avoid communicating with one another.

"Come on, make up your mind," said the Blind Piano Tuner. "There are other people waiting, you know."

Jay turned around in a daze, half expecting to see a line of people behind him. There was no one there, though his weren't the only footprints in the dust. There were the muddled footprints of himself aged four, aged five, and so on, up to twelve, though all Jay saw was a mess in the dust.

"I don't understand," he managed to say at last.

"To speak to the operator, press zero," said the Blind Piano Tuner.

Jay did.

The Blind Piano Tuner changed the handkerchief for a golfing sock and said in a new voice, "What?"

"I don't understand," said Jay.

"What?"

"How can I talk to myself?"

"Everyone does it all the time."

"Yes, I know that, but that's just thinking aloud," said Jay. "I mean, how can I talk to myself when I was younger?"

"Your past follows you everywhere. Everyone's does. It's with you for your whole life. Talking to your past is just like looking at photographs of yourself."

"It doesn't make sense," said Jay.

"Try it and see," said the Blind Piano Tuner. "Please."

Jay couldn't. The idea of talking to himself was just too scary.

"Do it. *Now!*"

"No, I can't, man," said Jay, and dropping the receiver, he ran back in what he thought was the direction of the door.

Back in the kitchen, Douglas and Merlin had finished cleaning up and the old wizard was showing Douglas just how much fun could be had running around the flagstones pushing a wet mop and bucket. Douglas may have been transformed by his swim in the Gene Pool but he was still, in many ways, a child. He had also taken quite a shine to Merlin and was anxious to please the old wizard.

"Okay, okay," said Douglas, "let me have a turn."

"Well, my child, I am not sure," said Merlin. "'Tis not for all, the call of the sacred mop."

"Please, please."

"Oh, very well, little one, I will give thee leave to mop, but venture no farther than this room," said Merlin, "and those twenty-four through there, and remember to keep changing the water like I showed thee." He paused, then, "Come, child," he said to Kay, "needs we must talk."

The wizard and the most beautiful girl in the world walked out into the morning sunshine in the courtyard garden. It was the most exquisite place Kay had ever seen, though when she thought about it, she couldn't remember having actually been in any other garden before. White roses grew everywhere, filling the air with their gorgeous perfume. The white peacocks came rushing over and Merlin fed them tiny white crackers he carried in a white pouch around his waist. And high above them, for the first time in 270 years, a skylark twittered sweetly in the clear summer sky. If there had been any poets present they would have been transported to ecstasy and written pages and pages of maudlin doggerel. Thankfully poets had become extinct in the twenty-first century.

"I say, chaps, what about The Oracle?" said The Oracle, sticking her head out of the jar. "Are you just going to leave her here?"

Merlin picked up the jar, carried it to a round pond, and tipped The Oracle out into the clear water. There were other goldfish swimming between beautiful blue water lilies and they all began to smile.

"There, my child, and when I say 'my child' I don't mean *my* child, I mean 'tis just a figure of speech, forsooth. Go talk with thy sisters, little fish," said the old wizard.

The Oracle looked up through the water at Merlin and wanted to cry. She knew he was her father, yet he would not acknowledge her. And because fish can't cry, she wanted to cry even more.

"And forsooth, nay fivesooth even—sorry, ye corny medieval joke—venture not outside these very walls, little fish, for beyond there lies the stuff of terror and thistles and all manner of beasties," said the wizard. "Verily I say, darkness shall cover the land, pestilence shall visit thee, and weird thingies shall fall from the sky."

"Like, what the hell are you talking about?" said Kay.

Merlin took Kay's arm and, leading her through the garden, told her about his life. How he had arrived on Earth and how Ethel had saved him from his burning ship. How he had built Camelot and, for a while, turned it into the center of the kingdom, from where his protégé Arthur and all his playmates had ruled the world.

"Forsooth, they were such hard times," said Merlin. "The cleaning up alone was horrendous, but it was a lot of fun, especially Nimiane, the Lady of the Lake, though thou couldn't have called her a lady, not with some of the things we got up to. She looked just like thee, thou know, same hair, same—"

"Yeah, right," said Kay, taking her arm out of Merlin's, which was beginning to sweat a lot.

"Thou know, sometimes we—"

"I don't think I want to, like, hear about it, thank you," said Kay, cutting him off. "I wonder where Jay's gone."

"I know not," lied Merlin, "but the phone has stopped its infernal ringing."

Kay walked off to explore the wonderful garden, while the old wizard sulkily went back to the kitchen. He knew exactly where Jay was, which was more than Jay did. He had run until he could run no more. He sat on the floor, his heart pounding in his chest like a hammer, while he got his breath back. All he could see on every side was a soft white mist. The polished parquet floor shone like a becalmed sea, reaching away flatter than water into infinity. The dust had gone out like the tide, but at least the wretched phone had stopped ringing. The seagulls had stopped calling too. There was total silence, as enveloping as the mist.

He was completely and absolutely lost. The Blind Piano Tuner focused his thoughts and guided Jay to the next step. The primary motive for getting Jay into the ballroom was to show him the Great Flaw. He would be part of a great journey soon and without the Great Flaw they would never reach their destination.

The Great Flaw is this: A year has 365 days yet a circle has only 360 degrees. As Jay walked away from the phone it hit him. He found himself wondering why there were five more days in a year than there were degrees in a circle. In thinking this, he had unwittingly stumbled upon the Great Flaw. It was a discovery of enormous significance, elegant in its simplicity yet, as its name implied, a basic fault in mathematics that had been there since time began. Except Jay had got it backward. There were not, as he thought, five more days in a year than there should be; there were five too few degrees in a circle.

Something went *click* inside Jay's head. More things fell into place than he realized he even *had* inside his head. No answers came out but a lot of questions formed an orderly line. Unknowingly, Jay had taken the first step on the path to higher wisdom.

There was something on the floor ahead of him. It was a skateboard. After penicillin and the shopping bag, the skateboard had been the fourth most useful invention of the twentieth century. Jay hadn't seen a skateboard for years. It looked just like the one he'd had, the one his sister, Sue, had thrown on the bonfire. It had the same picture on the top. It even had the same scratch along the left-hand side from the time he'd raced the garbage truck and lost. He still had the scar on his elbow. He picked the board up and turned it over in his hands.

It even had his name written on the bottom.

"Oh, man."

As he skateboarded across the endless floor in what he hoped was the right direction, his scared confusion turned to calm acceptance. Yes, he had had a skateboard. It had been exactly the same as this one and he had seen his sister throw it on the bonfire and watched it burn so ferociously that even the steel wheels had melted. It had been the day before his family went away. And now, twelve years later, here he was skateboarding across a floor that was too huge to be real on a skateboard that couldn't exist. He wasn't dreaming. Maybe this was one of the alternate futures that Ethel had been talking about. Maybe somehow he had slipped from one to another where his skateboard hadn't got burned.

"Okay," he said to himself. "Okay, chill out, man. Stay cool." And later, as the fog grew darker, "Everything's cool."

One of the chandeliers had fallen from the ceiling and lay in a mound of broken crystal and wire. Twice the height of a man, the once elegant creation was now a pile of garbage. It had obviously been there a long time. There were cobwebs all over it and the ninety-eighth generation of a colony of tiny blue spiders living in a world of what to them was crystal castles and spires.

There was something on the other side of the mound. He could hear it clattering about and muttering. He walked around the chandelier and there was a boy aged about ten.

It wasn't just any boy aged about ten. It was Jay.

"Oh, cool, you found my skateboard," said the young Jay.

"What? Oh, yeah," said Jay. "Like, what the hell's going on?"

"Well, you wouldn't talk to me on the phone."

"I don't understand," said Jay. "I'm going mad, aren't I? Is this, like, a flashback? Don't tell me, you're going to give me some really important bit of information?"

"No, I thought you were going to give *me* some really important bit of information. You know, to help me in our future," said the young himself.

"Hang on. Listen. If either of us says anything, it could alter the future."

"Or the past."

"You can't alter the past," said Jay.

"Can I have my skateboard back? I said I'd lend it to Sue."

Jay opened his mouth to tell himself to stick close to his parents all the time because they were going to vanish, but as he opened his mouth to give the young himself the advice, the young himself vanished.

But the skateboard didn't.

Jay sat down. His heart was beating like it was going to burst out of his chest and he felt as if he was going to faint. The phone and the skateboard had been weird, but he could handle them. They were just like funny dreams. But meeting himself in the flesh, face-to-face, was too much.

He skated on into the darkening mist. The smell of decomposing hedgehogs filled the air. It spiraled around and around him until Jay felt himself retching and barely able to breathe. The darkness rolled over him and he felt scared. Far away in the darkness a lonely bell began to toll, not the frantic ringing of the telephone, but a deep resonant sound, lost and frightening yet hauntingly irresistible, like the warning bell that guides ships through fog down deep dark rivers, the bell that would guide the ferryman across the Styx. It echoed through the darkness, drawing Jay toward it like a sleep-walker, except that he was wide awake, or thought he was. He seemed to be watching himself as if he were two people, an observer and the observed. The skateboard seemed to be sticking to the floor, making it harder and harder to move, until he picked it up and began walking.

"You know your worst nightmare?" a soft voice whispered in his ear.

Jay spun around but it was totally dark. Something could have been right beside him and he wouldn't have seen it. He waved his arms frantically, but there was nothing within reach, nothing except the creeping cold.

Jay knew the worst nightmare of his childhood, but he had a strong feeling he was about to discover an even worse one. As a child he had woken screaming from dreams where he had run as if through heavy molasses while something huge, dark, and unseen had slowly gained on him, something so huge that it used up all the air around him so that he had none left to breathe. The nightmare had always ended before the invisible terror caught him, but that had made it no less terrifying each time it came. Now he had the terrible feeling that today was the day the molasses would set thick around his ankles like toffee and the horror would envelope him.

Something wet slid down his leg.

Into his shoes.

Hot breath parted the hairs on the back of his neck and he dropped his skateboard. Before he had time to bend down and pick it up, the voice began again.

"That's right," it whispered. "That's the one. Only the molasses isn't molasses and it goes on forever and ever. Pick up your skateboard and keep walking."

The molasses that wasn't molasses was warm, exactly the same temperature as blood. But it couldn't be blood. Sure, blood was thicker than water, but not as thick as molasses. At least, human blood wasn't.

Jay wanted to turn and run, but it was so dark he wasn't sure which way to go. He wanted to lie down and curl up into a ball, as if by making himself as small as possible all the bad stuff might go away. But to lie down would mean lying in the molasses that wasn't molasses. He thought about dipping his finger into it and tasting it, but couldn't bring himself to do so.

"Where are we going?" he said.

"You know the place where all the clouds went when the chicken cleared the sky?" whispered the voice. "Far, far away, so far away you'll never be able to come back. But you will come back. You'll come back and kill everyone, even Kay, and then you'll feel so indescribably terrible that you'll want to kill yourself, only I won't let you because that would be too easy. Ready? Get on your skateboard and off we go."

Of course, being knee-deep in thick molasses stuff that wasn't molasses meant the skateboard was totally unable to move.

"Shit, shit, shit. Crap, crap, crap," said the voice. "We'll have to walk."

Progress through the thick molasses stuff that wasn't molasses was incredibly hard going and slow.

"Oh, crap," said the voice. "At this rate you'll have starved to death by the time we get there."

Jay stopped.

"I'm going back," he said.

He turned and tried to walk in the opposite direction, only it wasn't the opposite direction, because the molasses that wasn't molasses was getting deeper. It reached the top of his legs and stroked him. The voice that had been sharp and threatening now turned soft and enticing.

"Come on," it said.

Another dream from Jay's childhood flowed over him and he struggled to get a grip on it. The sun was shining and he was by a river.

"Keep the sun shining, keep the sun shining," he said to himself.

It flickered. The river turned to molasses, dark clouds covered the sky. Jay bit his lip and concentrated. His lip began to bleed and he focused his thoughts on the taste of the blood. He tried to remember the last time he tasted his own blood. He'd been seven or eight, playing by another river. He'd tripped on a tree root and bitten his lip. He remembered wanting to cry, to run home to his mother, but she'd forbidden him to play by the river, so he'd wiped his eyes and sat in the sunshine until the pain had subsided. The river sparkled and danced, reflecting the bright blue of the empty sky.

"Bastard," muttered the voice.

It felt weak and distant. Something wet slid out of Jay's sock, up his leg, and flew limply off into the darkness, something as cold as death, something that could only have been a liquid vampire bat. Then Jay was free.

"I'll let you go this time," said the voice as it trailed off into the distance. "I'll be back."

By the time he reached the wall of the Grand Ballroom, Jay's heart had slowed down. Incredibly, the door was only a yard or so to his left. In fact the door had been following his erratic progress across the dance floor and was waiting for him. There was no point in keeping him inside the room longer than was necessary. The main thing was that he had discovered the Great Flaw, even if at the moment he didn't realize just how important it was going to be and he had got it backward. Soon the day would arrive when it would all become clear. The five missing degrees in every circle would no longer be missing. This is not to say that the 360 degrees would shuffle up to let the missing five in. What it meant was that for as long as humans had played with mathematics their circles had been too small.

Far away in the mountains the Blind Piano Tuner smiled. Jay was the only one who had ever come back.

Jay pulled the door of the Grand Ballroom shut behind him and collapsed against the wall at the top of the stairs. He put his head between his knees and took long deep breaths until his breathing was back to normal. He couldn't get the image of himself aged ten standing in front of him out of his mind. It should have been a dream or a hologram, but it had seemed totally real. Jay wished he'd reached out and touched the figure. He'd thought of it at the time, but he had been too scared. It was like he had been in two realities at once and touching the child would have made the two collide and vanish.

When he felt calmer, he started back down the stairs to the exit. Noises, colors, and smells tried to lure him into other doors. Names appeared on them:

RUNNING THROUGH MOLASSES
FALLING
THE DREAM THAT DARES NOT SPEAK ITS NAME
FLYING THROUGH WATER
PARADISE
THE DREAM THAT NOT ONLY DARES SPEAK ITS NAME,
    BUT SHOUTS IT FROM THE ROOFTOPS
THE LAST-CHANCE SALOON
HEARTBREAK HOTEL
THE HERMITAGE
LIFE WORSE THAN DEATH
THE REALLY CLEVER LABORATORIES
DEATH WORSE THAN LIFE . . .

Name after name, the sum total of humankind's dreams and nightmares. As Jay passed them, they changed their names in last desperate attempts to catch his attention. THE ROOM OF TERROR became THE ROOM OF TERRIBLY WONDERFUL CUPCAKES, for example. But Jay's experiences in the Grand Ballroom had been more than enough for him and he ignored everything, finally staggering out onto the roof, exhausted.

He lay flat out on the warm lead sheeting and stared up into the sky. High above, skylarks danced on the air, their excited twittering song drifting down like soft rain. He heard Kay singing to herself in the garden and went down to her, to hide in her arms and tell her about the Tower of Dreams.

He found it hard to put into words what had happened, meeting himself as a child and the terrible voice in the darkness. If he hadn't been clutching the skateboard, clutching it so tightly that his knuckles were white, he would have persuaded himself it had all been a dream, but the skateboard was hard proof.

"I'm going to see Merlin," he said. "See if he knows what it was all about."

Kay said she would stay in the garden for a while. She

188

Colin Thompson

needed to be out in the air away from everyone. Jay's experience in the Tower of Dreams had disturbed her and she needed to think. It wasn't what had happened to him— that was too weird to be frightening, at least, not secondhand. What bothered her was the sudden realization that she knew almost nothing at all about Jay. He had spoken so little about the past that he seemed to be as devoid of one as she was.

Back in the kitchen Merlin, furious with himself at his pathetic attempt to flirt with Kay and even more furious that he had grown so old he couldn't actually remember why he wanted to flirt with her, was making stew. He was peeling onions and the tears were pouring down his face all over the vegetables. On an old wood-burning range as wide as a small house an enormous cooking pot was slowly coming to the boil. What effect the tears of a two-thousand-year-old intergalactic wizard would have on mere mortals like Jay and Kay or mere mortal-cocktails like Douglas was anyone's guess, but no doubt everyone would find out that night at dinner.

Douglas, who had washed the twenty-five floors until the flagstones were as bright as the day they had been cut from the quarry, was now drinking the water from the mop bucket and singing quietly to himself in the corner.

"Where's Ethel, man?" said Jay. "Still away?"

"Ethel has left the building," said Merlin.

Ethel had not actually left the building, just the time. She was still in Camelot, still in the very same room as the rest of them. She was there, just two hundred years earlier, and amazingly Merlin was making vegetable stew, the same recipe he had been trying to re-create since that haunting night centuries before when, too drunk to know what he was doing, he had thrown handfuls of things into a pot and produced a stew that King Arthur and all the other knights had said was the best stew they had ever tasted. Of course, they had all been very drunk too, so even Douglas's mop bucket would have tasted wonderful.

And here in Merlin's kitchen, as he attempted to re-create something that was no more than a distant memory, was

189

illustrated one of the great frustrations of life. Your memories always tell you the past was much better than it really had been. The sun shone every day when you were a child and everyone loved you, when in reality it rained a lot and you wet the bed during endless terrible nightmares. It's the same on every planet in every galaxy. Everyone sees the past through rose-colored glasses. You then spend the rest of your life chasing dreams that never existed. Pathetic, isn't it?

Over the centuries, Merlin's stew seemed to him to have got worse not better. He had begun with a simple list of ingredients, basic vegetables in hot water, and over the centuries had added and taken away different herbs and spices. He had even used exotic ingredients from far-off galaxies, like the screaming lettuce of Xargon, and priceless herbs with leaves that took seven centuries to grow an eighth of an inch and tasted like the perspiration of the Gorlag fusion fish. He had seventeen rooms piled high to the ceiling with cookbooks, but still the perfect recipe eluded him, still no one else had ever said, "That was the best stew I've ever tasted."

Screw quests for the Perfect Hour, this was far more important. This was a real quest with real benefits, the Perfect Stew. The recipe that Merlin was using was this:

Ye Perfect Stew, No. 17857

3 tablespoons—the silver one with the bent handle that did once grace the very kitchen of Queen Guinevere and was used by her to partake of stewed prunes—of olive oil pressed from ye fifth tree south of ye blue summer house sometime between Midsummer Eve and the following Tuesday

3 carrots that do weigh no more than 2 ounces each and have been fertilized with manure from white leghorn chickens that has been rotted for six months in the sporran of the noble Scottish knight Grummor McGrummorson. (Note: We be running low on manure.)

2 large onions from halfway up the string that does

hang by the old butter churn in ye seventh vegetable store that have been chopped fine with the sharpened jawbone of a rat that has been soaked this past six months in a stone jar of 1827 Napoleon brandy

2 stalks of celery that have been blanched with the red cardigan of Queen Guinevere

5 ounces of split red lentils that have been split with the penknife of Odin (in the tall jar behind ye pot scourers)

2 cloves of garlic crushed with a fresh oak branch that has been stripped of its bark and rolled on the thigh of a Mexican cigar smoker

9 ounces of ripe tomatoes that be too ripe to hold in the hand lest they do burst and run down thy apron into thy very shoes

5 gills of unsalted water from the streams of Tristan da Cunha

1 tablespoon of Dead Sea salt

1 gill of cabernet sauvignon from the cellar of a left-handed friend

1 bay leaf

1 sprig of thyme, unless it has grown fed up waiting for no man and has gone away with the tyde

1 jar of ye Ancient Herbalist Kitten Tonight cook-in sauce

There were other ingredients that are really too obscure and disgusting to mention, although they will be listed for the sake of completeness:

1 teaspoon of ye toenail clippings—left foot only— from the oldest spinster who does live by the lake of Titicaca

2 cupfuls of dust from the bottom of an Arab stallion's nosebag. If ye stallion have the croup, then shall thou also add 1 peppercorn.

1 handful of ants that have been marinated in toilet water for three days—thou shall use water from the toilet by the kitchen maid's pantry.

Ye lint and skinne flakes from the jockstrap of ye jumbo family-size sumo wrestler. Make sure ye wrestler is removed before adding.

Ye leftovers, provided they have not been eaten more than once

1 lizard bouillon cube—low-salt

Some mud

Saliva to taste

**Throe the Lotte
In Thy Potte
And Stir a Lotte.**

If Jay had had the slightest interest in cooking, and had looked at Merlin's recipe, cold shivers would have run down his spine, not because of the recipe itself or any of its ingredients or methods, but because of the typing. It was exactly the same as the writing on the piece of paper. The piece of paper in his pocket moved, flexing against him like a familiar caress.

The old wizard had a sneaking belief that the vegetable stew had actually been dead animal stew with vegetables and, though he didn't like to say anything when Ethel was around, he reckoned the dead animal had been a chicken. He had a vague memory of the air being filled with feathers and something warm struggling in his hands, though that could have been another memory altogether and had nothing to do with cooking.

"Look at this," said Jay, holding up the skateboard. "I found my old skateboard."

"Verily, so thou didst find the Grand Ballroom, then?" said Merlin.

"Yes. It's a seriously weird place," said Jay. "Do you know what it's all about?"

"And foundest thou the telephone?"

"Yeah, man. It was unreal."

"And spake thou with thyself?" said the wizard.

"Not on the phone, no."

"Great mercy for that."

"Why, what would've happened?" said Jay quickly.

"Methinks thou wouldst have either vanished in a puff of nothing or changed back to the age of thyself thou wast talking to. I know not for certain," said the wizard.

"I met myself in the flesh, man," said Jay. "I spoke to myself."

"And nothing happened?"

"Yeah. The second I opened my mouth to speak and, like, warn myself what was going to happen, I vanished."

"And think on, my child, didst thou discover the Great Flaw?" said Merlin.

He leaned forward in anticipation and held his breath. What if the boy hadn't found it? Telling him would not be the same. It would just be hollow words. The Great Flaw is something that has to be discovered for oneself or one can never use it.

"Of course, I walked across it for ages, man," said Jay.

"Nay, not the great floor. The Great Flaw, the degrees of a circle, the days of a year," said Merlin.

"Oh, yeah," said Jay. "It's weird, man."

"Wouldst thou offer me explanation of the Great Flaw? 'Tis many years since I heard of it and my memory doth play tricks on me," said Merlin.

Jay explained how he had discovered that a year had five more days than a circle had degrees and the old wizard cleared up the last bit of the puzzle.

"Nay, it be not so," he said. "The year hath the very number of days it should. The circle it is that hath too few degrees."

"So, the Tower of Dreams," said Jay, "why's it called that?"

"Verily, it is the place," said Merlin, "where dreams come true."

"Not for me it wasn't," said Jay.

"Though not necessarily thine own dreams," added the old wizard.

"That's for sure," said Jay.

"Potato," said Douglas.

Chapter 21
Fluffy's Story

When Merlin tipped The Oracle into his garden pond, the other six goldfish that were just goldfish all came rushing over. Now, the thing about regular goldfish, as opposed to goldfish being occupied by other life-forms, is that they are dumb. In fact, they are a good many stages below dumb, the famous "goldfish memory" being a perfect example of just how totally complete their dumbness is. According to scientific research, the goldfish has a memory span of 2.6 seconds. This immediately brings up two questions: How do you find this out and why would you want to find this out? The third question is, what sort of a goldfish-brained idiot would waste part of his or her life trying to find out this sort of thing anyway? An eminent professor highly qualified and gifted in conning his government out of totally useless research grants, no doubt.

Anyway, suffice it to say, goldfish have an almost nonexistent memory capacity, so it was no surprise to anyone when the following encounter occurred between Fluffy and the six goldfish.

"Hello," said the first goldfish.

"What?" said The Oracle, who, not being a goldfish, couldn't understand a word the creature was saying.

"What?" said the first goldfish.

"Go away," said The Oracle.

"Who said that?" said the first goldfish, spinning around.

"Go away," said The Oracle.

"Hello," said the first goldfish.

And so on and on and on and on, times six, until Fluffy stuck her head out of the water and screamed at the top of her voice, which, being a goldfish's voice, barely echoed across the next five lily pads, "HELP!"

"Ah," said a passing kingfisher, hearing The Oracle's cry for assistance, "lunch." And he swallowed her.

By now the liquid from the Gene Pool that had been in Fluffy's jar had worked its magic on all the other goldfish in the pond. They were now floating on their backs smiling at the sky. They had all grown young for a brief instant then died of complete happiness. Their ghosts hovered above the water for a moment and then sank to the bottom of the pond.

Oh, crikey, not again, thought The Oracle from inside the kingfisher as they flew together up to the roof.

"Hello, pretty bird," said Douglas, who had finished drinking the mop bucket and gone outside to find someone to play fetch with. "I don't suppose you want to play fetch, do you? No, of course you don't. You're just a bird and members of the feathered fraternity cannot speak, except for parrots, and they, poor things, only mimic. They don't understand what they're saying. Anyway, you're not a parrot."

"Douglas, help The Oracle, there's a good chap," shouted Fluffy from inside the kingfisher's stomach. "Kill this damn bird!"

Of course Douglas couldn't hear her and by then the acid juices inside the kingfisher's stomach had begun to eat away at Fluffy's body. Her tail was gone and her fins were fast disappearing too.

"Oh, gosh, not again," she said, and for the 127th time since she had been born, she transferred her mind into the body of another creature and became the kingfisher.

"No, Douglas, The Oracle does not want to play fetch," she said, and flew up into the air.

Fluffy had been a bird before. She had been a partridge, a parrot, an ostrich, and a duck, none of them particularly good at flying, and the best thing about being a bird was the flying. It was amazing. You could soar up into the sky away from everything. It gave you such a wonderful sense of freedom.

196

Colin Thompson

The kingfisher's body flew splendidly, maybe not so great going upward but expert at diving down like a rocket. The worst thing about being a bird was that it usually ended in you becoming someone else's dinner.

But then isn't that always the way? she thought. *Whatever body you occupy, there's always some bugger who wants to eat you.*

Fluffy, like Ethel and her father, Merlin, had been the worst student in the whole history of oracle school, so like them she had been sent to Earth. There was an old joke about a place being so bad that if the galaxy needed an enema that was where it would be plugged in, but in the earth's case it was beyond a joke. Earth was the place that had inspired the joke to begin with. The human population of the planet thought that because they were so aggressive and self-destructive, everywhere else must be just as self-destructive. In fact most planets lived peaceful happy lives, but then on most planets the population's brains had evolved at the same rate as their bodies.

Because Merlin had also been such a poor student he'd been sent to Earth too. The authorities on Morphine had been pretty pleased with themselves at the huge savings in cost they'd achieved by sending a wizard and an oracle in the same spaceship. "After all," their old headmaster had said, "we don't want them coming back here."

And so Merlin's spaceship had crashed on Earth. It had been designed to run out of fuel as soon as it reached there. If Ethel hadn't rescued them, Merlin and Fluffy would have become extinct centuries before. It seems incredible, doesn't it, that she just happened to be in the right place when the spaceship crashed?

Fluffy's career as The Oracle had been brief. As soon as her looks had started to fade and she had changed from occupying a human body, it had all gone out of the window. Once she moved into other life-forms, no one ever listened to her again.

All in all, she thought as she preened her newly acquired feathers, *it's been a total waste of time, really.*

Fluffy was the only oracle who had been able to move from

species to species. Normally they just went to a planet, found the main life-form, adopted it, and stayed young and beautiful, or hideous, depending on the planet, forever. Although Fluffy had thought changing species seemed like a brilliant idea at the time, a really democratic thing to do, to give every living creature the benefit of her wisdom, it had proved totally useless because she had never been able to speak or communicate with any species other than humans, and once she had ceased to look human virtually no human had ever listened to her again. I mean, if you were strolling casually along and a warthog came up to you and started talking, you'd generally tend to faint or run away and sober up. If you were openminded enough to accept a hideous-looking pig trying to have a conversation with you, you'd be unlikely to take any advice that it might give you seriously. And even if you were one of those incredibly rare people who were so open-minded as to actually take notice, the minute you tried to tell anyone else about it, they'd tend to lock you up in a room with padded walls and no sharp objects.

So apart from a few years at the beginning, Fluffy's career had been a disaster. Ethel the chicken had been the only creature who had taken her seriously, but Ethel knew far more than Fluffy ever would so never needed her advice anyway. She just pretended, to keep The Oracle happy. If only she'd stayed at Delphi. If only she could find a way to become a beautiful woman again instead of a beautiful kingfisher.

Chapter 22
Spider, Spider, Burning Bright

Kay was sitting by the pool gazing at her own reflection. It was the first time she had ever seen herself and she was fascinated. She turned her head from side to side and made funny faces.

"What are you doing?" said Douglas. "Trying to frighten the fish?"

"No," said Kay, blushing. When she realized he had been watching her she felt rather silly.

"Do you want to play fetch?" said Douglas, picking up a broken branch.

"Okay," Kay sighed, and threw it as far as she could.

There were questions in her head, questions that until now had been vague, as if her brain didn't know how to ask them. Her memories seemed unreal, as if she had seen them in a movie, not that she really knew what a movie was. The last one—*Star Wars: Episode 47, The Alzheimer's of the Jedi*—had been made almost two hundred years before. But she felt as if someone else had written the script of her life and someone else had experienced it.

When Ethel had cloned her from Jay's rib, she had tried to clone his memories, too. She had done her best to change them so they became female memories, but memory management was one of the subjects that Ethel had failed at school, so the results had been muddled and patchy. The part of Kay's memory that should have been full of memories— childhood games, her father carrying her home when she was tired, her first kiss, pictures of people and places—was empty. Her brain was full of knowledge, like a library packed with information, but she had no memories.

The thoughts that kept reoccurring in her head were, *What am I doing here?* and *What on earth's going on?* and *Why do I feel so empty?* Endless thoughts kept filling her head, merging together into the word *What?* or sometimes *Why?* She looked at Douglas running back with his stick and almost envied him his simple uncomplicated, albeit totally screwed-up, brain.

"Oh, man," she said, "what are we, like, doing here?"

"Playing fetch," said Douglas.

"Yeah," Kay sighed, "maybe you're right. Though, like, are we the ones throwing the stick or are we the sticks?"

She leaned back and threw the stick high in the air. It seemed to fly with a life of its own. It soared above the seventh story, hovered over the roof for a second like a humming bird, and then fell over the far wall into the dense forest below. Douglas stared at the space where it had been and ran toward the far end of the garden.

"Douglas, no," Kay shouted. "You mustn't go outside. Merlin said it's dangerous."

"I want my stick," said Douglas petulantly.

"Hey, man, we'll find you another one," said Kay.

"Don't want another one. I want that one," said Douglas.

The dog bit of his brain seemed to be in total control and, like a dog, he had one idea fixed in his head and that was to get his stick.

"HEEL!" Kay screamed, and Douglas came to a dead halt. "SIT!"

"No," said Douglas, getting up again.

There was a stone arch leading out of the garden through the castle and Douglas headed for it, with Kay running after him. He might have been two hundred megabytes short of a gigabyte, he might have been built of bits of body that had once belonged to at least seven different people, but when he was fixed on a single thought, he could move very fast and Kay had to run as quickly as she could to keep up with him.

The arch led into a dark tunnel that ended in a pair of

massive oak doors that had been shut for centuries. There were mountains of junk piled up against them and those in turn were buried under layer upon layer of cobwebs, huge thick cobwebs as thick as rope, that were all tangled up with the bones of animals that had been caught in them and had thrashed about horribly until they had died and become some enormous spider's dinner. There were the skeletons of goats and sheep half hidden in the deepest layer. Kay was sure she could see human skulls staring out at her in empty-eyed terror. Even Douglas stopped in his tracks and began to tremble.

"Listen, Douglas," said Kay, "I'll come with you and look for your stick, but let's, like, find another way out."

"Have to go this way," said Douglas.

"Well, maybe the spiders aren't here anymore," said Kay. "The cobwebs look really old, all broken and covered with dust."

And of course, as soon as she said that, something moved in the darkness above them, sending stale clouds of dust down onto their heads.

"Come on, let's get out of here," said Kay, tugging at Douglas's sleeve. "Let's go and ask Merlin. He's cool. He'll know what to do."

Much as she wanted to keep away from the lecherous old wizard, right then he seemed a better option than whatever it was up in the tunnel roof, the whatever it was that had silently dropped a giant cobweb between her and Douglas and was waiting in the darkness for her to walk back into it.

Fluffy, who had been flying up in the air and soaring down as fast as she could, saw them entering the tunnel and flew after them. As she reached them she saw the cobweb come falling down.

"The Oracle says look out behind you," she shouted as she landed on Douglas's shoulder.

Kay spun around just in time. There was a bird hovering in the air and it was talking to her.

"Not another talking animal," she shouted, beginning to panic.

"It's she, The Oracle," Fluffy shouted as another cobweb

dropped down on the other side of Kay. "Look out behind you." Then, "Oops," said The Oracle as a spider the size of a Shetland pony slowly lowered itself toward its victim.

"Douglas, do something," shouted Kay.

Douglas did. He began to cry. "Stick, potato, Mommy," he sobbed.

"Oh, shit, man," said Kay.

"It is all right, The Oracle will save the day. She will go and get help," The Oracle said, and flew off back into the garden.

"Get Merlin," Kay shouted after her. "It's all right, Douglas, Merlin will come and rescue us."

"I want my mom."

"Go and see if you can find a nice big stick," said Kay.

"Stick, bash, bash, bash," Douglas said between his tears, and went back into the garden.

Porcanella the spider dropped slowly down toward Kay, taking her time and savoring the experience, tenderizing the meat by letting it stew in its own adrenaline. In fact she couldn't move any faster. She was very, very old, as old as Merlin, for she had arrived on Earth in Merlin's spaceship and, like the wizard, had been partly protected from aging by the spaceship's force field that now encircled Camelot. But she had aged, albeit very slowly, and now had terrible arthritis in all her joints, except the one she occasionally smoked for purely medicinal purposes to ease the pain. Even if the most gorgeous spider in creation had sidled up to her, and sidling is something spiders do better than anyone else, and given her an adoring gaze with more than 70 percent of his eyes, Porcanella would have taken an hour to reach him, if she made it at all. If she had tried to move any faster, her legs would have snapped like matchsticks with dry rot.

Merlin obviously realized how slow Porcanella was. Either that or he was incredibly callous, because when Fluffy flew back a few minutes later, she said, "Merlin said he'll be about ten minutes. He's just put a soufflé in the oven and he can't leave it."

"I don't believe it, man," shouted Kay. "I mean, like, I could be dead by then, you know?"

"He said not to worry," said The Oracle.

"Can't find a stick," said Douglas, running back in with a rusty metal bar.

"What's that, then?" said Kay.

"It's not a proper stick," said Douglas, looking miserable. "Rusty stick, all dirty."

"Good boy," said Kay. "Clever boy. You bash up the cobweb with the rusty stick."

Porcanella had stopped moving. She had forgotten Kay completely and was staring at Douglas, openmouthed.

"My hero," said Kay as she stepped through the chopped-up cobweb.

"My God," said Porcanella to herself as she struggled slowly to the ground.

"My soufflé," said Merlin in the kitchen, staring dejectedly at his crumbled creation on the kitchen table.

"Douglas is a clever boy," said Douglas.

"What's going on?" said Ethel, reappearing. "Who called me back? Cluckin' hell, where did you get that?"

"Over there," said Douglas, pointing at the stone. "Sorry, Mommy."

"Kill the damn spider," said Kay, "quick, before it comes after us."

"No," said Ethel, "that is Porcanella, the sacred spider of Morphine. If you kill her, you kill a living legend. Anyway, she's completely harmless, unless you're a slug, that is."

Chapter 23
The Legend Returns

Merlin came out of his kitchen into the garden. Something wasn't right. He couldn't put his finger on it but something was missing. The balance had changed. And then he saw it.

"Oh, my God," he said.

The sword was gone. Excalibur, that once proud symbol of all that was noble and great, which had stood rusting out in the middle of the courtyard garden, stuck in its iron anvil on top of the stone, forgotten and streaked with stains, was no longer there. For more than one thousand years, through ten thousand storms, through ten thousand lightning strikes, it had refused to budge. Seven hundred seventy-six people had tried to pull it from its prison, but to no avail. The mighty Excalibur, which was in reality no sword at all but the hyperactive fusion drive from Merlin's crashed spaceship, the single thing that might one day take him home, was no longer there.

For well over a millennium the remains of Merlin's spaceship had lain almost forgotten in the deepest cellar below the castle, a cellar far below the lowest dungeons that only Merlin and Ethel even knew existed. You may wonder why the old wizard would go to the trouble of carting several hundred tons of broken machinery down into the bowels of the earth. Sure, he might have wanted to keep it well hidden, but there were places just as suitable for that, places that were nowhere near as hard to get to. The truth is that Merlin had not dragged the wrecked ship down there, but that this was where it had crashed in the first place. It had hit the earth at 1,249 miles an hour, one mile an hour too fast, and made a very deep hole. Merlin had then simply built Camelot over the hole. He had removed the force field to enclose the castle and embedded the precious fusion drive Excalibur in solid iron and stone where no one could make off with it. No one, until that young upstart Arthur had come along.

The trouble was that he hadn't been concentrating when he put the sword back in the stone after Arthur had chopped loads of heads and other body parts off with it, and he had completely forgotten the spell to get it out again. For hundreds of years he had been waiting for another Arthur to come along so he could finally go home to beautiful Morphine. In fact, Morphine was no longer beautiful, but the old wizard didn't know that, and beautiful or not, it was home, the place where the heart is supposed to be.

Although Merlin had not seen Excalibur go, he knew instantly who had taken it. He felt an excitement in his heart that he hadn't felt for centuries, not just the wonder of someone else with King Arthur's magical powers, but with Excalibur free from the stone, the anticipation that he could go home.

As he reached the rest of them on the other side of the garden, he felt as though he was awakening from a long, long hibernation. Adrenaline that had grown opaque and stagnant from lack of use began to stir in the old wizard's ancient body. It surged to his head, making him feel dizzy. The world began to spin around and around, his legs turned to Jell-O—not the red wobbly stuff in a bowl but the little packet of crystals you add the water to—and he fainted.

He woke up to find a chicken on his chest, staring deep into his eyes.

"Hmmm, interesting," said Ethel.

Merlin sat up slowly, thinking maybe he had dreamed the whole thing, but no, Douglas was holding Excalibur.

"How gat thou that sword?" said the old wizard. He knew the answer but after so long wanted to savor the sweetness of the words.

"Found it," said Douglas, sticking out his bottom lip.

"And where didst thou find it, sweet child?"

"Over there," said Douglas, pointing at the stone with the great anvil sitting on top of it.

"O noblest of creatures, thou are truly blessed," said the old wizard, stroking the confused idiot on the head.

"Mommy," said Douglas, getting agitated, "what have I done?"

He couldn't tell if everyone was pleased or cross that he had pulled the sword out of the stone. The intelligent part of his brain was struggling to take over. He had been a baby too long. His rebirth had begun with his passage through the big potato and now drinking the mop bucket had been the second stage. There was only one more stage to go and Douglas would become the genius that Ethel had dreamed of.

"Hush, baby," said Ethel, "it's all right. You're a very good boy."

"What the hell's going on?" said Kay.

Only Ethel knew the full implication of the event and she wasn't pleased. The last thing she needed was for Merlin to go home, but as always she was ready and one step ahead of everyone else. While Merlin had been unconscious, she had taken the golden key that hung around his neck. The key that most people would have imagined locked some wonderful door or treasure chest in Camelot, or some great lady's chastity belt, was the ignition key for Merlin's spaceship. She had replaced it with another key that looked almost identical but would open no more than a broom closet. There was no way the old wizard could repair his ship and fly off, but there was no point in taking risks. Ethel had taken too many risks; now it was time for cool calculation.

They all went back to the kitchen for a strong cup of tea. Porcanella, her old arthritic joints creaking at every step, followed them. She sat in the corner eating Merlin's collapsed soufflé and feeling old and sad. Kay's terror at seeing her had rekindled thoughts of the old days, when all who saw her had quaked. They had had good reason, for in her prime Porcanella had sucked the insides out of Morphine's enemies at the rate of two a day. She dreamed of those days, when she had lived in a beautiful garden not unlike the one at Camelot. How relieved and surprised the prisoners had looked when they had been locked in the garden, the garden with the thousand trip wires of Porcanella's almost invisible web. What happy days they had been, being a hero, a living legend. And now, old and toothless, she was reduced to sucking up soufflé and eating slugs.

After dinner Kay asked Ethel where she had been, if she had found any clues to the Perfect Hour. The old chicken was evasive and vague because she couldn't admit her travels had been completely useless. Her first attempt had taken her to a remote Scottish laundry in the 1950s, where seventeen old women were washing an endless mountain of kilts. Her second attempt had taken her into the future. She had been to more than fifty places and none of them were remotely where she wanted to be. But because members of her race were genetically incapable of admitting they had made a mistake, Ethel told herself that she had simply gone to those places to eliminate them from the search.

"Since I left, I have traveled far and wide," she said grandly. "I have been to the heights and the depths. I have been to every country in the world and possibly a few on another world. I have seen so much that even with my amazingly powerful brain, I have barely had time to analyze a thousandth of what I have seen. Another report will follow shortly."

Night crept over the forest and wrapped Camelot in darkness like a thick security blanket. Out in the tall trees, as the other birds fell silent, the owls began to call to one another as they started their day. The fading light brought a chill to the air and everyone followed Merlin back into the castle. In the Great Hall a fire the size of a small forest burned in a fireplace as wide as ten beds. Its smoke crept around the edges of the room, filling it with the scent of pine needles and timeless oaks even though only in one small hidden valley far away in the Himalayas where no one had traveled for more than two centuries were there any ancient trees. Nowhere else on Earth, not even on the remotest island or the highest Patagonian mountain, was there a single tree that was more than 150 years old. The last of the ancient trees had been cut down by then, replaced by dust bowls and unswerving rows of conifer farms. It had been incredible—Ethel had hardly been able to believe that a race of creatures could be as blind as man.

Dangerous dreams visited Jay that night: the unfinished business of the skateboard. He had been pulled back to reality by powerful magic when Douglas had found the sword, but the Tower of Dreams never left business unfinished and while Kay slept beside him as peacefully as a baby, Jay tossed and turned and groaned as he returned over and over again to the darkness of the room and the voice whispering in his ear.

The next morning over breakfast Ethel gave everyone their instructions. She'd been busy inside their heads during the night, so no one questioned anything she said except Douglas. She'd been inside his head but had got lost in the jumble in there.

"Today we must begin the pre-quest," she said.

"I thought you'd just been away on the pre-quest," said Kay.

"No," said Ethel, "that was the pre-pre-quest."

"So what's the pre-quest?" said Kay.

"Well, it's a sort of quest before the main quest. It's like going shopping for groceries before you make the cluckin' stew," said Ethel.

Douglas began jumping up and down in his excitement, and broke three glasses waving Excalibur around.

"No, baby, you must stay here with Uncle Merlin," said Ethel in a very calm but very, very-you-could-die-if-you-defy-me voice.

Amazingly, Douglas said nothing. For the first time in his short life, wheels inside his head, and there were a few of those that Ethel had put in as a temporary measure, turned smoothly and he sat quietly in his chair and fiddled with his

Colin Thompson

crusts. Time and Excalibur were beginning to work their magic on him.

"Good boy," said Ethel, quite taken aback by the creature's easy acceptance. "Eat up your crusts so you grow big and strong."

"I am big and strong," said Douglas.

"You will stay here with Merlin," Ethel continued, "for training."

"What do you mean? Like, to become a knight?" said Jay.

"Yeah, whatever," said Ethel, who in reality just wanted a break from Douglas. Keeping an eye on Jay all the time was more than enough. "We must head north," she said.

"North, why north?" said Kay.

"That's where you head when you're on a quest," said Ethel. "Everyone knows that. You go west if you're a cowboy looking for a new life in unspoiled lands free from trouble and cares, apart from hordes of marauding Indians, syphilis, and gunslingers. You go south if you're escaping from stuff or want cheap drugs, and you go east if you're seeking spiritual enlightenment and colorful clothes. If you're on a cluckin' quest, you head north. Not travel north, not go north, but *head* north. Everyone knows that."

"Okay, but why?" said Jay.

"We have to get the Tabernacle," said Ethel.

"What's that?" said Kay.

It's always Kay, thought Ethel. *Why can't she do anything without questioning it?*

"It's something we need for the quest," said Ethel, who actually didn't know what the Tabernacle was, just that the Blind Piano Tuner had told her she needed it.

"Yeah, so what is it?" Kay persisted.

"It's a magical sort of mystical thing," said Ethel.

"Yeah, go on," said Kay.

"Well, it's actually secret chicken's business," said Ethel, "a powerful force that we have to harness."

"Well, you can make stuff appear," said Kay, who was beginning to enjoy annoying Ethel. "Why can't you just make it fly here or however you do it?"

209

"The Tabernacle is in a mystical place and is guarded," Ethel snapped. "We actually have to go and get it."

Jay did not want to fly out over the forest again. He was frightened of the Virus. He tried to persuade Ethel to go on her own, but she said she needed him to fly the hovercar. She wouldn't explain why she needed Kay to go too, but she obviously had her reasons.

Chapter 24

North

So Jay, Kay, Fluffy, and Ethel the chicken headed north, while Douglas stayed at Camelot with Merlin.

As the hovercar rose up over the castle walls, the sun rose above the distant mountains. The deep golden light of the new day poured across the dark green of the forest. Pools of soft mist lay in the shallow valleys, the tops of the tall trees breaking through to catch the warmth of the new day. Flocks of white birds lifted themselves out of the trees and began the day's work. It was incredibly beautiful, a view that said all was well in the world. And everything should have been well, all the ingredients were there. It was hard not to relax completely and be taken in by the beauty of it all. Yet the Virus was out there, hiding in the gloom of the forest floor, hiding in the secluded parts of almost every living creature's brain, a giant global feeling of unease. The beauty of the new day, the reawakening of nature since Ethel had cleared away the choking canopy of dirty clouds, was so far only skin-deep. It felt as if everything could snap at any second.

Looking out across the world as they flew low over the treetops, Ethel felt a great weariness in her heart. It had all gone on too long, the constant hassle, the constant endless list of unfinished business. And since she had spoken to Jay back in the elevator, the list seemed to have got longer and longer, as if her making contact with the human race had been a trigger that had sent signals across the galaxies inviting every troublemaker and deadhead out of the galactic woodwork to

211

come and screw around with everything. Deep inside, the old chicken sighed, a sigh that reached down into the very foundations, and even the crumbling rubble below the foundations, of her soul, a bottomless sigh that would have made her shoulders drop below her elbows if she'd been inside a human body.

I am so cluckin' depressed, she thought, glaring down at a grove of beautiful old oak trees and making all their spring leaves turn into autumn.

A tiny voice in the back of her head kept telling her it was dangerous to repress her feelings, that doing so would only mean they would come back magnified a thousand times. Yet right now she needed to be strong and not give in to her depression. There was so much to do and she seemed to be the only one able to do it, to organize everyone. Although she didn't like to think ill of him, and she knew it could be a dangerous thing to do, the Blind Piano Tuner hadn't been much help so far, stuck in his snow cave with his mind on higher cluckin' things all the cluckin' time.

Jay stared fixedly ahead, refusing to look down into the forest. The Oracle sat quietly on the backseat, thinking about her father and struggling to re-form the buried memories that the authorities had taken from her before they had sent the two of them off to Earth. Kay, who had not been totally convinced that the Virus was evil, scanned the forest floor for signs of human life. She still ached to meet other humans, to hear their voices, see the expressions on their faces, just to say hello. And it was her that the Virus focused on. Because she was so desperate she was the easiest target.

This was even more tempting than their flight to Camelot. The Virus opened clearings in the trees and filled them with the images of happy smiling people, whole family groups that made Kay's heart ache for all the sweet memories that she had never had. She begged and pleaded with Jay to land, but Ethel had filled his head with white noise so he couldn't hear her. As long as he kept his eyes on the horizon, they would be safe. Ethel reached out ahead of them and as the distant air grew cooler she could sense the Virus was not there. Its own planet was hotter than the equator, so the

Colin Thompson

Virus would take longer to cover the colder parts of Earth.

Only a few more minutes, Ethel said inside Jay's head. *Hold tight. Left hand down a bit.*

Kay felt as if her heart would break. Tears poured down her face, turning the world into a blur, and she felt a terrible loneliness that she would never be able to share with anyone.

If only we could find some real humans, Ethel thought.

But there were no signs at all. As the population had grown smaller and smaller, everyone had gradually drifted toward warmer climates. There was no point in living in the cold unless you had to and there was more than enough room for everyone. There were so few humans left they all could have fitted comfortably on one medium-size tropical island.

They came to the coast and the Virus was behind them. Everyone could take it easy as they flew across a wide blue sea dotted with islands. Jay relaxed and tried to comfort Kay, but she felt drained. It was impossible to explain to him how she felt. She was the only person who, at the age of twenty-four, had met only one other human being, two if you counted Douglas.

They reached land and continued to travel north. There were no lush forests here. The land was parched and worn out. Man had stripped it bare and nature had been slower to reclaim it. The outlines of fields could be seen and the muddled patterns of ghost towns. There seemed to be no signs of life at all, not even a single plume of smoke.

Ethel looked down into the grass and there was nothing living there either. This was radioactive wasteland, the theater of the last nuclear war. No one would be able to live here for centuries. Plants would grow distorted and wild. Cockroaches would thrive and evolve, but mammals that came into the area would grow sick and die. Even Ethel could do nothing about that. But the devastation had its merits. The Virus was unable to cross, so the land ahead was free of it.

In the distance, at the edge of the wasteland, the tallest mountains on Earth, the Himalayas, rose up toward the sky. Their peaks were white with snow and half hidden in clouds. Ethel reached out and scanned as far ahead as she could and

213

there, in the heart of the mountains, was what she was looking for, a faint almost imperceptible signal, weaker than an amoeba, but it was there. At least what she was seeking existed. The legend was true.

"We have to cross the mountains," she said.

"We will freeze to death," said The Oracle. "You know that."

"We have to go up there," said Ethel. "It's a risk we must take."

So Kay tucked Fluffy inside her shirt, Jay tucked Ethel inside his, and the two humans clutched each other as the hovercar flew up into the clouds. As they moved deeper into the mountains it began to snow, large wet snowflakes that clung to everything and then froze.

"I can't see a thing," said Jay. "We'll crash into a mountain and that'll be the end of it."

Kay curled up into a ball. She pulled her hands into her sleeves and buried her face in Jay's clothes. The cold felt like a hundred knives. Jay's hands were so cold he couldn't feel the controls. Ice formed on his eyelids and he wanted to curl up too and go to sleep.

"It's no good," he said.

"Stop looking with your eyes," said Ethel. "Close them tight. Let yourself go and everything will be all right."

"This is farcical," said Jay. "You can't see your hand in front of your face."

"Let the farce be with you," said Ethel. "Use the farce and you will be able to see through it."

The old chicken seemed to have taken on a strange, almost mystical quality since they had reached the mountains. She had gone to a higher mental plane as well as a physical one. Her voice, which had always been hard to disobey, now held a deeper, more powerful quality that was impossible to question, a voice that was much larger than a chicken.

Jay closed his eyes and tried to focus on the clouds and as he did so he felt his hands move the controls as if by magic. The hovercar rose and turned to the left. It broke clear of the clouds and they were flying high above the Himalayas in the clear thin air beneath an endless blue sky.

"Can you feel it?" said Ethel.

"Yes, it's over there," said Jay breathlessly as the ship flew deep into the heart of the mountains, where only one man had ever been before them, beyond Everest into the unfashionable lesser peaks that seemed to go on forever. The thin air made breathing difficult and the travelers felt themselves grow light-headed.

They dropped into the clouds again and Jay, with his eyes closed tight, somehow knew exactly where to go. The cold air tried to reach in through their clothes but there was now an aura around the hovercar that kept them warm.

"Look," said Ethel, and far below them through a gap in the clouds a tiny valley shone like an emerald in the unending blanket of snow.

This was the Valley of the Tabernacle.

As they flew down in small spiraling circles, the air grew as warm as a summer's day. All around, the Himalayas were frozen in the grip of an almost eternal winter but here in this tiny valley it was summer. The grass was fine and brilliant green and through it ran streams of clear water born out of the millennia-old layers of ice high in the mountains above. The streams curled and twisted until they all ran together into a perfect lake and in the middle of the lake was an island covered in soft trees and daffodils and in the middle of the island was an ivory tower. And through the clouds above, from a small opening of blue sky, the sun shone over the whole valley and not one inch more.

Jay brought the hovercar down by the edge of the lake, beside a man in a long orange robe who didn't even look up as they approached.

"I thought you would never come," he said, not turning his head to look at them.

"Sorry, got held up," said Ethel.

"For two hundred ninety years I have been here, waiting," said the man.

"It's only two hundred eighty-eight," said Ethel.

"Well, it feels like two hundred ninety," said the man.

"Yeah, well, I had places to go, things to do," said Ethel. "If you only knew the cluckin' half of it."

"For two hundred eighty-eight years I've been standing here, staring at the island where my beloved Thora lies sleeping," said the man. "Every day from dawn till dark I have waited for you. Time has hung heavy on my shoulders."

"Who are you?" said Kay.

"My name is Kalang," said the man. "I am the Keeper of the Tabernacle."

"What is the Tabernacle?" said Jay.

"The most sacred of the sacred relics," said Kalang. "I am the Keeper of the seven hundred seventy-seven most sacred relics and the Tabernacle is the most sacred of them all."

"Yeah, right, man, but what is it?" said Jay.

"I don't know," said Kalang. "I am only the Keeper, I'm not allowed to look at it."

"You mean, like, you've been here two hundred eighty-eight years and you don't even know what it is you're guarding?"

"It's not for me to ask such questions," said Kalang.

"So you don't know what it looks, like, like?" said Kay.

"Well, it's a cardboard box all tied up with magic rope that only the Chosen One can cut," said Kalang, "with something inside it."

In the 1980s Kalang, like many other Westerners, had come to the Himalayas seeking enlightenment. For ten years he had wandered the mountains, a thin solitary figure seeking out the most spiritually elevated gurus in the most physically elevated caves. As the years had passed, most of the wisdom seekers had returned home, finding their enlightenment in mortgages and E-mail. But Kalang had stayed, never losing faith, always feeling there was something greater than he was guiding him through the mountains. Time had passed and he had grown older but none the wiser. His clothes, his shoes, and his dreams had all worn thin. And then one day, when he was about to give up and go back to his old job at the meat counter in the supermarket, as he was wandering through a narrow gully higher in the mountains than he had ever been, far beyond the reach of maps, where the air was so thin you could fold it up into nothing, he had fallen into a deep crevasse, but instead of dying he had found his guru.

He had landed on a bed of snow and there in the blue-ice glow was a tiny cave. In the back of the tiny cave was a tiny figure, no larger than a five-year-old child. The figure sat, cross-legged, in the air, three inches above a golden cushion surrounded by liquid crystal computer screens and 420 pairs of worn-out open-toed sandals. This was the Blind Piano Tuner and he had been waiting for Kalang.

It had been more than ten years since the guru had planted the seeds in Kalang's mind that had made him leave the security of his simple suburban life and go to the Himalayas. Ten years had been a long time for Kalang. But in all that time the Blind Piano Tuner had kept the thought of enlightenment alive in his mind. He had surrounded him with a protective aura that led him through blizzards, found him food and shelter, and kept him safe from all harm. He had then made him the Keeper of the Tabernacle and Other Assorted Relics, with the promise that it would lead to his own personal ultimate nirvana. Then he had sent his disciple into the beautiful valley to keep watch over the sacred box until the day came that the world was ready to reclaim it. That day had arrived.

Fluffy flew out of Kay's shirt and soared up into the sunshine. The lake was thick with bite-size trout and Fluffy knew she had found her own paradise.

"So who's Thora, man?" said Jay, "and why can't you go and get her?"

"She is my princess," said Kalang, "and I cannot swim."

"So why not make a boat and sail across?"

"I cannot. I am forbidden to set foot on the island," said Kalang. "And besides, I am aquaphobic. Even the rain terrifies me."

Kalang was a fatalist. That was why the Blind Piano Tuner had chosen him as the Keeper of the Tabernacle. No one else would have been able to spend hundreds of years in a remote Himalayan valley guarding a cardboard box without even wanting to look inside it. Kalang had not even thought of doing so. That was not his role in life. The Blind Piano Tuner had made it perfectly clear that his role was to watch over the Tabernacle, nothing more, nothing less, until the day a chicken came from the sky to claim it.

"Okay, man, so where is this Tabernacle?" said Jay.

"I'm not allowed to tell you," said Kalang.

"If I went and got Thora, would you tell me?"

Kalang looked confused. The looks of fear and happiness fought for control of his face at the same time and both lost. He had shut down most of his feelings ages ago. He had concentrated his mind on the one single thought of his undying love for Thora so that he could keep her face in his memory. Two hundred eighty-eight years is a long time to be away from someone, but Kalang could still recall her smile.

Although Kalang appeared dumb, he wasn't. He was stuffed to the brim with the sort of deep yet largely useless wisdom that comes from spending years selfishly seeking personal enlightenment. It was just that hundreds of years of standing still in the same spot, day in, day out, staring fixedly at the Ivory Tower, had put his brain into hibernation. Ninety percent of Kalang's thoughts had simply filed themselves away for future reference. And now the future had just arrived.

"Come on, then," said Ethel. "First of all we'll fly you over to the island and find Thora, then we'll look for the Tabernacle."

"I can't move," said Kalang.

And he couldn't, not one inch. The Keeper of the Tabernacle was literally rooted to the spot. Not only had grass and roots grown over his shoes and wrapped themselves around his legs, but he himself had grown roots and they went deep into the ground, so deep that their ends were roasting in the fire at the center of the earth. That was how he had managed to stand there all those years without starving to death and that was how he, a mere mortal, had managed to live so long. Kalang was becoming a tree.

"I don't suppose anyone's got any pruning shears, have they?" said Ethel. "And a flowerpot."

This presented a chicken-and-egg situation. Inside the Ivory Tower, Kalang's true love, Thora, lay asleep in one of those enchanted-rose-thorn-finger-pricking deep sleeps that only her one true love could wake her from. Meanwhile, on the bank of the lake Kalang was changing into a tree, a cruel fate that could be reversed only by a kiss from his one true love.

"Bummer, man," said Jay.

"The Tabernacle is why we're here," said Ethel when she had led them out of Kalang's earshot.

"Why do we need it?" said Jay.

"Yeah, come on, chicken, I bet you know what it is," said Kay.

"All will become clear in good time," said Ethel.

So they flew across to the island and walked up the path to the golden door of the Ivory Tower. But it was locked.

"Go on, chicken," said Kay, "you can unlock doors."

"Not this one," said Ethel. "Look, there's no keyhole. In fact, there's no lock and it isn't actually a door. It was never made to open."

"So how did Thora get in there in the first place, man?" said Jay.

"I think she was made to fall asleep and then the tower was built around her," said Ethel.

There was one tiny window, no bigger than a man's hand, high in the wall, the only real window in the whole building. Jay made the hovercar hover outside the window while he peered through it. In the middle of the almost dark room was a bed and naturally in the middle of the bed was a beautiful princess in the traditional lying-on-a-large-bed-dressed-in-white-with-very-long-blond-hair style, except her hair was short and brown and she had only a rather grubby T-shirt on and the bed was quite small, hadn't been made in years, and was home to several families of mice.

Meanwhile, Fluffy was flying back and forth collecting grass for the nest she had decided to build in Kalang's pocket. She didn't want to be The Oracle any longer and thought she'd like to spend the rest of her life as a kingfisher. It never occurred to her that she had no say whatsoever in the matter.

When they got back Kalang was crying. Every time they looked at him, he seemed to be more treelike. His handsome features were growing gnarled and an owl was looking into his mouth with a view to turning it into a rather desirable residence.

"I know . . . ," he stammered through his tears, "there's only one window and it's no bigger than a man's hand. Not only that but the tower is carved from a solid piece of the hardest stone in the universe that no tool can touch."

"So how did they carve it in the first place, then?" said Kay.

"They didn't," said Kalang. "They dripped water on it for seven million years until it was hollowed out like a big bowl and then they turned it over. The window is only there because there was a weak spot in the rock."

"You mean Thora's been in there for, like, seven million years?" said Jay.

"No, only three hundred," said Kalang. "Once the tower was ready they went and got the most beautiful woman in the world, made her prick her finger on a special rose that had taken seventy-seven years to bloom, and when she was asleep, they put her in the tower."

"How?" said Jay. "And who did? I mean, who's they?"

"Gravox the wizard, Thora's father. He built a wooden scaffold with a bedroom at the top and then lowered the Ivory Tower over it. And before you ask, it's the heaviest thing in the universe and no one can lift it. The only way she can be freed is if she wakes up, then the tower will turn to dust," said the sad Keeper of the Tabernacle. "It's hopeless, we're both doomed. The Blind Piano Tuner was right, you can't fight destiny. I'm going to have owls living inside my mouth and Thora's just going to keep on lying there forever. I don't suppose you could go over and reach in through the window with a long brush to dust her a bit, could you?"

When Kalang had come to the secret valley to watch over the Tabernacle, Thora and her father were already living there. They were the only two humans left in the valley. Thora's father, the wizard Gravox, had turned the rest of the small population, including his own wife, into trees. It wasn't that everyone had been evil or even bad. It was that Gravox had a very short temper. His wife had dropped his newspaper on the floor and before she could bend to pick it up, Gravox had turned her into a eucalyptus. From then on it was all downhill. Racked with remorse and grief, Gravox had plucked out his own eyes so that he would never be the victim of his own anger again. The trouble was, it was too late by then. There were only he and Thora left.

Gravox did not like young men with long hair, or short hair, or any sort of hair, or no hair. Being blind, he couldn't see Kalang's hair, but the young man spoke as if he had long hair and that was enough for Gravox. He hated young men who were kind and gentle like Kalang, and young men who weren't, and middle-aged men, and old men, and any men who were breathing. No one was ever good enough for his daughter, so he had turned anyone who came near her into a tree. Finally, having incarcerated Thora in the tower and cast his last spell on poor Kalang, he died of a heart attack, lost in the middle of a dense forest of his own making. With the mad wizard's death, Kalang, instead of becoming a tree in an instant, had changed slowly.

"Have you tried, like, loud noises?" said Jay. "That always wakes people up."

"Not when they're under an enchantment," said Kalang. "I've tried everything. Nothing can wake her except a kiss from me."

"I have a plan," said Ethel, who had wandered off in deep thought. "The Tabernacle is essential to our quest. If we are to have the slightest chance of re-creating the Perfect Hour, we need the Tabernacle."

"Come on, then," said Jay.

"Tell me quick, while I still have blood in my veins and love in my heart," said Kalang.

"You must lose your blood," said Ethel, "and all trees have love in their hearts, you will never lose that."

"Why must I lose my blood?" said Kalang, trying to wipe his eyes but only poking a twig up his nose.

His skin was turning into bark and the sap was beginning to rise. The transformation that had taken two hundred years to turn a man into a tree was suddenly accelerating toward its conclusion. The arrival of Ethel and the others had made time, which had slowed almost to a stop, run at normal speed and the spell that had been put on Kalang, which the mystical valley had tried to protect him from, was running its course.

"Here's my plan," said Ethel. "Soon you will be a tree,

unable to speak, unable to see, but still able to think and feel. When that happens we will prune you. We will cut off all your branches, except the one pointing toward the Ivory Tower. We will feed your roots and you will grow. Your one branch will reach out across the lake, wrap itself around the tower, reach in through the window, and wake your princess."

"Brilliant," said Jay.

"Come on," said Kay. "How long's *that* going to take?"

"Yes, well," said Ethel. "I know it's not the greatest plan I've ever had, but it's the only cluckin' one we've got."

"I have to say something," said Kalang, struggling to speak as his mouth turned to wood.

"What?" said Ethel.

"I've remembered where the Tabernacle is," he said. "It's under, it's under . . ."

"Where?"

"It's under the b . . ."

"What? It's under the what?"

"Bed," said Kalang, and the Keeper of the Tabernacle became a tree.

Birds and mice appeared from everywhere and began fighting over his branches. The owl flew into his mouth. Fluffy snuggled down in his pocket and the others squabbled over his every nook, cranny, and orifice.

"All right, get the saw from the hovercar," said Ethel, "and start pruning."

"Are you sure he won't, like, feel anything?" said Kay.

"Of course he will," said Ethel, "but we all have to suffer for love."

"I haven't," said Kay.

"You will."

It took two days to cut Kalang back until there was only one branch left. They chopped and sawed, but there always seemed to be a branch they'd missed. New branches appeared as soon as they turned away. The spell that had made Kalang a tree had been designed specifically to keep him away from Thora, so it was strong and it was not going to give up without a struggle.

Over the next two weeks Kalang's remaining branch grew slowly across the lake. Ethel fed his roots, Jay and Kay kept him pruned, and Fluffy laid three eggs in his pocket.

It was a peaceful time, the first time Jay and Kay had really had time to get to know each other, the first time for Kay, in her short existence since Ethel had created her out of Jay's rib, that she had ever felt peaceful. They walked along the lake's shore hand in hand and talked about the deep meaningful things of life, like "What's your favorite color?" and "Why do we, like, keep saying 'like' all the time?"

They found a deserted cottage at the far end of the lake, the closest thing they had ever seen to Jay's dream of living in the country, and while Ethel and Fluffy fussed over Kalang, they stayed there on their own and finally became the lovers that Ethel had dreamed of all those years ago when Jay had been a baby. This was why Ethel had wanted Kay to come with them to the Valley of the Tabernacle.

"If only this could last forever," said Kay, but no sooner had she said it than The Oracle flew down and said it was time to go.

"You know," said Jay as they walked back to where Kalang stood, "I'd like to bring you back here one day, when all this quest stuff is over."

At last the branch had reached the island and you could almost hear the poor Kalang tree sigh as it was finally released from the effort of holding a two-hundred-yard-long branch up in the air. Its tip curled down onto the ground, crawled up the grass toward the tower, and began the climb to the window. Around and around the tower it curled as it slowly crept higher.

"Why on earth couldn't it just climb straight up the wall, man?" said Jay.

"Come on, now," said Ethel. "There are times when no matter what is happening, no matter how urgent the situation, times when art is more important than anything else. Supposing one day in the future someone wants to draw some pictures to illustrate this momentous event. What do you think would look best, a branch artistically curled around the tower or one just shooting straight up the wall? We have to consider history, you know."

As it neared the window, the branch grew so fast you could almost see it moving. It curled back away from the window, hung still in the air for a moment, and then plunged into the tower.

"Eat your heart out, Sigmund Freud," muttered Ethel, but no one knew what she was talking about.

There was a long silence full of potential, followed by another long silence. Jay climbed onto the branch and followed it around the tower until he was outside the window. As he peered in through the tiny space the branch had left, he saw it reach across the pillow and touch Thora's lips.

Massive bolts of lightning flashed across the sky, followed by deafening thunder and torrential rain. But this is of no interest to us at all, as the storm was thousands of miles away in Australia, in a remote desert place where it hadn't rained for seven hundred years. . . .

Back in the bedroom of the Ivory Tower, nothing happened. The branch moved slowly across Thora's lips but she remained completely immobile. The branch then slid down her neck and into her T-shirt.

Meanwhile, back at Camelot . . .

"Verily, thou hast passed the Floor Scrubbings and Moppings Trial, O noble majesty," said Merlin to Douglas. "Thou mayst take a choccie cookie from the Great Tin of Goodies."

The floor was truly amazing. Not only could Douglas see his own reflection in every single flagstone, two flagstones were packed with faces all jostling for his attention. At first he'd thought the reflections were dirty marks and had spent three days trying to wipe them out. Only when they began to speak to him did he realize they were more than muddy footprints, or rather faceprints.

Merlin was confused. Something wasn't right. Only the Chosen One could see the Reflections of the Ancients, and that was Jay. Not even Merlin himself could see them, though he knew they were there and had great wisdom to impart. The reason he had got Douglas to scrub the floors until they shone was to get them ready for Jay's return, so that he could absorb all the wisdom of the Reflections of the Ancients. Douglas should not have been able to see them. There couldn't be two Chosen Ones. Had they all got it wrong? Was Douglas the Chosen One after all?

Merlin had grown used to the quiet life over the past centuries. The years with King Arthur and the Knights of the Round Table had been more than enough excitement for one lifetime, even a lifetime as long as Merlin's. Now Excalibur had been pulled out of the stone again and things had begun to get complicated with all the comings and goings. He'd been young last time, in his primo. Now he just wanted to take things easy for the rest of his life. He'd almost be prepared to give up the dream of returning to Morphine.

So while he waited for the others to come back, Merlin puttered about the great castle of Camelot, weeding the flower beds, cooking soufflés, fiddling with bits of bent wire that might one day help to get his spaceship going again, and playing double-handed chess with Porcanella.

At first Douglas didn't understand a word the Reflections of the Ancients said, or have the slightest idea of their importance. He generally viewed the world like a puppy, happy to see everyone and greet them as if their only desire in life was to play with him. All anyone or anything had to do was say hello and they became his best friend. So he sat on the floor and smiled while the Reflections of the Ancients began to impart their wisdom. And slowly a few words began to get through the fog between his ears and into his empty brain.

"Listen well, my child," said a reflection, "for we have waited these many long years to give thee our wisdom, wisdom that will help thee in thy quest for—"

"Potatoes?" said Douglas.

"Actually, I was going to say enlightenment," said the reflection.

"Oh, that," said Douglas.

"It is time to put away potatoes and other childish things," said the reflection.

"And sticks, not sticks surely?"

"Aye, the days of sticks have passed," said the reflection. "But don't be sad, my child, for thou will find that thou no longer crave such things."

"We have much to impart to thee," said another reflection. "Never wash thy whites with thy coloreds."

"Unless thou are in South Africa," said a third, "but that's another story."

"Gentlemen lift the seat," said the first reflection.

"And lower it again afterward," added another.

"Beware of Blind Piano Tuners bearing skis," said the first.

"And remember, no matter who tells thee otherwise, be it Merlin or even the very chicken who created thee, never, never, never look directly at the Sun through a telescope," said another. "Mark this well, for the day will come when thou will be asked to do this as if thy very life depended on it."

"And always, always look both ways before."

"Before what?"

"Everything."

They sat talking for six days and nights without stopping. Douglas never moved. He neither ate nor drank nor slept for 144 hours straight, and gradually all the combined knowledge of the Reflections of the Ancients made its way into his brain. The part of his brain that had come from a dog now became a vast storeroom where millions of ideas and thoughts were neatly filed away for future reference. Thoughts that had taken brilliant minds whole lifetimes to work out were piled up in Douglas's head until he contained the total knowledge of all mankind. The knowledge of great thinkers like Kant and Spinoza mingled with the thoughts and beliefs of great dreamers like Bob Dylan and Lewis Carroll. Their conclusions mingled with the ideas of great philosophers, of writers of fiction, of the great computer HAL, and of Bart Simpson. And as these ideas mingled inside Douglas's head, they spoke to one another and gave birth to new ideas, ideas so brilliant that even the Blind Piano Tuner had never thought of them. A chain reaction had begun that nothing could stop.

*   *   *   *

Meanwhile, back in the Himalayas . . .

The branch crept down the inside of Thora's T-shirt, negotiated a couple of tight curves, and came out on her left knee. Still nothing happened and autumn was approaching rapidly. Almost overnight Kalang's leaves had turned golden and begun to fall. Time was running out. Soon his sap would stop rising, let out its breath, and begin to sink into the ground. It was the first autumn in the valley for 288 years and it was making up for lost time. Things began shriveling up and falling, while small creatures that had never slept before began to hibernate.

"We need to give Kalang a sort of kick," said Ethel, "something to make him move faster. Get your penknife out."

Jay made a deep cut into Kalang's bark and began to carve:

k ♥ t

As he made the last cut, sap began to ooze from the timber. The whole tree shuddered, the tip of the branch quivered, and a long string of angry swearwords poured out of the tower window.

And in the same instant the tower crumbled in a heap of dust and in the middle of the dust, perched high on a wooden scaffold, Thora sat up in bed.

"Shit," she said. "I was having a really good dream."

And in the same instant that the tower crumbled, Kalang turned back into a man. The spell was broken. He and Thora were free. "My leg's bleeding," said Kalang.

"Shit, shit, shit," said Thora, rolling out of bed. "Where are my damn shoes?" Then, realizing she was naked apart from a very dirty, old T-shirt and there was someone looking at her, she added, "Where are my damn bedroom walls?"

She wrapped herself in a bedsheet while Jay flew the hovercar over to her scaffold to bring her back to her long-lost love.

"Under the bed," said Ethel. "The Tabernacle, look under the bed."

"There's just a pair of old shoes and a cardboard box tied up with rope," said Jay.

"Bring them with you."

Kalang was beside himself with joy. At long last his one true love, his divine princess, the object of his every dream and desire, his sole reason for living, was standing before him, radiant, beautiful, and perfect, apart from the cobwebs in her hair, nearly three hundred years of dust on her skin, and her filthy bedsheet toga.

"My angel," he said, falling to his knees.

"Kalang?" said Thora. "Is that you?"

"Yes, my princess, it's me," said Kalang.

"God, you're a mess. Your hair's all full of leaves and your clothes look as if they've been dragged through a hedge backward," said Thora. "Did you get the bacon?"

"Bacon?"

"Yes, bacon, remember?" said Thora. "You were going to trek through the Himalayas and get me some bacon. It was a sort of quest to prove your deep and undying love. And I was going to prove my deep and undying love by eating the bacon and doing the cleaning up. Don't tell me you forgot?"

Ethel explained that 288 years had passed since she'd given Kalang his shopping list and her own father had put her into a deep sleep and turned her sweetheart into a tree. And for all that time Kalang had stood watching over the Ivory Tower, day in, day out, through hail and rain, thunder and sunshine, standing guard over her, keeping her safe from the ravages of time and Jehovah's Witnesses.

"There has been no bacon on Earth for two hundred years," said Ethel. "Still, I think you'll agree waiting for you by the lake all this time beats a bit of shopping as far as undying love's concerned."

"My hero," said Thora, melting into Kalang's arms. "I suppose that does deserve a bit of a cuddle."

Thora found the timescale somewhat hard to take in. It felt like she'd slept for only an hour or two. In fact she was still tired. People just don't sleep for that long, and why hadn't Kalang grown old and died? When Kalang told her about her father she almost fainted.

"Bastard," she said. "We must find him and chop him down, just in case."

"There are three thousand trees in this valley," said Kalang. "How shall we know which one is him?"

"It will be the one that is the most twisted and distorted," said Thora.

"We must be going," said Ethel. "We have what we came for."

"Not so fast, chicken," said Kalang. "You seem to forget that I am the Keeper of the Tabernacle. That is 'Keeper' as in 'keep,' which means I keep it."

"Who says so?" said Jay.

"Well, uh, I can't actually remember," said Kalang. "But that's not the point."

"And you seem to forget that I am Ethel the chicken and I am about three thousand million cluckin' times more powerful than you are," said Ethel. "So if you try and stop us, I'll turn you back into a tree and give you Dutch elm disease and I'll stick your girlfriend in a cluckin' tower with no little window and no central heating and no cluckin' bedclothes or bed."

"Fair enough," said Kalang. "Take the stupid thing. It's only a cardboard box. Nirvana can wait."

"Look around, idiot," said Kay. "You're living in the most beautiful place on Earth with a beautiful woman who adores you. How much more nirvana do you want?"

"Oh," said Kalang.

"Typical man. Can't see anything under his nose," said Kay.

"What's that supposed to mean?" said Jay.

"You're just as bad," said Kay. "I bet *you* wouldn't trek through the Himalayas to get me some bacon."

"What's bacon?" said Jay.

Fluffy struggled out of Kalang's pocket. Now that he was no longer a tree, it was a fairly useless nesting site. The first time he sat down he broke her eggs and it had taken Fluffy all this time to get her legs out of his key ring.

The four travelers climbed into the hovercar. Kay stuck the Tabernacle in the glove compartment and they set off south back across the mountains. As they passed over Everest a face peered out from a tiny snow cave just below the summit. It was the Blind Piano Tuner. He took out a notebook and pin and pricked a hurried note. A few minutes later a gray carrier pigeon with the note tied to its leg flew north.

"Can we, like, look inside the box?" said Kay.

"Not until we're safely back in Camelot," said Ethel. "Only Excalibur can cut the rope and only Douglas can hold Excalibur."

Kay shook the Tabernacle. There was something inside the box that rattled.

The Blind Piano Tuner smiled. Another circle was complete, not the big circle of course, but just one of the radiating rings that Earth had made when it had been born and fallen out of the Sun.

Kalang and Thora spent the next fifteen years measuring every tree in the Valley of the Tabernacle. It seemed that no matter where they looked there was always another tree just that bit more distorted. And then one day, out in a small clearing all on its own, they found Gravox. They cut him down and seasoned him for three years and then Kalang made him into a boat and the two lovers spent every day floating on the lake. Watching Thora bathe in its pure waters soon cured Kalang of his fear of water. They spent their nights doing all the things the evil wizard had despised, like reading poetry and threading flowers into each other's hair and making babies.

Chapter 25
Open the Box

When they got back to Camelot, Douglas was on his knees in the central courtyard garden completing the Weeding ye Rose Beds Trial. When they had left he had been a lumpy ungainly idiot with a heart of gold and a brain of mixed parentage. Now he moved with a careless grace. He had a heart of gold, a brain of mixed parentage, new shoes, and a head full of incredible information.

"Mother," he cried happily, walking over to Ethel as the hovercar came to rest by the stone and the anvil.

"Hello, baby," said Ethel as her creation picked her up and patted her. "Have you been a good boy for your Uncle Merlin?"

"Ah, Mother, you would not believe what has happened while you have been away," said Douglas. "Do you know about the Reflections of the Ancients?"

"Yes, of course," said Ethel, "but you shouldn't."

When Merlin told her what had happened she couldn't believe it. Far from explaining things to the old wizard, she was as confused as he was. Jay was the Chosen One, not Douglas. There was only one thing to do. They had to see if Jay could see the Reflections of the Ancients too.

"Can it be possible?" said Merlin. "In all my life I never heard tell of two Chosen Ones in a single galaxy. That is not the way. Verily, it contradicts all the ancient rules."

"Maybe it's time to do just that," said Ethel.

"Aye," said Merlin, "we have followed the rules these

231

many centuries and to where has it brought us?"

"Exactly," said Ethel.

"I don't know what you two are talking about," said Kay, "but can we open the box?"

"Box, of what box dost thou speak?" said Merlin, whose short-term memory kept forgetting itself. "Surely not the most sacred of all ye relics, the very Tabernacle, the treasure of the ancients?"

"The very same," said Ethel.

"So let's open it, man," said Jay. "The suspense is killing me."

"Is that it?" said Merlin in obvious disbelief.

"Yes," said Ethel.

"Methinks thou have been taken for a very ride, my friend," said the old wizard.

It wasn't surprising, for the box that now stood in the middle of the kitchen table, the sacred box of the Tabernacle, was no ornate camphor-wood chest with a brass keyhole and secret runes carved all over it. It was more your small brown cardboard affair, held closed by Scotch tape that had lost all its powers of adhesion and gone brittle and crumbly. The whole thing was wrapped around and around with a strange rope that seemed to have no knot or ends.

"How the hell do you undo that?" said Kay, pulling at the rope.

She turned the box over and over, and the more she pulled and twisted the rope, the tighter it seemed to wrap itself around the box. She tried the kitchen scissors but they turned blunt as soon as they touched the rope. She tried several knives but they did the same.

"Douglas, my child, we have need of the mighty Excalibur," said Merlin. "That alone may cut the ropes that bind."

And that was exactly right. As soon as the tip of the great sword touched the rope, it parted and dissolved away. There was mysterious writing on the box, a great mystical word in red lettering on all four sides that no one understood. And the word was

FedEx.

"Open it, man," said Kay, too nervous to touch it.

Merlin reached out and, with an air of great reverence, slowly peeled the ancient Scotch tape away. He opened the flaps and small beads of polystyrene flew everywhere. He reached in and withdrew a small cylinder, which he stood upright on the table.

"Is that it?" said Kay.

"What is it, man?" said Jay.

"A sacred container," said Merlin.

Ethel said nothing. She walked down the table and peered at the cylinder. Time had ravaged its surface. Rust had eaten away most of the paint, and through the rust two tiny words were all that remained of the ancient hieroglyphics that had once covered the entire vessel. And the words were

WD-40

"Well, well, not exactly what I expected," she said, unwilling to admit she hadn't the faintest idea what it was.

It's interesting to think how values can change so much over time. To the caveman the most desirable object in creation was probably a lump of wood. To mankind in the twentieth century it was colored folding paper and shiny metal, and now in the twenty-third century it appeared to be a small but incredible can of lubricant, though no one present, not even Ethel, had the faintest idea why they needed it.

The Blind Piano Tuner, watching from his cushion of gold in the mountains, knew.

"Hmmph," said Kay, which seemed to sum up everyone's feelings.

With all the traveling and the waiting for Kalang to grow, it had taken them almost a month to fetch the Tabernacle and the whole thing seemed an enormous anticlimax. They sat dejectedly while Merlin went back to his Perfect Stew quest.

He had twenty-seven white bowls on the table in front of him, the smallest containing seven strands of saffron, the largest containing seven pounds of potatoes cut into pieces of identical weight (.77 ounces), and the others with a variety of mundane, exotic, or just plain ridiculous ingredients. He was in the process of throwing I Ching cards into the air to decide in what order the bowls should be emptied into the pot, a pot that he had filled by leaving it below a rainspout seven inches in diameter for seventy-seven seconds, seven minutes after it had started raining.

"Methinks that all our problems did begin when we began to count in base seven," he said. "The cards speak to me and they say we should count in base random. Douglas, put the sacred Excalibur down before thou have an accident and go wash thy hands. Not in the soup pan, thou fool. Needs I must start all over again."

"Maybe that's, like, your missing ingredient," said Jay.

"Yeah, like, perhaps dirt from an idiot's hands is just the thing it needs," sniggered Kay.

"Be not so . . ."

Merlin was about to say "ridiculous" but it suddenly all made sense. Douglas was the new king. Hadn't he been only the second person in history to pull Excalibur out of the stone? And hadn't the first one, Arthur, been staggering around the kitchen drunk as the lord he was on the night that Merlin had made the Perfect Stew? Yes, that was it. Arthur must have washed his hands in the stew pot.

"BRILLIANT," he cried.

"I was, like, kinda joking, man," said Kay.

"No, no, in thy wit thou art speaking the very truth. It all cometh back to me," said the old wizard. "For I see a vision and in the vision the noble Arthur takes his hands from the pot, wipes them on his tabard, and then empties the bowls into the pot, and then, and then . . . Ye gods, Douglas, grasp the noble Excalibur and stir the stew."

And so it sort of came to pass, Merlin re-created the Perfect Stew, so perfect that everyone was allowed only a thimbleful and had to fill up on beans on toast. The rest of the stew was placed in an ancient hallowed container with the magic word *Tupperware* on the lid and taken to the cold store, a cellar deep below the castle kept cool for centuries with ice blocks from the last ice age.

At last, thought the Blind Piano Tuner, *it's all coming*

together—the stew, the Tabernacle, Excalibur freed. At last everything is coming together.

He sighed. Soon it would be time to leave the cave, the cave that had been his home for almost as long as he could remember. Thirteen thousand years in the same place, you get kind of attached to it. You wear your own grooves in the place, put up your own coat hooks. Life had been so peaceful. He had known this day would come, but he had managed to put it to the back of his mind with his seven times table. He began to pack his bag.

"I've been thinking," said Douglas, the wisdom of the Reflections of the Ancients beginning to kick in, "about the Tabernacle. I don't suppose you've got such a thing as a very large machine in need of repair, a tractor or a spaceship maybe?"

"Clever boy," said the Blind Piano Tuner to himself.

"Spaceship, what spaceship?" said Merlin evasively.

"You know cluckin' well," said Ethel. "Your spaceship, the one you and The Oracle came here in."

"The Oracle came here in a spaceship?" said The Oracle.

"Yes," said Ethel, and she explained to The Oracle how she and Merlin had crashed on Earth, how their memories had been erased, and that, yes, Merlin was indeed her true father.

"The Oracle knew, the minute she saw him," Fluffy said, and flew over to the old wizard.

She sat on his arm and he stroked her feathers. It was a poetic but sad reunion, difficult for both of them. They thought of all the lonely times over the past centuries when it would have meant so much to have had someone to turn to, someone to love. And now that they were reunited it was ironic. The natural act of reaching out and clinging to each other was impossible.

"Spaceship," said Kay. "What spaceship, where?"

"Deep below here, in ye very bowels of ye earth, where it has lain these past centuries," said Merlin, wiping the tears from his eyes, suddenly remembering.

"Have you, like, been down there recently, man?" said Jay.

"Verily," said Merlin, "I was there in 1757."

"Man, that's like over, uh . . ."

"Five hundred and thirty years," said Douglas.

Everyone turned and stared at him. The Reflections of the Ancients had certainly worked some amazing magic on him. His brain seemed to be as sharp as a knife. He looked almost presentable. All the colors of his different body parts had melted into a rather gorgeous shade of tan, with only a very faint hint of green, and bits of him that had kept falling off were now as secure as anyone else's.

"Seven hours and nine minutes," he added. "Come on, we'll go and fix the ship. If I'm not mistaken, little chicken, we need to leave Earth to fulfill the next stage of our quest for the Perfect Hour."

Ethel was speechless. Even she didn't know that. Everyone else just stared at Douglas openmouthed.

Brilliant! thought the Blind Piano Tuner. *Who knows just how to control the strings? Who's the smartest Blind Piano Tuner in the world?*

"But first," Douglas added, "there is something I must do."

"What?" said everyone almost simultaneously, though not exactly simultaneously, so that it actually sounded like "Wwhhhaawwhaaaatt?" But Douglas got the message.

"I have to bring my notebook," he said, and began digging up the floor.

"You've got your notebook hidden under the floor?" said Kay.

"No, of course not," said Douglas, pulling up two flagstones. "My notebook *is* the floor. Look."

"Yeah, man, two shiny slabs of stone. They're lovely," said Kay.

"The faces, can't you see them?"

"I can see my face," said Kay.

"Jay, what can you see?" said Ethel hesitantly.

It was time to put him to the test. It was a test she hadn't wanted to do. Only the Chosen One could see the Reflections of the Ancients. She had created Douglas to help them on their quest. He was to have been their strong man, not the Chosen One. That was Jay's role. She held her breath.

"Oh, wow, man," said Jay. "Who are they?"

236

Oh, my God, thought Ethel. *There* are *two Chosen Ones.*

"They are the Reflections of the Ancients," said Merlin, "and they are here to give thee of their deep wisdom."

It was too good to be true, two Chosen Ones. Merlin felt like dancing, though his old bones were too stiff. Ethel, forever the pessimist, dreaded the day when Douglas and Jay might be locked in deadly battle. She pushed the thought out of her mind, though, and tried to tell herself that two was better than one, that at last everything seemed to be going to plan. After all the mistakes and unplanned events—like the Virus arriving when she accidentally moved Fluffy's jar to the exact dead center of the universe and left the door open, and letting herself get trapped by Nigel, things were looking good.

"Wow."

"What are you talking about?" said Kay. "There's nothing there."

"The Oracle can see nothing, therefore it cannot exist," said The Oracle.

"So, like, tell me something cool, Reflection Man," said Jay to the flagstones.

A face, timeless, creased with wisdom yet sparkling with a mischievous glint in its eye, looked straight at Jay and said, "The stew needs more salt."

"Yeah, I know that, man. I mean something, like, really cool and important," said Jay.

"No, my child, thou do not understand. The stew *needs* more salt," said the reflection. "Take the salt and the stew with thee when thou go down to the deep cellar to repair Merlin's craft."

"But—," Jay began.

The reflection cut him short. "I have the wisdom of all those who have lived before me. Do not question my words, for thou have only the wisdom of five minutes," it said.

"Believe," said the second reflection. "Remember how thou closed thy eyes and saw thy way over the mountains? Thou must live thy life like that from now on. Thou must see with thy eyes closed. Thou must hear with thy ears blocked. Thou must smell with thy nose full of grass."

"Not that sort of grass," said a third.

"And thou must speak with thy mouth full, in spite of what thy mother told thee," said a fourth.

"Only a Chosen One can see us or hear us," said the first reflection. "Look deep in my eyes. Look through them into the mind of history."

Jay stared as if hypnotized. His mind, which had always coasted along about two yards behind the rest of him, was running to catch up. Lights came on all over the inside of his head. Whole areas of his brain that had slept since the day he had been born suddenly woke up.

Before he could do or say anything the reflection held up its hand.

"Keep this to thyself," it said. "The powers we have unlocked in both of thee are all the more powerful for being known only to thyself and Douglas. The chicken can no longer read your mind."

But I can, thought the Blind Piano Tuner.

Yes, and I can read yours, too, Piano Man, thought Jay.

"Wait," said the reflection. "We can fix that."

"Shit," said the Blind Piano Tuner.

I can still read yours, Piano Man, thought Jay. *And everyone else's.*

He could feel the Blind Piano Tuner roaming around the outside of his mind, trying to find a way in. God, the Reflections of the Ancients were good. He tried to read someone else's mind. Ethel's was like the biggest library in the universe, with not only every book that had ever been written in every solar system but every magazine, newspaper, school blackboard, letter, and shopping list. It was unbelievable. There was so much, he didn't know where to start.

He reached out beyond Camelot and tried to look for his parents. He could sense them, sense they were still alive, but couldn't tell where they were. Besides, he'd lived without them so long, a bit longer wouldn't matter.

This is, like, so cool, he thought.

Fantastic, isn't it? he felt Douglas say.

And it was, ten billion times cooler than anything else had

ever been, and he wanted to tell everyone about it but he knew he couldn't. He looked around the vast castle kitchen and slowly the dishcloth rose in the air, just an inch or two, so no one would see it, but enough for Jay to know that with a little practice he could move mountains and very probably would.

The Blind Piano Tuner saw the dishcloth move and was not happy, not because he lived in a mountain but because he now no longer had complete control of everything. But there are those who would argue that he never had it, that he was not the puppet master but just another puppet. Ethel, on the other hand, was very happy.

"Come on, then," said Jay, "let's go and fix this spaceship."

"Aye, well, verily, there's a bit of a problem," said Merlin. "I cannot remember the way. The path is lost to me."

Jay reached into the old wizard's mind. He had never seen such a cluttered mess. It was like a delinquent child's bedroom, except here and there were blank spaces, empty areas where the cells had died and memories had been lost forever. In the back of a small locked cupboard hidden behind a thousand recipes for stew, Jay found a complete map of the castle, including all the cellars and dungeons, and at the very bottom some steep stone steps that led down to the spaceship were marked.

They were very steep steps and Merlin had built them that way deliberately, to make it as hard as possible to reach the ship. They were built like a spiral staircase except with knots added. For Douglas, who was carrying the two heavy flag-stones, it was particularly difficult, especially as he had Merlin sitting on his shoulders.

"Steady, my dear," said Ethel from inside Douglas's shirt, "we don't want to fall."

They reached the bottom and there in a dimly lit cave were the remains of Merlin's crashed ship. It was not a pretty sight. Apart from the immense damage it had suffered when it had hit the ground at 1,249 miles an hour, a millennium or so in a damp cellar had not been kind to it.

"Ye are the first people to set eyes on the *Desperalda* in many, many years," said Merlin.

"Oh, cluck," said Ethel, looking at the wreckage.

Shit, thought the Blind Piano Tuner.

"Listen," said The Oracle, "The Oracle has something to say."

But no one was taking any notice of her. They were walking around and around the ship, shaking their heads in disbelief.

"Man, do you, like, really think this pile of junk is ever going to move again?" said Kay, pretty well summing up everyone's thoughts.

"Yea, verily," said Merlin. "It just needs a few things straightened out and a coat of paint."

"Yeah, right," said Kay.

Chapter 26

Fit Tab A into Slot B

It took several weeks to repair the ship. Douglas pulled and pushed, hammered and unfolded things until they were pretty well the right shape and size. It was full of dents and rust spots, but they were just cosmetic. Jay, with a little help from the Reflections of the Ancients, rewired, reprogrammed, and rejigged all the insides of the ship until little lights came on when you pressed buttons and confident humming noises came from what are commonly described as "the bowels" of the ship, not a particularly good description, though in the case of the *Desperalda* very apt.

And all this time no one had been inside the ship because the one thing they hadn't managed to do was open the door. Jay had done all the internal repairs using his new telekinetic powers. But no matter how they tried, the door would not budge. The trouble was that there was nothing to get hold of, no handle, no rivets, not even a gap wide enough to get a screwdriver into.

"The Oracle has something to say," said The Oracle, but no one was listening.

"Use the force, Luke," said Merlin.

"Luke? Who the hell's Luke?" said Jay.

"Sorry, another lifetime, I was dreaming," said Merlin. "What I meant to say was use the Tabernacle."

And of course that worked. A sickly damp smell of thousand-year-old air poured out of the cabin. . . . There was a thousand-year-old cheese sandwich lying on the control panel.

"So that's where I left it," said Merlin.

There were then only two major problems left.

The first was that there wasn't enough room for everyone inside the ship. It had been designed to hold two people, Merlin and The Oracle. Now there were four people plus a chicken and a kingfisher, five if you included the Blind Piano Tuner, who as we speak was skiing down the Himalayas toward India.

The second problem was the one that The Oracle had been trying to point out ever since they'd reached the cellar, and it was a big-time problem.

"The Oracle has something to say," said The Oracle, "and now is a good time to listen."

"WHAT??" said the rest in unison.

"How are you going to take off?"

"Well, first you turn the ignition switch—," Jay began.

"No, wait, there's more. How are you going to take off with a hundred feet of solid rock, cellars, and dungeons above your head?" said The Oracle.

"Ooops," said Merlin.

"Shit," said everyone else, including the Reflections of the Ancients.

"There's always cluckin' something," said Ethel.

She wasn't happy anymore. It was always the cluckin' same. You get things running smoothly, organize and plan for every eventuality. You coax, force, coerce people and other creatures into doing exactly what you want, even make them think it was all their own idea, and then there's some picky little detail that screws the whole thing up.

"It's not, like, exactly a detail, man, is it?" said Kay. "It's, like, pretty final."

"Every problem has a solution," said Jay.

God, I hope he comes up with one, thought Ethel. *I can't think of a cluckin' thing, apart from entirely dismantling the whole cluckin' ship and carrying it piece by piece up all those cluckin' stairs and rebuilding it in the garden.*

"Well, we could entirely dismantle the whole ship and carry it piece by piece up all those stairs and rebuild it in the garden," said Jay, "but there must be an easier way."

And of course there was.

The Blind Piano Tuner's mind had reached the southernmost tip of India and was staring out to sea. It traveled the oceans until it reached land. It dried itself off and scanned back and forth across the countryside, looking for churches, searching for his apostles, the Thirteen Hooded Figures of Ancient Legends and Times Gone By.

He found them in a sorry state. If you remember, they had been turned to dust when Ethel and her sisters had destroyed Nigel's earthly body. Over the ensuing weeks the dust had struggled pathetically to regroup itself. It had formed one pile and then pathetically tried to divide itself back into the thirteen individual piles, even though there was only enough to make eleven and a half. Each time they had gathered themselves together, a breeze had blown through the open door and muddled them up. Birds had trampled through them, rats had sat on them and scratched themselves, carrying bits of them off to drains many miles away. Now there were only the remains of seven.

"My poor children," said the Blind Piano Tuner. "I blame myself, sending you out into the world and not keeping an eye on you. If only I'd realized how wicked that cockerel was!"

Reaching out with the power of his mind, the Blind Piano Tuner slowly tried to re-form his apostles. They had been so badly damaged it was an impossible task. He took the remains of their souls and formed them into a single entity.

"Come, my child, we are needed at Camelot," he said.

The Patchwork Quilt of Ancient Legends and Times Gone By flattened itself out, rose slowly off the ground, and floated like a magic carpet out of the church. It climbed into the sky and flew over land and ocean to India to collect its master. The last time he had traveled, the Blind Piano Tuner had flown first-class. He had sat cross-legged in the air while his thirteen disciples had flown around him in a magic circle that had levitated him far above the earth. For years all those who had seen him pass overhead had talked about it and the vision had passed into folklore and legend. Now he crossed the great ocean and the forests on a rug and no one gave him a second glance. For thousands of years he had dreamed of this day, the day that he returned to the world, and it had all become a terrible anticlimax.

He landed in the castle garden and walked across the grass toward the cellar steps. It was the first time he had touched grass since he had arrived on the planet. There were times when the Blind Piano Tuner wished he could have been a simple mortal, able to enjoy the simple things of life and death.

"There's someone coming down the stairs," said Jay. "I can hear footsteps."

"It's the Blind Piano Tuner," said Ethel. "He's coming with us and he can help us get the ship out of here."

"Is he, like, good or bad?" said Jay. "It seems that most people we meet want to hurt us."

"He is neither good nor evil. He is the Blind Piano Tuner," said Ethel. "He is older than time itself, the oldest being in all of the galaxies. The echo of the big bang still rings in his ears. Today he will help us. Tomorrow he may try to kill us."

"Great," said Jay. "So what you're saying is, like, we shouldn't trust him."

"Not one billionth of a micron and yet for him to help us we must trust him implicitly," said the old chicken. "That is the irony of the Blind Piano Tuner. Today we have no choice because only the Blind Piano Tuner can help us."

The steps grew near enough for everyone to hear. The door opened and the Blind Piano Tuner entered. His tiny figure, dressed in a white robe, looked like a Buddha and his eyes seemed to peer right into your soul.

The Blind Piano Tuner was a true immortal and yet surely if someone is immortal, they should never age? To be a true immortal, then, one must look the same as a newborn baby and that was what the Blind Piano Tuner almost looked like, yet he was grotesquely old. He was pale and hairless like a newborn baby, no taller than a three-year-old child, yet his face was lined with age and wisdom like old corduroy. His hands were as tiny as a child's, yet they were thin as if time had worn them down. He had no teeth, or any need of them, since no morsel of food had ever passed his lips. His only sustenance was water that wasn't water from the Fountain of Youth that trickled from a crack in the back of his dark cave in the Himalayas. Every day since the birth of the mountains he had licked the wet rocks, catching the precious liquid before it vanished through a crack in the cave floor to trickle halfway around the world and drip from the roof of another cave, the one below the exact dead center of the universe, into the Gene Pool.

"We have need of thy talents, O ancient one," said Merlin.

"I know, I know. I've been watching," said the Blind Piano Tuner.

"Yeah, right," said Kay, looking at the weird little creature in complete disbelief. "What's he going to do, man, split the world open so we can, like, fly out?"

"That is exactly what I am going to do," said the Blind Piano Tuner. "Earthquakes are my speciality."

"Wouldst thou rend the world in twain, ancient one?" said Merlin. "Verily, thou will shake and break Camelot to its very foundations."

"If you want to fly to the stars, what else can we do?" said the Blind Piano Tuner.

"Why can't Ethel, like, shrink the ship down really tiny and then we could carry it upstairs, and then she could, like, make it big again?" said Jay.

"The fusion drive would implode," said Ethel. "They have to be an exact size. One fraction of a millionth of an inch too big or small and they implode. For intergalactic travel they're the only way to go, but they are so cluckin' unstable hardly anyone ever comes out the other side."

"Okay, so this earthquake, like, shouldn't we sort of get out of here?" said Kay.

"No need," said the Blind Piano Tuner. "I'm an expert."

"Still," said Ethel, "put these on just in case."

"Paper bags?" said Kay.

"Keep the dust out of your eyes."

There wasn't so much a loud bang as a dull distant cracking noise. The ground moved. It shivered and shook and far above them the soufflé that Merlin had left on a low temperature collapsed. A few seconds later Camelot shivered and settled back down on its foundations, which were now seven yards deeper in the ground than before. The castle was now only six stories high and the whole ground floor had become a cellar. But above their heads, where many levels of cellar and dungeons had once been, was clear blue sky.

"I say, old chap," said The Oracle, "well done."

She flew up through the opening, her bright blue wings flashing in the shafts of sunlight that peered down through the dust in the darkness. As she reached the garden there was another loud *crack* and the Tower of Dreams came crashing down on top of her.

"Oops," said the Blind Piano Tuner, peering up at the sky through the gaping hole. "Still, you can get the ship out now."

Merlin struggled up the stairs as fast as his frail legs would carry him, his old heart beating frantically in his chest until he thought it would break. After all these centuries to have found his daughter and then have her snatched away from him seemed the cruelest fate he could imagine and he felt his heart was breaking.

Douglas and Jay ran up ahead of him and they began frantically picking through the rubble until they found her. In her final moments The Oracle returned to the body she had been born with, a beautiful young woman. Merlin held her in his arms and wept. Nothing mattered anymore, the Perfect Hour, the human race fading to extinction, going home to Morphine. It was all meaningless. Without his daughter, the child that had been kept from him for so long, he wanted to die.

"I love thee, my child," he sobbed. "I am truly sorry we were apart for so long."

"Father," The Oracle said, and died.

"Can't you bring her back to life?" said Jay to Ethel.

After all, she had created Douglas from leftovers and made Kay from one of his ribs. She had even claimed earlier that she could clone someone from a single cell.

"No," said Ethel. "I am sorry, old friend."

Camelot seemed empty, just another three-hundred-room castle, beautiful beyond dreams. Merlin felt it was no longer his home. Tiny flakes of his dead skin lay in every room, his breath had touched every wall for so long the place had become part of him. Its walls were filled with the memories of great times gone by when King Arthur and his knights had held court there. When Douglas had come along and pulled Excalibur from the stone, Merlin had dreamed of those great days returning, of new knights, of new quests, of new boldly going just like in the good old days. Now, like the Tower of Dreams, the old wizard's dreams lay in ruins. Without his daughter, The Oracle, the beautiful Apollonia, Camelot to him was an empty shell.

Merlin reached down and from around his dead daughter's neck he took a golden chain. On the chain was an ancient Egyptian amulet, a scarab beetle carved from green jade with eyes of lapis lazuli.

"Wear this around thy neck," he said, giving it to Kay. "It will protect thee from evil."

But not from falling masonry, Kay thought.

"We have to go, Merlin," said Ethel gently.

"Right," said Jay, brushing the dust away from the two flagstones and taking charge. "There is room in the ship for two people. Who's going, who's staying?"

"I care not to go," said Merlin. "I cannot leave Camelot, where my beloved daughter lies."

"Come on, old man," said Douglas, putting his arm around Merlin's shoulders and leading him away.

"I shall stay here and build a shrine to my beloved daughter, and King Douglas must stay, for new legends are about to be born," Merlin added. "And this time . . ."

All eyes were on the old man.

"This time shall the Round Table be square."

And so it was. Jay and Kay climbed aboard the *Desperalda*. Ethel shrank the flagstones containing the Reflections of the Ancients until they could fit into Jay's pocket and then hopped up on his lap. The Blind Piano Tuner, wrapped in the Patchwork Quilt of Ancient Legends and Times Gone By, squeezed in behind the two seats. Douglas took Excalibur and slid it into place in the fusion engine. Ethel took the ignition key from a secret place under her wing and they were ready to leave, ready at last to leave Earth on the first part of their quest for the Perfect Hour.

"Does anyone know where we're actually going, man?" said Jay.

"Oh, yes," said Ethel, pointing to the sky. "Up there."

"By the way," said Kay in the split second before the *Desperalda* left Earth, "I'm pregnant."